SUREFOOT

The Adventures of a Warrior Princess
An Interactive Game Book

Akpoebi Nora Ojeke

SUREFOOT

Copyright © 2024 by

AKPOEBI NORA OJEKE

All rights reserved.

Designed & Published in Nigeria by

TEBEBA Global Publishing Ltd.

ISBN: 978-978-789-152-0

PUBLISHER'S CONTACT:

www.tebeba.com

Info@tebeba.com

PRAISE FOR SUREFOOT

Surefoot is a coming of age story about a woman who had lived in the towering shadows of her father but now experiences the intrigues that come with making mistakes and learning from them, from growing and succeeding. I have thoroughly enjoyed the book. I like the nuances as Surefoot goes on adventures to save her father and experiences the world through a new lens. The book will appeal to readers of all genres but especially young adults and people with an interest in the excitement that goes with gaming. Overall, it is a well-written book and I'm privileged to be one of the people to see it before it hits the market. I believe very strongly that it will be successful.

~Onem Sandra Osuoka ~

Surefoot is unlike any book that I have read. This is my first game book and it was an exciting read from start to finish. I am impatiently waiting for other adventures from Surefoot. This book will test your character and also make you think critically before making decisions. It's a beautiful book and a must-read for anyone who wants something fresh, exciting and unique.

~Francisca Egebrike~

Surefoot takes the reader on an odyssey, and like the Greek Odysseus, Surefoot's journey is long and eventful. This book will appeal to the adventurous reader, the reader that is open to new experiences and readers for whom reading is in itself a journey. Prepare to immerse yourself in a world of possibilities as you enter the pages of Surefoot.

~Dr Edem Onofeghara~

Surefoot is my very first read of an interactive story and everything about this book is written with incomparable precision. One story, several outcomes. Surefoot embodies survival, bravery, determination, desperation and much more Surefoot is crafted with intentionality and the journey to each end is an exciting one. This book actively engages the reader's mind as you have to remember your choice at every point. Action, adventure, imagery, Surefoot brings with it a roller coaster of encounters that you don't want to miss.

~Shallom Makanjuola~

Surefoot, the adventurous tale of a warrior princess. The diction and style of storytelling is captivating and interesting. It is filled with themes of love, family (in Vin Diesel's voice), courage, action, culture, suspense and so much more. I particularly like the belief and confidence of the main character and her undying nature to never give up. That character should be emulated by youths in my current generation.

I.E. Austin Esq

Surefoot indeed. I will call this game a novel like never before. It's one of a kind. A story with several game adventures. You will be in a hurry to get to the end of one adventure so as to continue with the next. The adventures are very exciting and interconnected. I wonder how the author was able to connect them all. This is going to be a bestselling adventure-game novel. Years will pass before anyone will be able to understand and learn this writing style.

More grace.

Dr Chinasa Mba

CHARACTERS IN
THE BOOK

CHIEF ZIZA

QUEEN COHANI

PRINCESS SUREFOOT

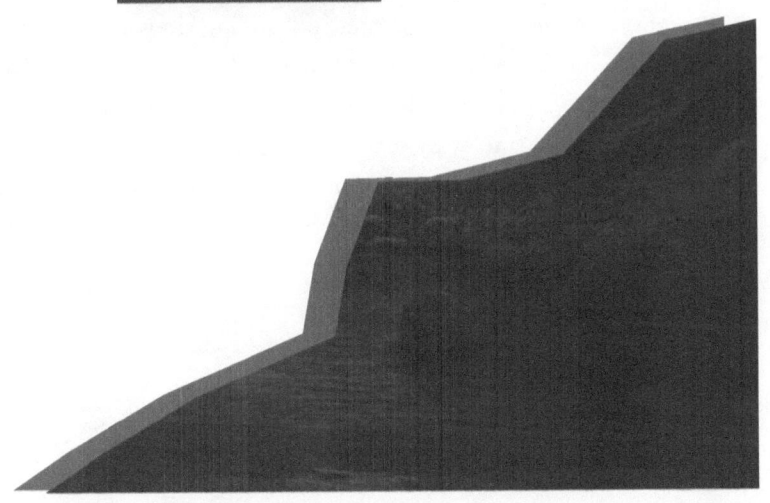

PREAMBLE

Y ou are Princess Surefoot, daughter of Chief Ziza, the great leader of the Omahi tribe of warriors, who controlled The Great Plains, a broad expanse of flat lands in the West African region. Chief Ziza was renowned for leading his people in great battles against the Akuka tribe who were fond of looting and killing other tribes across the plains in neighboring villages without mercy, sparing no one, including suckling children.

Chief Ziza alone held the great staff, that endowed him with the power to lead his people to battle and emerge victorious, which was given to him by the seven spirits of Ebinome River. Your mother, Queen Cohahi was a strong woman, standing beside her husband. They ruled their people with wisdom for many years. Queen Cohahi was a warrior in her days. In the Omahi tribe, both men and women were taught the art of war in order to defend their people from the Akuka invaders. She stopped going to battle after she became pregnant with you. Together, both parents had raised you, their daughter and only child, to be a strong and highly-skilled warrior.

The Omahi tribe had watched with trepidation as the Akuka tribe became more daring in recent times, expanding their raid to more territories and killing entire villages without mercy. The drums of war had begun to echo in the hearts and minds of every man, woman and child. Preparations were being made and warriors trained ceaselessly. You, Surefoot, were part of the daily excursions out of the village to stop some of the invaders from coming closer. The attacks were getting more frequent and it was clear that the Omahi tribe had to retaliate.

Then Chief Ziza was suddenly struck with an incurable disease and the tribe began to lose hope as they usually relied on him to lead them to battle. No one else could wield the great staff that would secure their victory, other than him. The staff was to be handed over to a male heir and you were their only child. Although you had proven your skill time and again in battle, the staff could not be handed down to you by the tribe's seer and elders. It was simply against all the traditions that the Omahi tribe believed in.

The seer had foretold that the only means of saving your father's life was for someone to journey to the Mountain of Lanogoza to get the healing stone, guarded by an ancient dragon.

Will you go on this journey to save your father's life and ultimately the lives of your people? If you choose to do so, tread carefully for danger lurks in every corner. The penalty for making a mistake whilst on this journey is... DEATH.

DISCLAIMER

This book is a fictional story. The Omahi tribe, the Mountains of Lanogoza, as well as character names like Surefoot, Ziza, Cohahi, Nadum and Strongheart do not exist.

Most of the information in this book including names, characters, languages, places and locations are figments of the writer's imagination or researched, as stated in the references section of this book. Any resemblance to actual events, locales or persons living or dead, is entirely coincidental.

Surefoot character illustrations were drawn by S. Esemjay Jonathan.

The author has mentioned mythical characters like ogres, vampires, witches, Medusa, the dinosaur, tyrannosaurus in the book. She has blended them with imaginary characters she created, like cravuners which are vampire birds, zepenters, which are large flying birds with the head of a snake and an enchanting lady called Mimanto.

The author hopes that this book captures the beauty and strength of African warriors and the main character, Princess Surefoot, in her search for the healing stone.

Join Princess Surefoot as she goes on this exciting and perilous journey.

Information about Medusa used in this book was adapted from an article *'Dangerous Beauty: The Real Story of Gorgon Medusa* written by Sree Kaya and can be found in the link: **https://medium.com/paperkin/what-does-it-take-to-feel-sympathy-for-a-monster-3f88a2727boc.**

NOTE FROM THE AUTHOR

It all started sometime in the late nineties, when there were no sophisticated computer games like what exists today.

There were very few interesting programs on the television back then, except for the news from the very efficient Nigerian Television Authority (NTA) and some tele-novellas.

Sitting down in my parents' living room and bored out of my wits, I imagined and toyed with the idea of writing my own adventure story. I had read an adventure book back in the day and sadly, I can't for the love of me remember the author or the title of the book. With that idea in mind, I got an old exercise book and pen and started to write.

I wrote three game books and in a couple of months, an adventure story was born. I know the last line made it seem like writing this book was an easy task.

No, it wasn't. The first point of call was to even get a storyline and the next thing was imagining how each decision taken by the players in the adventures could lead to multiple endings.

Isn't that how life is, anyway? Every decision and action that people take could have ended up in so many different outcomes.

I present my first game book to you, my dear reader, and hopefully the others will follow soon.

Please ensure you go through the game instructions, before you start reading this book as the chapters of the book do not flow into each other.

Enjoy!

INSTRUCTIONS TO GAME PLAYER

This adventure book chronicles the adventures of a warrior princess called Surefoot, played by you the reader. In addition, it presents several games and riddles for you the reader, to play and unravel.

Once you embark on an adventure, there will be questions asked of you after Chapter One.

Kindly note that you can't read this book chronologically. After Chapter One, your selection will lead you on to your next adventure. To put this simply, after Chapter One, you could be heading to Chapter 99 and then back to Chapter 46 etc.

Pick your storyline until you get to the end of your adventure.

Depending on your selection, you will embark on different adventures because this book has multiple endings.

Congratulations means you have reached a victorious end and **Adventure ends here** sadly means you lost and might have to start all over again.

Choose wisely and make sure you don't pick the wrong adventure, or it's all over.

Have fun playing as many adventures as you like, after each end of your selected adventure.

Good luck, **Game Player!**

DEDICATION

To Biboye Ojeke, now my husband, Dr Obraori Adiela, Francisca Egberike, Rosemary Egberike, Onem Sandra Osuoka, Ineware Alex Wells and Egwono Oriji. The oldies who enjoyed reading my stories from way back then.

I still got it.

Never lost it.

To Dr Edem Onofeghara, my friend turned beta reader. You have been exceptional in fine-tuning my manuscripts. Thanks so much for your wealth of wisdom.

To my brilliant son, Josh, the true gamer in the family.

To my darling daughter, Doubra, the teenage half of the writing duo. Love the way you analyze each aspect of my story and give me new ideas in the course of discussing the drafts.

To my darling friend, Lolade Shakioye, the one person that made me resurrect my gift for writing and constantly checks on me to be sure that I don't drop the ball again. Love your spirit and drive. Always pushing me to be the best version of myself.

To my editor, Ify Omeni, who had the pleasure of editing my first game book. I know this book isn't a conventional one but your excitement in bringing my ideas to life and your genuine feedback were vital in polishing my work.

Thank you, everyone

CONTENTS

CHAPTER 1

Father

The Omahi villagers made way as you walked with Queen Cohahi down the path leading to your father, Chief Ziza's mud hut. Today, everyone had congregated around the hut as the seer tried unsuccessfully to restore the ailing chief back to health. Your father had been struck with a sickness that came with high fever and night chills and didn't seem to be getting any better. His state was a constant source of worry to not only you and your mother, but the entire village.

There was also the issue of who to wield the staff of authority.

The staff of authority was a large, ugly-looking wooden stick. No one, not even the seer, knew what type of wood it was made from, though it looked like oak. The wood was twisted and woven into each other in a contorted gnarly mass, with a large bulbous tip that formed the head and glowed with a red orange fire. The glow sometimes emitted a flame that destroyed enemies when it was pointed at them. The staff still glowed intermittently as it lay on the holy altar, a shrine that had been built in honor to Andogun, the fire god. The altar was made up of five stone steps, barren except for beads and feathers carefully laid on each step. On the last step the staff lay, ominous and glowing in the native ancestral hut.

No one was permitted to touch the staff except the seer who had the power to perform the rites to appease the seven spirits of Ebinome River. Anyone else who touched the staff immediately disintegrated into nothingness. This had happened to a child who picked up the staff out of curiosity. Since that day, no one else attempted to touch the staff. The adults avoided it and all the children were warned to stay clear of the ancestral hut. A dull glow from the inside was an indication that the staff lay within its mud walls.

The villagers had heard the legend of how the staff came to Omahi Village. The great Chief Ziza had fallen into the sacred Ebinome River one day during his journey alone from one of the trading villages. He was on his horse, going across the bridge that was situated just above the sacred river, and the horse panicked when they came across a cobra on their path. The horse raised its legs as the cobra poised to strike and the chief tried to control the horse but it jerked and he fell off its back into the sacred river.

The seven spirits of the sacred Ebinome River didn't welcome visitors and immediately challenged him to battle. Chief Ziza was not one to back down from a fight and his strength had matched theirs as they fought for three days nonstop. The spirits were so impressed by his fighting skills and determination to win that they gave him the staff of authority. With that staff in hand, no one could defeat him in battle. But the gift had to be handed down to a male heir. Chief Ziza often wondered if he could give it to his only heir which was you, Surefoot. The seer consulted with the seven spirits who insisted that it must be given to a male heir. Your father had decided that the staff would go to whoever you married. The only problem was that you were not interested in any of the men in the village.

~ FATHER ~

The Akuka invaders had been coming into the Omahi land across the grassy plains where your village was situated, within a vast expanse of grasslands. They were getting bolder with each attack and although the Omahi warriors, which included you, succeeded in fighting them off each time, it was obvious that a major war was brewing. The elders and warriors needed your father's leadership and the help of the staff, to lead them in battle and end the incessant attacks once and for all.

Though you were a known and fearless warrior, you couldn't lead them into battle by wielding the staff of authority, since you were a female. Already, the warriors were wary of the outcome of the impending war with the Akuka invaders who wanted to rob them of their land and they also knew how merciless and ruthless these warriors could be. The Akuka invaders wouldn't just stop at killing the warriors. They would kill every man, woman, child and suckling infant in their bid to take over Omahi Village.

It seemed like time stood still as you strode down the path to your father's hut with your mother, Queen Cohahi by your side. Your feet moved as if in slow motion, making thumping sounds while you marched along the pebbled path. A slow chant rose from the villagers lining the path, hitting the ends of their spear to the ground in unison. The sound of the spears hitting the ground in harmony came to you like a dream as you looked up to the clear, blue sky. A lone eagle flew ahead and for a while, you watched it glide away in the distance. Your mother said something to bring you back to the present and you turned to look at her sad face as she glanced at you.

Queen Cohahi was a very strong woman and usually held her emotions in check. This was a necessary trademark of a queen, to be able to stand and rule beside the chief of the land. Her calm words of wisdom in his ears over the years had helped him to lead the great tribe of warriors and extended to the other tribes across the plains.

"Mother, you said something?" you asked, since you did not hear what she had said.

"We have to be strong. They are watching our every move," she whispered back to you.

You nodded, observing that the faces of every man, woman and child was furrowed with sorrow, as you walked alongside your mother. She had learned to speak few words from when she was little, as she was being trained to be a queen. She had learned the art of keeping her emotions in check. Your mother was a strong woman and had been acting as the chief since your father fell ill, managing your father's illness quite well and supporting the elders in making decisions, especially about the incessant attacks at the Omahi Village borders.

She had borne all the challenges that came with ruling this great tribe, with grace and strength and right now, she looked ahead, marching steadily to your father's royal mud hut as you followed behind.

The sound of chanting increased as you approached your father's hut and you observed the warriors standing silently on both sides of the entrance leading to the hut. The feathers on their headdresses moved slightly against the wind and they stared at you with a mixture of sadness and respect as they watched you approach the red and white painted hut situated at the center of the grassy plains.

They bowed their heads in unison to your mother, the acting chief and you, Princess Surefoot, as you both entered the hut, raising the flap of the cloth that covered the door and bowing your way in.

The smell of death hit your nostrils once you entered the hut. It was a difficult smell to describe. All you could say was that it was the same smell you had perceived many times when you watched the light slowly fade from the eyes of a deer that you just hunted and killed. That faint smell of dead leaves, mixed with blood. You shuddered to perceive it on your father who was wrapped up in animal skin, his face covered in sweat. His eyes were closed, but he was whispering in a fevered haze, words that you could not understand. You studied his face that was now sunken from the sickness that was sucking the life out of him. This face wasn't that of the father that you knew. Your mind went back, way back, years ago. You remembered the times you had spent hunting with your father.

"Hold it like this," Chief Ziza had said gently. He had adjusted the bow in your hand and positioned your shoulders to remain level with the line of the arrow.

Your thirteen-year-old self had been looking ahead at the animal in front of you. It was a wild boar and it was unaware of your presence.

"Now take a deep breath, look ahead and aim," he whispered calmly in your ear.

You had drawn a deep breath and watched the boar as it was feeding. It had turned around and seemed to stare at you. It seemed like you could read its mind, and it seemed to question you with its gaze. Your hand started to shake and you had let go of the arrow, just as your father Chief Ziza screamed, "No…not now." You missed the timing and the arrow had pierced the boar on its side. The arrow was sticking out of the boar that was enraged and running towards both of you. You had seen the smoky breath from its nostrils as it barreled through the shrubs heading towards you with great anger, as you opened your mouth in fear.

"Bring out your knife, Surefoot. You have to kill it," Chief Ziza had shouted at you but you were in shock. Your hands hung limply to your side. You were frozen to the spot in fear as you watched the beast running hard and fast, kicking up sand as it lowered its head, ready to charge at you. You had just closed your eyes, terrified. You had heard a loud squeal and opened your eyes to see your father holding the large head of the boar and twisting it.

Chief Ziza had grunted as his muscles bulged with the force of holding back the wild boar. With some effort, as the animal struggled to get out of his grasp, he had twisted its neck. With a loud grunt, he had snapped the neck of the wild boar that lay dead at his feet, with its hind legs twitching in death throes. He quickly turned to you and had held your cold hands, rubbing them in concern. You were practically frozen in fear. It was the first time that your father had asked you to hunt and take a life and it was shocking to see the animal you wanted to kill, try to kill you as well.

"Surefoot, you cannot afford to make mistakes like this. You always have to be ready and fearless. I will not be with you all the time to protect you."

You had looked at his eyes and there was no condemnation or disappointment in there, only love and you knew he wanted you to be strong and fearless. That was the last day you had let him down. You had over time watched his admiration and love for you grow, with each successful hunt and every battle you returned from.

The face lying on the bed didn't seem like the face of the father you knew and you were heartbroken to see him this way.

The old seer was sitting beside your father and he stood up, as two of you approached him. He was a tall, shriveled-looking man with a sharp hook nose and dark eyes. He wore a long, leather robe and a headdress of deer antlers and his gaze was unflinching.

"Queen Cohahi and Princess Surefoot," he acknowledged and bowed his head.

You both bowed your heads to him. When you looked around, you noticed that the elders were also in the room. They had been coming for a while to check on the health of their chief and they stood up and bowed as well and she acknowledged them before they sat down. Your eyes also made its way around the room, looking at the familiar faces of the elders and some of the young warriors that were in there as well. Your eyes caught those of Nadum and he held your eyes with an unreadable expression on his face. You turned away as the seer was speaking to your mother.

"Chief Ziza is not doing any better."

"I can see that, but what can we do? There must be something we can do, your greatness," she pleaded respectfully.

"I have tried all that I can and it seems that he might… not make it," the seer replied calmly watching the queen.

"What about the seven spirits of Ebinome? Have we consulted them? They can come to our aid. After all, they gave him the staff," your mother suggested.

The seer smiled sadly and turned away as he responded, "Do not forget that although the spirits gave our chief the all-powerful staff of authority, they also feel slighted at being beaten by a human…"

"Could it be that this sickness is from…?" she asked.

The seer turned around sharply. "Let us not get carried away with accusations. Do not forget that Chief Ziza is also not a saint. He has killed and offended many people outside the Omahi tribe."

"My father has always done what was right for his people," you interrupted. There was no way you were going to listen to anyone speak ill of your father.

The seer turned to you and his features softened. "I understand, dear princess, but I just want us to realize that this illness might be coming from anywhere."

"Including someone from our tribe?" you questioned, just as your mother held your hand in caution. You turned to look at her as she turned her head

slightly, her eyes pleading with you not to go any further. Two of you had talked earlier about not unduly provoking the elders and right now they were whispering amongst themselves and you could feel the tide of favor slipping away. They were not happy that the queen was leading the tribe on the chief's behalf and were ready to put a man in the helm of affairs even before Chief Ziza's death. You turned to see them watching you, anger etched on their faces and you bit your lips to stop the torrent of anger that you were about to spew out.

"I hope the princess is not accusing anyone in particular?" the seer asked, calmly walking towards you.

"No, she is not. She is merely being emotional and wants her father to get better," your mother spoke on your behalf.

"Yes, indeed as a true daughter would," the seer added.

One of the elders called Maraba stood up and interjected. "Display of emotions is not the mark of a warrior of Omahi and the future queen." He walked with slow steps towards both of you.

You were going to say something, but your mother replied, "Indeed, I agree with you wholeheartedly. It will not repeat itself."

Elder Maraba nodded and looked at you. "I want to hear her say it."

You felt anger rising up your face and your heart started to beat at a fast pace. Then your mother squeezed your left arm. You knew this was not the time to stir up trouble and give the rank of elders a reason to dethrone your father before he died.

"It will not...repeat itself," you said through clenched teeth. All you could think of was ripping the satisfied smile off the face of the bald-headed Elder Maraba.

"Good princess," Elder Maraba said with a satisfied smile and he turned around and looked at the people in the room.

"Unfortunately, the chief cannot be cured. He was a good, kind chief and we all love him. However, the Akukas are coming and we need a leader who can wield the all-powerful staff. We know that the chief has no male heir…"

Your mother interrupted Elder Maraba and you were surprised at what she said. "He has no male heir but our daughter, Surefoot is stronger than three warrior males put together."

Elder Maraba turned around and looked at the queen, "That might be true and yes, she has proven herself in battle, but she is not a male," he said, looking Queen Cohahi in the eyes.

"But she can…" your mother began.

"She cannot wield the staff and you know it," another elder interrupted and everyone started talking at once. Whatever support two of you hoped to gain from the people in the hut was definitely gone as you could sense hostility in the room.

"The chief will die and we will not be able to pass on the staff if we do not do it now," someone said.

"Well, he is not dead yet!" you cried.

"Oh, but he will be dead very soon, as you can see," Elder Maraba said.

"There must be something we can do," your mother protested.

"Nothing can be done, do you not see? We are wasting precious time," Elder Maraba added.

"On the contrary, there is another way," the seer remarked quietly.

"What do you mean by another way?" Elder Maraba asked, surprised.

The seer had a thoughtful, faraway look in his eyes and he turned to look at everyone. "The healing stone," he whispered.

Elder Maraba laughed. "The healing stone in the Mountain of Lanogoza? No one has ever returned from that journey."

"Indeed, that is the only way. A dangerous but certain way to make our chief survive this illness."

"Well, no one will ever go on that dangerous journey," Elder Maraba said, laughing and looking around as the elders all smiled and nodded in agreement.

Queen Cohahi turned to the men, desperation in her voice, "Will no one go to save my husband, your chief who has served every one of you and guided you all with wisdom?" She looked at the men who turned away, avoiding her gaze. Her shoulders bent dejectedly. Indeed, no one dared to go on this journey to save the chief because it was a long and torturous journey. All the people that had attempted the journey never returned.

You looked at the lineup of strong warriors who were in the hut and were surprised that not one of them wanted to go on this quest. Your father had been proud of his warriors and would do anything to make sure they were all safe, yet they chose to repay him with cowardice. Except they were not cowards and this was their plan all along – to watch their chief die.

Your gaze rested briefly on Nadum who avoided your gaze. He was a vibrant and headstrong young man who usually led the warriors in battle. He had the favor of the elders who had suggested him to your father several times as the best suitor for you. He had made some romantic advances towards you, which you rejected. Nadum knew what was expected of him, played his part very well and won the favor of your father. You noticed that your father had been showing a lot of confidence in Nadum and giving him more royal duties to perform, which you used to do from when you were much younger. It seemed like he was being groomed to be the next chief, by your father. You hoped that your father could see that his golden boy wasn't willing to make any sacrifices for him.

The journey to the Mountain of Lanogoza is a feat that he can accomplish with ease, you thought to yourself, except he had other plans. The more you thought about it, the more you realized that the death of your father would mean an easy access to the throne for Nadum and you immediately volunteered, without thinking twice about your decision.

"I will go on the quest," you replied calmly and the chatter slowed to silence, as everyone stared at you in surprise.

Your mother turned to look at you in alarm and you could tell that several thoughts were going through her head about how to dissuade you from the decision you had made. She did not want to lose her only child as well as her husband. She turned to the elders and tried to reason with them.

"My lords, we can ask some of the warriors to go on this quest...," she started, but Elder Maraba raised his hand and quieted her.

"Indeed, a warrior has already shown interest in going on this quest," he said pointing at you.

Your mother looked up at you but you were staring at Elder Maraba intently. She could tell what you were thinking and knew it was not good.

"She is my only child. The only heir to your chief. Surely, you will not let her go on this quest?" A horrified look filled her face.

Elder Maraba turned to the elders and they started talking, while you both watched. "We need someone to lead us to battle. The chief's heir is a female and cannot do so. Maybe it is better that she goes on this quest," he replied, smiling coldly. His disdain was just enough to break your resolve to be calm. You moved forward with your hand holding onto the knife at your waist, but your mother held your hand. Nadum and three other warriors walked towards you and stood in front of Elder Maraba protectively, as he laughed.

"What were you planning to do, Princess? Kill me?" he asked mockingly.

You were about to say something, but your mother interrupted, "No, she was not trying to do that. I implore you, elders."

"We have made up our minds," Elder Maraba replied coldly.

Just as your mother was about to say something, you interrupted her by holding her hands firmly. She looked at you and you smiled reassuringly at her. You understood why your mother was worried and did not want you to embark on this journey. You recalled the stories and experiences about the mountain and though you shuddered, you put up a brave front. As though one of the elders read your mind, he stood, and looked at your mother and said calmly, "We cannot afford to lose any of our men to a foolhardy cause. No one has ever returned from the Mountain of Lanogoza."

"You will sacrifice your princess instead?' she asked the group of elders and the men turned away from her, refusing to meet her gaze.

"She volunteered. We did not force her to go," Elder Maraba replied defensively.

"I volunteered to go because I do not see any man here brave enough to take up the task of saving their chief," you spoke in a cold voice.

The room filled with chatter as they all started talking at once. It was obvious they were not happy that you had called all of them cowards to their faces.

The situation was hopeless and time was racing. You turned back to the seer who had been quietly watching the entire proceedings.

"My lord, what must I do to get to the Mountain of Lanogoza on time?" you asked him, ignoring the stares of the people in the room as they turned to hear the seer's response.

The seer sighed, walked up to you and gently placed a hand on your shoulder as he spoke, "You have to cross so many seas and mountains to get there and finally face the stone's guardian, a huge ancient dragon."

Your mother opened her mouth to protest and you quickly turned to her and held her shoulders firmly.

"Mother, I will be fine. I have been trained in the art of war and the way of the warriors."

"But, Strongheart…," your mother whispered.

"I am not Strongheart, I am Princess Surefoot and I will return," you replied firmly, pushing away memories of Strongheart to the back of your mind.

Squeezing her shoulders, you continued, "Do not worry, Mother, I will go on this quest and bring back the stone on time to save Father."

Her lips firmed up in a straight line. She quickly kept her emotions in check, nodded at you and smiled. You smiled back at her, turned around and looked at the five elders seated on the floor of the hut. You stared at Nadum who turned his face away, still unable to meet your eyes, probably out of shame, you imagined, and looked at the seer.

"What is expected from me?" you calmly asked the seer.

"You really intend to go to the Mountain of Lanogoza?" one of the elders asked and you nodded at him. He turned back to the others and they continued their whispers.

~ SUREFOOT ~

Elder Maraba nodded and spoke for the rest of them. "You have very little time to get the stone and return. If we do not see you in the next high moon in five days, we will give the staff of authority to Nadum."

You nodded at them. It was clear this was what they had wanted all along. It was also obvious that they did not expect you to come back alive. The journey to the mountain appeared to be a death sentence and it seemed you had sealed your fate.

"My daughter will return to us with the stone," your mother said bravely. You turned to look at her and for a moment were overwhelmed by the pride you saw in her eyes.

"Very well then, your highness, let us proceed with the arrangements for her departure," Elder Maraba said. He went out with the elders and the other young men, out of the hut.

The hut became quiet. The only sounds were the whimpering from the feverish Chief Ziza and the sounds of chanting by the warriors outside the hut.

The seer nodded at you and put his hand in a bag that was lying on the floor by your father's bedside. He gave you the contents, which were an egg and a feather.

You looked up at him, puzzled, as you accepted the items and he said, "Your journey, Princess, is no easy task. You will need these to aid you along the way."

"How will I know how and when to use them?" you asked.

"When the time comes, Princess, you will know," he replied. He continued in an ominous tone, "You will meet witches, monsters and ogres, and many other creatures that are not known in these parts, but you must not show any sign of fear. You will see great mysteries and cities that you have never seen beyond the great plains, but this evening, the fire god will reveal these mysteries if he approves of the journey"

You felt your mother clasp your hand and squeeze it hard in a comforting manner. This was what you had trained for all your life as a warrior. To be ready and victorious in any battle. The journey was going to be tough, but you had to be brave. You smiled at your mother to comfort her, because you could imagine the emotional turmoil that she was going through. Then you turned back to the seer who was still talking.

"You can go either to the north, east or west, to find the pathway leading to the abode of the ancient dragon," the seer told you.

"You mention so many places. Which of them will lead me there?" You had a confused look on your face.

"Any of them could lead you to the desired place. You have to find the right path," he told you, in that same ominous tone.

"I will find it." You tried to sound determined, even though his directions confused you.

The seer nodded at you and proceeded to attend to your father who had begun whimpering. He placed his hand against your father's head. There was a calabash containing water by the side of the chief's bed. The seer took a rag, wet it with water from the calabash and started wiping the sweat rolling off your father's forehead. Queen Cohahi watched her husband thrashing uncontrollably and let out a low sob, whilst you held her comfortingly. The seer made a paste from some items that he ground in a plate and forced it through the clenched teeth of your father. In a few moments, Chief Ziza's thrashing stopped and he drifted into a troubled sleep.

"I will find that stone, Father and I will come back," you said with quiet determination.

The seer looked up at you solemnly and said, "We do not have much time. You need to get ready to leave."

You left the hut with your mother and were met outside by the chants of the warriors as they hailed two of you. You both acknowledged their greetings with nods and walked to your mother's hut.

Inside the hut, your mother broke down in tears. She had been trying to be brave while in your father's hut. She did not want the elders to think she was weak. Your mother clung to you in tears. You stroked her face as you studied the wrinkles that were tell-tale signs of aging on her beautiful face and noticed how her grey hairs had significantly multiplied since your father fell ill.

"Surefoot, I am not sure about this," she said as she sat down by the bed and held her face in her hands, struggling between her emotions and her sense of duty as a queen, to be calm. You had to admit that in all the years of growing up, you had never seen your mother cry. Her outburst, although expected, was very surprising to you.

"Mother, it is the only way. You know everyone there expects father to die and they plan to make Nadum the chief," you replied.

"I can see that. Elder Maraba mentioned that they will give him the staff of authority if you do not return."

You quickly knelt by her side and took her hands, "Mother, you have to be strong."

"I...I used to be strong, but I guess I am getting old and tired," Queen Cohahi said, sniffing back tears.

"You are not old, Mother. You are the bravest queen I have ever known. Strong in battle and killer of Raka."

She smiled through her tears. "You know I have almost forgotten my time as a warrior."

"Exactly, Mother. That is the woman Father married and that is the mother that taught me to fight. You killed Raka, the six-foot giant who terrorized everyone in the plains."

Your mother calmed down and looked at you as you said, "I am my mother's daughter and I intend to return, Mother."

She looked at you with big eyes full of sadness and quietly said, "We shall hold prayers for you."

Your mother reached out and held you in a tight embrace. You let go of all the emotions that you were holding back and wept on her shoulders as she slowly rocked you.

Turn to Chapter 109.

~ SUREFOOT ~

CHAPTER 2

Jump into the Sea

As the waves rose and loomed dangerously ahead, you were afraid they would break your boat into a million pieces. The waves rose, each one higher than the next and pushed you and the boat, around. The boat was being tossed about endlessly by the waves. You were no longer able to control them and decided that you might have to jump into the sea. You stared in alarm as a huge wave started to build. This particular wave was taking on a life of its own like a huge monster, rising and rolling just ahead of you and threatening to land on the boat at any minute. Just as the huge wave was about to descend, you dived into the ocean and started swimming away from the direction of the waves, with as much strength as you could muster. The waves kept pushing you back but you fought to keep yourself afloat. You knew that if you gave in now, you would surely drown and so you kept swimming away from the boat and the monstrous wave.

After a while, you dared to look back and watched in horror as the monstrous wave crashed upon your boat, submerging it in the dark, merciless sea. The ripple effect of the wave suspended you above the sea for a moment before plunging you into the depths and you struggled to swim up to the surface.

You came up for air and gasped as the waves continued to toss you about. Although you were exhausted at this point, you continued swimming until your hands ached. Some distance ahead, you noticed a dark object in the waves ahead of you and as it got closer, you saw that it was a fin.

The fin was prominent above the waves and you wearily turned around to avoid the creature that owned the fin and was making its way towards you. Just then, you noticed another creature right behind you, its fin tearing through the sea in your direction. You started swimming in the other direction and saw a shark dive out of the water right in front of you. You ducked and narrowly missed its snapping jaws as it splashed in the water beside you.

You had to think really fast because the sea swarmed with sharks. It was their habitat and you couldn't outswim them.

A snapping jaw just missed your face by inches and you dived once again to the side. The sharks were circling you, taking their time as though playing a dangerous game. You were their meal and they had all the time in the world. In desperation, you took a gulp of air and went back into the water and started swimming with all your might. Your arms ached with each stroke and you were almost out of breath but somehow you hoped that you could outswim the sharks. Something went by your left very fast and you turned to see a shark coming in your direction. You tried to reach for your dagger. It was coming closer and you were fumbling with your waist band.

Where is that blasted dagger? You were sure that you had placed it right there. It was hard to keep holding your breath and the shark was very close now. It opened its mouth and you could see its razor-sharp teeth. You felt the dagger, pulled it out just in time and sliced at the shark. You gave the shark a wide gash across its head and blood was spilling around you, almost blinding you in the water. You were almost out of breath and immediately started swimming up to get some air. The water around you and the shark was turning red and it was widening out into the ocean as the animal thrashed about in pain. It seemed that was a signal for the others, as they started swimming closer, attracted to the blood as you swam even faster towards the surface.

You were almost above the surface and hurled yourself up, gasping desperately for air. You looked around and saw no land for miles out. Your head began to spin and you collapsed in exhaustion. You felt a sharp pain on your leg and looked down to see blood floating around you. *What just happened? Did something bite me?* you wondered. You felt another sharp pain on your other leg and then you went back into the water to find more sharks circling you. They looked vicious and were taking turns to bite at your thrashing feet. You slashed at one of them that just made a move again and then all of them came towards you like they had received a silent signal. They started biting and tearing at you. You tried fighting back but you were outnumbered. The pain was unbearable but after a while you felt nothing. All you saw was the face of your father lying on his bed shivering, murmuring and in pain.

I am sorry, I failed you father, you thought one last time as the world faded into a watery darkness.

𝔄𝔡𝔳𝔢𝔫𝔱𝔲𝔯𝔢 𝔈𝔫𝔡𝔰 𝔥𝔢𝔯𝔢.

Poor Game Player. Remember it's an illusion.

You can return to Chapter 27 or start the game again from Chapter 1.

CHAPTER 3

You thought about the riddle for a while and wondered what could possibly fit that description.

What is long and short?

What is fat and slim?

What is short and tall?

All of a sudden you smiled, as realization dawned on you. Then you answered, "You are the one."

"Why?" Hippo asked, smiling.

He smiled, you thought to yourself, *I must be on the right track, then.* With that assurance, you told him why you gave that answer.

"Well, because you want to be long, but you are short and you want to be slim, but you are fat and you want to be tall, but are short."

The idea to the answer had come to you when you realized that Hippo had

given the answer away in the body of the riddle. He had described himself as he was – short and fat. It made sense that he desired to be the opposite of what he really was. It was a lucky guess that you hoped would be the right answer.

His smile was like a sneer. He opened his mouth, revealing sharp, brown teeth and for a moment you thought the answer was wrong, but he reassured you by saying, "Wise Princess, I'll let you pass. No one has ever given me the correct answer. For getting it right, I'll give you a gift."

He snapped his fingers and wings appeared on your shoulders. You tried to look behind you at the gorgeous white spread on your back and you laughed as you realized that you could control the wings with your mind. You flapped them and momentarily lifted yourself in the air.

"These wings are a gift, to aid you to fly over the remaining six mountains and seas," Hippo said.

"Thank you," you said and smiled at him with so much gratitude.

"When you arrive at the Mountain of Lanogoza, the wings will disappear. My magic does not work on the mountain," he told you.

You thanked him and he stepped aside to let you pass. You ran past him and jumped over the side of the mountain. You initially closed your eyes but soon realized that your wings were fluttering and suspending you in the air. Out of excitement, you twirled around in circles, testing the wings and then proceeded on your journey. The view above the seas and mountains was breath-taking. Clouds parted to reveal a long stretch of blue sea, with a little scattering of rocks. Seagulls flew underneath you in a well-arranged formation and dived into the sea for their day's catch. You saw migrating humpback whales diving in a uniform manner and occasionally expelling spouts of water from their blow holes in the sea below.

After a while, you flew over a forest and the large spread of green lay below you with the trees looking so small, like tiny ants. All of a sudden, you noticed that you were not alone in the air. A group of flying centaurs approached you. They were about fifteen half horsemen, with wings.

As they approached, they flew around you, talking animatedly amongst themselves and laughing. They were surprised that you had wings and you noticed the leader, a well-built muscled centaur with long, flowing black hair and straight moustache, steal admiring glances at you.

He questioned you but you were in no mood to entertain this distraction. You had already lost a lot of time and had to make it back home in time to save your father. The leader mistook your quietness for agreement and asked you to follow them, as he intended to make you his bride.

You were enraged by his arrogance and at the six laughing centaurs. They seemed to be in a lively mood and prevented you from moving any further. They were flying around you, laughing, their tails flapping in the air, along with their massive cream-colored wings.

What will be your next action?

Will you fight the leader and wipe that arrogant smirk off his face? Turn to Chapter 76

Will you take the feather that the seer gave you from your pouch? Turn to Chapter 61.

~ SUREFOOT ~

CHAPTER 4

You were quite exhausted from the earlier fight with the zepenter and this recent one with the snake. You decided to wait and see who was coming. Leaning against the wall of the cave, you tried to catch your breath. You thought to yourself that if there were other people in the cave, you intended to approach them so they could help you in your quest. With that in mind, you tried to make yourself comfortable and waited for the person approaching.

The footsteps sounded closer now and seemed quite loud for one person, you thought to yourself. The walls of the cave that you leaned on vibrated slightly and you looked down to see the pebbles on the floor jump up with each step. *This person has to be huge,* you thought, observing the vibrating stone pebbles. You looked up in time to see a giant ogre striding towards you.

His large feet made a loud sound as he stomped on the ground. Suddenly, you realized your mistake and started to get up from the floor to find a way of escape. Ogres were not reasonable creatures and would rather bite your head off, than talk with you.

The ogre stopped mid-stride and started sniffing with his large nose pointed at the ceiling of the cave. You were moving slowly sideways, against the wall of the cave, but his keen sense of smell found you.

He looked in your direction and his bushy eyebrows rose up in surprise to see you there. The muddy slide and the water had camouflaged you a bit, but you started moving fast as he approached you.

You decided to stay very still. There was a chance that he might not see you as you leaned against the cave. The ogre came closer, his large feet thundering as it moved, causing boulders of rock to shake and roll off the sides of the cave. Your heart was racing very fast, but you felt you could fight it. You were extremely exhausted with all the travails you had experienced and an ogre was not an easy opponent to kill. He was closer now and stood tall in front of you and eventually bent down until he was looking straight into your eyes.

You were very still and almost held your breath. Perhaps the ogre would think you were a statue and move on, but the ogre was now sniffing and coming very close to you. Up close his facial features loomed up at you, large eyes peered at this mound of mud leaning against the cave. The ogre was ugly, with large, broken teeth. His mouth opened up in a snarl, boils all over his face and sparse hair on his bald head. The ogre reeked and the smell nauseated you to a point where you felt you would pass out. He sniffed again and started reaching out a large, stubby finger to your face and you held your breath as he pressed against your face.

"Human....me smell your blood!!" the ogre roared in anger.

"I smell you too, you dirty, horrid thing." you shouted back at him.

The ogre pulled back his hand and aimed for your face with force, but you ducked as he made a hole in the cave where your head would have been, raising dust that filled the narrow passageway.

"Missed me!" you taunted as you rolled away and went in between his legs as the ogre bent down and looked at you, roaring in anger.

You raced across the cave and jumped to the side as a huge rock went past your side. The ogre was hurling rocks at you in anger and you dodged until you fell against the side of the cave, almost knocking yourself out.

"I crush... I crush you human," the ogre yelled in a sing-song manner as it stomped in your direction and raised his hand to smash you to the ground. You quickly got out your dagger and ran towards it and sliced it on the foot. The ogre screamed and held his leg, hopping from one side to the other, holding his cut leg as blood poured down. He was in so much pain and making such a ruckus with his stomping that the cave started shaking and rocks started falling down from the cave ceiling. You ran in a zigzag manner, avoiding the rocks and the ogre that was jumping with one leg held in his hand, still howling in pain. You had to be careful that he didn't jump on you and moved aside just narrowly missing his leg just, as you looked up to see a huge boulder heading in your direction. You tried to jump away but you were not fast enough and the boulder landed on your leg, crushing it to the ground.

Your cry of pain made the ogre stop. He turned to look at you and suddenly started laughing as you struggled to get the boulder off your leg.

"Human!!" he roared and made for you, making you desperately push at the boulder that didn't look like it was going to budge. The ogre towered over you and you reached for your dagger that had fallen to the side, but this time he was quicker and tossed the dagger out of your grasp.

He fixed his angry eyes at you and smiled. His smell was overwhelmingly disgusting but at this time you didn't notice it as you couldn't think of a way out of this predicament.

He pushed the boulder aside easily and grabbed your hand just as you were about to run.

"No! Please, stop!" you screamed as he picked you up gently, bringing you to his face.

"Please!" you begged again, squirming in his large hands but that only made the ogre laugh even more as he levelled you to his face so he could take a closer look.

"Me squeeze human,' the ogre smiled, looking at the delicious morsel he held in his hands.

"No...no!" you screamed as you felt his hand close in on your waist, **y**our breath sucked out of your body. The ogre laughed as he pushed you, wriggling and screaming into his mouth.

𝔄𝔡𝔳𝔢𝔫𝔱𝔲𝔯𝔢 𝔈𝔫𝔡𝔰 𝔥𝔢𝔯𝔢.

You were not fast enough.

You can return to Chapter 89 or start the game again from

Chapter 1.

CHAPTER 5

Fight with Vanotica

You felt your strength waning as the tails kept hitting you from all sides. You stretched your hands on the sand, desperately searching for a weapon, as Vanotica continued to pull you towards the pool. You grabbed a stone and with it you started hitting at one of the tails. The action appeared futile, as it only angered her more. Her face contorted in rage and her green eyes sparked fires of hatred that you could feel across the distance. You watched as her tails stretched out of the water towards you and you desperately looked around. Somehow, your pouch had fallen off your body and was lying a few feet away.

"Here," the seer handed you the egg and a feather. That memory came to your mind as you were struggling to get the tail that was holding tight and squeezing hard, until you felt that your bones were going to break, off your leg. You noticed the other tails making for you as you screamed in pain.

"How will I know when to use them?" you had asked.

"When the time comes, Princess, you will know," he had replied.

This time is as good as any, you thought, as you kicked the tail with your left feet and smiled as Vanotica screamed in pain. You did it two more times and she let go. With a cry of triumph, you stood up and started running towards the pouch, stretching your hand to grab it. It was just in sight when you felt Vanotica's tails encircle your waist and turn you around, lifting you in the air and slamming you back on the hard ground. That action seemed to drain the last drop of energy from your body. Your vision started drifting away as pain erupted from the left side of your head, which had taken much of the impact.

"Surefoot, wake up," you heard your mother cry. You heard Vanotica laughing triumphantly as you felt consciousness drain from you. You saw yourself being dragged into the pool of water and everything went dark as Vanotica swam into the depths of the pool to drown you.

𝔄𝔡𝔳𝔢𝔫𝔱𝔲𝔯𝔢 𝔈𝔫𝔡𝔰 𝔥𝔢𝔯𝔢.

Sorry, poor Game Player.

At least you had lots of water to drink!!!

You can return to Chapter 62 or start the game again from Chapter 1.

CHAPTER 6

Fight the Water Demon

❧❧❧❧❧❧❧ ❧❧❧❧❧❧❧

The water demon had just smashed the boat with its numerous hands and you narrowly missed dying by diving into the sea. You swam up to the surface and took a deep breath and looked around at the furious waves caused by the thrashing of the demon's multiple arms. Fragments of what was left of your boat were floating around you but the demon was nowhere in sight. The beast erupted in front of you with a terrifying, loud scream emanating from its seven mouths. It stretched its hands towards you as you swam across the sea, terrified and calculating your chances of survival.

There was no place to hide in this open sea and you had no boat to attempt to make an escape. The sea was unrelenting and the water demon was making its way towards you. You decided to fight it, even if it meant your inevitable death. You grabbed your knife that was held firmly by your waist belt and held it in your hand. Looking around desperately, you saw a large part of the boat floating close to you. You swam towards it and climbed on and tried to balance yourself on it, despite the persistent waves.

'Come on!" you growled at the water demon as it came closer, all fourteen red, bulging eyes trained on you while you stood on a part of the boat, with feet spread apart.

With a large scream and your knife held in front of you, you leaped on the huge demon. It growled in anger and its many hands tried to attack you as you climbed on its body, continuously stabbing it while you used the knife to propel yourself up its huge frame. You made your way close to its neck and it tried to shake you off its body, but you stubbornly held on. As you brought out your knife to stab it on the neck, it disappeared and you fell back into the sea.

It seemed your suspicions were right all along, although everything seemed so real at the time it was occurring. The water demon was also an illusion, just meant to frighten you. Your boat materialized back in the sea as though nothing had happened earlier. You swam back to your boat and climbed into it and observed that there were no signs of it being burnt or broken. The fire and the demon destroying the boat, were just illusions. With that revelation, you lay on the boat for a while to catch your breath. The journey was proving to be very challenging, testing you not just emotionally but physically and at the moment, you were spent.

After lying down at the bottom of the boat for a while, you noticed that the boat wasn't being rocked by the waves anymore. The waves and thunderstorm had come to a standstill and the silence made you alert and suspicious. You sat up when you noticed something that looked like mist rising lazily up from the water just ahead of your boat. The mist came together, forming a large face made of mist floating just above the sea right before you.

The face looked like that of an old man with a long beard and hair billowing in the wind, all white like the smoke. You had fought many creatures but wondered how you would fight a smoky face. He interrupted your thoughts as his deep voice rang out across the sea.

"I admire your skills, brave warrior princess. You're indeed very brave. I'm the god of the Sea of Illusion and I'll let you pass through my kingdom with no more tests coming your way. However, as you approach the Mountain of Deception, beware of impending danger."

He disappeared as quickly as he had come, giving you no time to even react and you noticed the mist, melting away, revealing a dark, imposing mountain up ahead.

The boat slowly drifted towards the shore and came to a grinding halt when it struck sand. You promptly came out, pulling the boat along the beach littered with sharp rocks and pebbles. You tied it securely against a protruding wooden stick you found by the side of the beach, since you would need it on your way back.

You picked up your bag from the boat and tied it securely around your waist. You proceeded to climb up the dark mountain and approached the entrance shaped like a skeleton head. Getting closer, the mountain entrance seemed to have two holes like eyes opening into a dark cave inside the mountain. You peered cautiously into the closest entrance to the cave on the left and it looked damp, dark and uninviting.

Will you go into the dark cave? Turn to Chapter 46.

Or

Will you think of a way to light a fire and illuminate the dark cave? Turn to Chapter 22.

~ SUREFOOT ~

CHAPTER 7

The Discus

A lot of time had been wasted already with the delays you experienced fighting Arturech in Ishbatech's kingdom. Now, the mischievous cloud fairy was sending you on another quest. The weapons that Mother Cloud and Mira had shown you appeared to be flimsy, compared with the type of beast that you were going to fight. It was a beast with seven fiery heads and hundreds of hands. A bow and arrow and a spear didn't seem like good choices of weaponry, in your opinion. A discus on the other hand was a round and very heavy object that, for some reason best known to the cloud mother, was also a weapon fit enough kill this beast. You made up your mind and picked the discus. You were initially almost weighed down with its weight.

You started familiarizing yourself with it, swinging it from side to side and you turned back to both of them who watching you quietly. The perfect selection of a weapon was necessary to kill the fiery beast so you could continue on your quest. Time was running out.

"I will take the discus," you said quickly.

"You're sure about that?" the cloud mother asked and you nodded affirmatively.

You just had to be smart about your plan to use the weapon you chose. You were in a hurry to leave the pink cloud and fulfill Mira's request for you to fight with the hydra. Although you were very reluctant to do this, you saw no other way of getting on with your quest.

"I guess we have our weapon. Thanks, Cloud Mother," Mira said, taking one more bite of cake and sipping on her tea. Then you both made your way out of the house after you placed the discus in your pouch.

Waiting patiently outside the pink cloud house was the flying horse that Ishbatech had given you and you climbed on it gratefully, patting its head. The cloud fairy stepped on her small cloud and floated away and led you up the sky towards the hydra's place of abode.

It started getting hotter as you flew up in the air and you could hear the heavy panting of your horse due to the strain of flying, reduction of oxygen with elevation and heat from the sun.

"Are we there yet?" you asked, as you started to sweat. You were worried that your horse might pass out soon.

"We are here now," she said, pointing ahead. Mira had taken you far above the clouds to a large, empty void-like space. *It seems as though there is no life here,* you thought to yourself. It seemed like you were all suspended in some weird way, like gravity was there and then not there and the horse was just floating, but it could control the direction it moved with its wings. The entire environment was grey and smoky and you looked down to see the clouds floating away underneath you. There was a dark, heavy feeling in the air. Your horse noticed it too and you could sense its tensed-up muscles. You had to start stroking the horse so it did not panic and cause you to fall. It was miles down to earth and you could not fly.

You noticed that Mira was beginning to act nervous. She started to wring her arms in fear as she floated slowly in front of you. You had almost forgotten how hot it was with the shock of finding yourself in this void-like state. Soon, you started feeling the intense heat and then you heard it. A loud, piercing shriek that made the horse want to turn back. It sounded like a sound of one voice and many voices at the same time. It was difficult to describe and it filled you with a sense of foreboding as the sound came from all around you. You just managed to keep the horse under control after it started turning this way and that in panic.

You managed to control the horse and Mira floated back to you.

"I wish you the best, Princess but I can't continue with you."

"Why?"

"My cloud will melt. Besides, the hydra will kill me on sight as it has done to all my sisters. Good luck," she said, quickly floating away in fear.

Watching Mira float away to the safety of the clouds until she was no longer visible, you tapped the horse and spoke to it gently, "It is just you and me, now. Do not be scared and do not let me down."

That last thought made you laugh as you clearly did not want the horse to let you fall down to certain death. It seemed strange that you could find humor in that statement, given the circumstances you were in now. The scream of the hydra came again from all sides and you took a deep breath and closed your eyes and listened. You tried to relax your mind and stay in tune with the silence that came in-between the shrieks of the hydra. Then the silence got shattered by the sound that came again. Then you isolated its source and realized it was coming from your left.

You urged the horse towards the sound of the noise and the heat grew more intense. The hydra drew its power from the sun, so it made sense that it would live in this hot zone. The sky in this zone was dark but suddenly became brighter as the hydra appeared from behind a dark cloud. Nothing prepared you for the sight of this monster that had several heads, all of its eyes locked on you with a look of pure hatred. Its fiery hands reached towards you, with flames pouring out of its red arms and body.

The beast appeared to be on fire but it wasn't. Its forked tongue slipped out of its several heads and it poured fire in your direction. You quickly pulled the reins, directing your horse away from the flames. It neighed in pain as a flame of fire went past and singed the tip of its right wing. You turned the horse around and made it fly over the beast. It seemed like you were above a large fire and the heat from the beast was so intense that you both were almost set on fire. The hydra shrieked, following your movements with its numerous eyes. Its hands stretched out towards you and the horse, with flames burning intensely in your direction.

You were a few feet away from the outstretched arms of the hydra and you spoke to the horse.

"Stay with me." You calmed the horse and it flew steadily in circles in that position at a safe distance above the hydra that was still reaching out to you.

You put your hands in your pouch by the side of the horse and retrieved the heavy disc. Looking down at the hydra that was very close now as it continued to reach out, you threw the discus down at the beast. The hydra saw it coming and sent a flame at it and you quickly flew out of the way. The discus was made of stone and so it didn't melt when it come in contact with the intense heat from the flames. It hit the beast hard on its chest and it roared in pain, letting out a high-pitched shriek that rang loud across the sky as it fell to its death.

You let out a shout of victory, patted your horse happily on the back and began your descent from the sky. As you approached the clouds, you saw Mira waiting, jumping from one cloud to the other in excitement. She floated towards you and jumping up to your horse, gave you a hug which you tiredly accepted.

"Thank you for saving us from the evil monster, the hydra." Mira chuckled with happiness.

You nodded wearily, sweating from heat and exhaustion, after the battle with the hydra. The cloud fairy noticed you were tired and urged you to retire with her to the pink cloud house and rest a while.

"The cloud mother will be happy to have you stay with us for a while. There are lots of sweets and treats and…"

"I have to continue with my quest," you interrupted and for a moment thought she was going into a mood again as she watched you.

"Alright brave warrior, you may pass," she said with a smile and a bow, jumped back on to her cloud and floated away.

You patted the tired horse and continued with your quest, flying away from Mira and the house in the clouds. Your mind was on the time spent so far on the quest and the health of your father. You wondered how your mother fared with the elders and if they had tried to convince everyone to hand over the staff to Nadum. The thoughts of happenings back home were almost making you to despair but you decided to focus on your quest.

You observed how the clouds parted as you watched the changing views from above, going past long fields of tall, green forest trees, and seas. You watched the white formation of sea gulls flying above the large bodies of water to mountainous regions and you knew you were very close to the mountain where your quest will end.

The Mountain of Lanogoza was very distinct from the other mountains in the area. From a distance it was shaped like the head of a skeleton. The base of it looked like a mouth wide open and frozen in horror. There were two holes at the top that looked like hollow eyes and you nudged the horse towards the base. The horse descended to the mountain and you came down and tied it securely by a tree close to the entrance of the cave. At least it would have some time to rest whilst you made your way inside the cave.

You entered the cave cautiously and after walking a while, your eyes got accustomed to the semi- darkness of the cave. Following a narrow passageway, you walked within this hollow mountain, and had no encounter with anyone except for rats crawling about the caves. The passageway opened up to a space with light pouring in from a large opening above it and your eyes were drawn to two stones sitting on a silver carpet.

Could one of these stones be the healing stone of Lanogoza? Why were they just lying there? Where was the ancient dragon that was the guardian of the stone?

This was too easy and you wondered if it was a trick by the guardian of the stone. You definitely had to pick one stone and you wondered which one you should take.

Will you pick one?

Turn to Chapter 73 or Chapter 14.

Good Luck!!!

CHAPTER 8

Jump behind the Rock

❧❧❧❧❧❧❧ ❧❧❧❧❧❧❧

You decided to jump behind a rock just in time as the figure passed by, looking for you. As the shadow of the figure slithered past, you cautiously peered through the crack of the rock and were shocked to see that figure was actually a woman.

You observed her as she moved slowly ahead, looking around for the supposed intruder in her abode. From the shadows it seemed like there were long, gnarly objects stretching out of her head and they moved in different directions, much like they were dancing. On closer look, you realized that there were snakes on her head. They slithered and coiled and made hissing sounds as their forked tongues slithered out and they also looked around like their mistress. Her feminine form ended on her waist. The second half of her was a long green tail that slithered back and forth as she checked every crevice, whilst holding a bow and arrow firmly in her grasp. One of the snakes on her head looked in your direction and hissed as you bent down quickly, holding your breath and listening for any sound that might mean that she was heading back in your direction.

Time seemed to stand still as you held your breath but after a long, scary silence, you heard her slither in the opposite direction to the cave. The movement from her tail made rasping sounds while the scales connected with the rough, pebbled floor of the cave. You had to change location when you saw her coming back in your direction.

You crawled away from the rock and thought about the creature that you just encountered. She used to be a woman called Medusa. Legend had it that she was once a very beautiful priestess of the goddess Athena. The priestesses usually took a vow of celibacy, but Medusa had broken it by having an affair with the god of the sea, Poseidon, which made Athena very angry. She had cursed Medusa, and transformed her to this hideous creature with snakes sticking out of her head. What was even worse about the curse was that anyone she looked at turned into stone. So, you had unknowingly made a wise choice by hiding behind the rock instead of waiting to find out who was approaching.

Scrambling quietly to the next rock, you peeked from the side and watched her approach, holding her bow and arrow. You were careful not to look directly at her and you were happy she wasn't staring in your direction. She held the bow and arrow steadily in front of her, the snakes were coiling wildly in the air and hissing in different directions. You turned back, trying to determine your next move to escape being caught.

You leaned against the huge boulder of a rock that you were hiding behind. Your gaze moved round the large cave, desperately looking for a way out. You noticed parts of skeletons scattered all over the floor of the cave and were disappointed that you had not noticed that the crunching sound you heard when you were walking was from skeletons littered about in the cave. Their appearance showed the untimely end of every adventurer that had made contact with Medusa. You hoped that your fate would be different from all those unfortunate souls that had met their end, either from Medusa's bow, or a bite from one of her numerous snakes.

As your eyes adjusted to the dim light of the cave, you noticed stones shaped like people, frozen in different postures of fear, with their mouths wide open and panic in their eyes. You had just discovered what would happen to anyone who stared directly into her eyes. There was no obvious exit from the cave without you coming out in the open so you both continued to play this hide and seek game. She must have sensed your presence but couldn't tell exactly where you were located and became very meticulous in her search.

Gratefully, there were lots of huge boulders of rocks in different sections of the cave and you narrowly avoided getting caught by moving from one rock to the other. Each time you moved two boulders ahead, once she turned to inspect a rock, you chose that time to move to the next rock.

You were fast running out of rocks to hide behind and soon, would have no other choice but to stand your ground and fight her. Just then, she turned around suddenly and saw you and quickly aimed, releasing her arrow with an angry growl. You heard the sound of its release and saw its flight in the air and instinctively dodged to the left. You felt it go really fast by your face with a sharp thwack sound, missing you by a hair's breath.

Medusa screamed in anger and frustration and you could hear the snakes hissing even more furiously as she slithered towards you, releasing arrows along the way. You started running zigzag down the cave to avoid being struck by the arrows that were missing you and getting Medusa even more frustrated. She didn't back down and it was a long way down the cave, with no visible end in sight.

You had to do something.

Will you try throwing your knife at her? With a good aim, the knife might hit her in one fatal blow. Turn to Chapter 88.

Or

Will you bring out the egg that the seer gave you? Turn to Chapter 103.

~ SUREFOOT ~

CHAPTER 9

Go East

⚜ ⚜

You rode East on your horse, Dusty, accompanied by the four warriors, including Nadum, to the outskirts of Omahi Village. The sound of the horses' hooves clumped on the soft earth, leaving a dusty trail along its path as you all rode in silence, caught

up in different thoughts. Your thoughts were full of your quest, the dangers that lay ahead and the conversation of the day before. You wondered what the warriors thought about your decision. It didn't take long for you to find out, as Nadum rode close to you and shouted out so you could hear him above the sound of the horses' hooves.

"You need to stop this madness," he yelled out.

"What madness?" you countered.

"This journey you are going on is certain death."

"Why are you so sure of that?" you asked, getting a bit irritated with his attitude. You despised the fact that he was not brave enough to go on the quest and now he was trying to dissuade you from going.

He laughed mockingly and replied, "Well, no one has ever returned from the quest. Where is Strongheart?"

"Strongheart is a braver man than you will ever be, so don't ever mention his name again," you said with a hiss, glancing sideways at him.

His face turned hard and he bit his lip, looking ahead. You all continued in silence until the group approached the outskirts of Omahi Village on the east side of the plain. The warriors were there to accompany you to the outskirts of the village and now you could see that the grassy plain ahead was filled with grass as far as the eyes could see. The men stopped their horses and you did the same and turned to them. You nodded at them deliberately, avoiding Nadum's angry stare.

They quietly bade you farewell and watched as you navigated your way down the grassy plain. The air was still and there was nothing in sight for miles, but grass. After what seemed like miles of riding with no other companion but trusty Dusty, you stopped by a solitary tree and led your horse to a nearby stream. The stream looked clear as it ran along brown pebbles. You and Dusty settled down for a long drink and you used the opportunity to fill up your water pouch.

Evening came by very quickly and you led your horse back to the tree and sat down to eat some roasted meat that your mother had placed in your food pouch the night before. As you brought out the meat, the spicy aroma of the roasted meat made your stomach growl in renewed hunger. You sank your teeth into it and chewed happily, but the neighing of Dusty distracted you before you heard the sound. The smell of the food had attracted a zepenter, which was a very large flying bird with the head of a snake, sharp fangs protruding from its wide mouth. Its sharp claws were pointing in your direction. You turned in desperation to pick up your spear, just as the creature descended, but Dusty galloped into its path, trying to protect you. The zepenter's sharp claws pierced the side of your horse and you could hear its bloodcurdling scream. Picking up your spear as the zepenter tore at your horse, you jumped high in the air and brought down the sharp metal point of your wooden spear in the middle of the zepenter's head. It let out a shrill screech and turned around, with the spear protruding from its head, its wings flapping slowly as life ebbed out of it. You stood, breathing shallowly as it slumped at your feet. You pulled out your spear, pierced it in the heart and it shuddered into a deathly pose.

"Dusty!" you screamed, running to your horse but the damage done by the zepenter was too much and he breathed his last in your arms. You sat beside your dead horse, too exhausted to move and eventually fell into a deep and troubled sleep.

The feeling came like a nudge and you woke up from your sleep and observed with alarm that your surroundings were different. This was not the grassy plain. You looked for the solitary tree but it was not there and the bodies of the zepenter and Dusty that lay not far from where you slept had disappeared. You were sitting on a sandy floor facing a huge stone gate that was resting on four massive pillars. Two stone images of ferocious-looking lions surrounded the gate on both sides and you stood up looking at their massive swollen faces, with huge stone fangs protruding from their mouths.

You felt someone watching you and turned your attention from the stone lions to the left of the gate where you sighted a tall, old man. His hair was all white and hung low to his shoulders and he wore a long white robe, with a staff in his hand. You stood up cautiously, not taking your eyes off him. You wondered how you got there. One moment, you lay beside the blood-soaked body of your horse with the dead carcass of a zepenter lying on the other side and the next moment, you found yourself here. This must be what the seer had warned you about.

Your thoughts were interrupted by the voice of the old man.

"Welcome, brave warrior, to the Land of Magic. I'm its keeper. To pass here, you must pass through me."

You approached him cautiously and watched as he stood up and leaned against his staff. You did not trust anyone that used magic and wondered what he meant by passing through him. This must indeed be the start of your quest to the Mountain of Lanogoza and you remembered what the seer said about not showing any sign of fear. The old man was watching your every move as you studied him quietly as well.

"How did I get here?" you asked.

He smiled quietly and leaning even further into his staff, said in a deep voice. "This is the land of magic and magic needs no explanation. I believe you are on a quest?"

You stood up tall and stared at him square in the face, ready to meet whatever challenge that came on your way towards the end goal. He nodded at you as if he had gotten your response from your body language.

"You need to pass through this gate to continue on your quest," he said, waving at the gate.

"How do I pass through the gate?" you asked.

He smiled at you this time and repeated what he had said earlier. 'Welcome, brave warrior, to the Land of Magic. I'm its keeper. To pass here, you must pass through me.'

After he made that statement, his smile slowly disappeared as he watched to see your response. *What does he mean by passing through him?* you thought to yourself.

Will you fight him, since he is a weak old man and you can easily defeat him? Turn to Chapter 54.

Will you try to walk in through him? Turn to Chapter 39.

Will you throw down the egg given to you by the seer? Turn to Chapter 89.

~ SUREFOOT ~

CHAPTER 10

Pick Something

✦✦✦✦✦✦✦✦ ✦✦✦✦✦✦✦✦

There was nothing wrong with helping yourself to this gold. It was so much that no one would notice that any piece was missing. After all, you did not plan on only enriching yourself and your family. Picking up a long, golden chain, you mused to yourself, *this chain will look good on the seer, as a gift.*

After a while you decided to drop the chain, as you thought it wasn't a wise thing to do. You turned around and were struck by how much gold there was in this chamber.

Pick something up, a voice in your head said.

No one will notice and no one will care, the voice in your head repeated.

Your eyes were immediately attracted to a beautiful gold amulet. You picked it up and a ring rolled to the floor. Bending down to pick the ring, you admired its glitter and smiled to yourself. There seemed to be so many attractive items to choose from and you did not know which one you should leave behind. A loud sound behind you made you spin around in alarm. You realized that you were not alone.

The eyes that watched you were cold and angry. The light from the gold reflected on the scales on his huge body, sending out a silvery sheen of halo around his face. He looked regal as he quietly moved across the gold littered around the room. A swish of his tail sent a chest of gold with its contents flying in all directions and you unconsciously dropped the chain and the ring.

It was the ancient dragon, the keeper of the healing stone in the Mountain of Lanogoza.

The ancient dragon stared at you and your previous excitement waned.

"You're a greedy princess, and you're not worthy of the stone," he said, in a voice that reverberated in the room. The walls actually shook with the strength of his anger, causing some of the gold to fall, making shattering sounds on the floor.

You opened your mouth to protest. How could you explain to the keeper of the stone that stealing was not in your nature? Your parents had brought you up to value your integrity above worldly riches. How could you explain what had come over you just now? There was no way the dragon would believe you. You had failed the integrity test.

Just as your mind was swirling in confusion, you noticed the dragon open his mouth and a ball of flame came in your direction. You flew to the side as it landed on the spot where you were. You turned to look at the mass of fire burning to the side and back to the dragon that stood even taller, his wings spread out as he opened his mouth and flames poured out of it. You ran to the side as he continued pouring flames out in an arch, closely following your trail.

The ancient dragon stood in your way. There was nowhere else to run to in the chamber of gold. The dragon had made sure that every exit area had been blocked by flames of fire. Maybe if you reasoned with him, then you might still find your way out of this dilemma.

"Please, I am on a quest to save my father," you pleaded, panting in exhaustion. The heat from the flames in the room was overwhelming.

"You should have thought of that before trying to steal from me," the dragon roared in anger as he opened his mouth and a ball of flame made its way towards you.

Adventure Ends Here.

Thief!!!

You can return to Chapter 45 or start the game again from Chapter 1.

~ SUREFOOT ~

CHAPTER 11

Wait and See

✦✦✦✦✦✦✦ ✦✦✦✦✦✦✦

The women tossed their baskets of beautiful flowers to the ground as they ran, blinded by fear. You were standing there but they all ignored you, as they ran in different directions screaming all the way to their various houses, which they shut behind them. You stood there, trying to guess what was happening. One moment they seemed happy and the next minute, the entire village of women was filled with chaos. You looked around in desperation to find the cause of their alarm. When the screams of panic intensified (which meant that whatever the danger was, it appeared to be getting closer), you decided to lie down in a section of the garden partially covered by flowers and leaves, to find out the cause of the panic.

You lay down among the flowers and miraculously managed to avoid getting trampled by the feet of hundreds of fleeing women. You finally saw the reason for their panic. There were figures in the sky, steadily advancing towards the village. They looked like small men flying with wings and to your alarm, they were gleefully shooting arrows at the fleeing women. The women screamed and fell to the ground all around as the arrows landed and you wondered why they were not fighting back. In Omahi Village the women were trained as warriors and went out along with the men to fight in defense of the village. These women were just running and trying to find places to hide from the unending attack and many were not successful in hiding away from the merciless hail of arrows that came after them.

The flying men were too many for you to attack in the women's defense, so you lay on the ground. You were beside yourself with anger, listening to the screams of death all around you. Sliding your arm to your back, you slowly brought out your pouch, placed it in front of you and pulled out your bow and arrow. Attaching an arrow carefully to the bow, you targeted one of the flying men and let go of the arrow. The arrow flew straight into the heart of the person you assumed was the leader of the flying men. His face registered his shock as the arrow pierced his heart and he fell from the sky with a dying scream. The other men looked at his falling form with surprise etched on all their faces. It seemed that no one from the village had ever put up a fight, as you could hear from their shouts of alarm.

"What's happening?" one of them screamed.

"It seems the arrow came from over there," someone else said and you crouched further into the bushes as more women ran past, luckily not trampling you in the process.

A scream of pain sounded just ahead of you and a lady fell just beside you. The lady's face was just inches from your own. Her brown eyes, filled with pain, stared at you unseeingly as blood gushed out of her open mouth. This was more than you could bear and you didn't understand why they would attack these seemingly helpless women.

You stood up with a scream, bow in hand and immediately started firing your arrows at the flying dwarf men, in quick succession. The suddenness of the attack caught them off balance and you succeeded in killing about four of them before they started evading your flying arrows by maneuvering away from them. Seeing that your arrows were not making much of an impact due to their evasive maneuvers, you brought out your spear and ran towards the line of the men flying in the air, still looking like they were in shock. One of them snapped out of it and fired an arrow at you. As it came towards you, you hit it aside easily with your spear, promptly bending down and simultaneously removing the knife out of your boots. You ran towards a hill and jumped on it, using it as a leverage to jump in the air. You threw your knife at the one that fired at you and the blow made him fall from the air. You went to him and pulled out the knife sticking out of his body and looked up at the group of men that had started descending, with their bows and arrows aimed at you.

The women had stopped running and were watching the scene in surprise. The ones still on the field stopped mid-stride and the ones in their houses were watching through the windows. To distract you, they started firing their arrows at the ladies still standing in the field. The women had stopped running when you started the counter attack and now with the resumed attacks, they were now running in your direction. The distraction that the flying men had caused, worked. You noticed too late that the flying men had a huge net which they quickly draped over you and they descended, hitting you from all sides. You tried to fight back but there were too many of them overpowering you. You lay back, panting weakly from all the blows that you had just received.

"What do we do with her?" one of them asked.

"Let's kill her," others chorused.

"No, wait! We have to take her to our master, Ishbatech. She's obviously not from here and he will know what to do with her," one of the flying men, that had now assumed leadership following the death of their leader, spoke.

You watched as one of them walked closer, hit you across the face with a wooden rod and everything went black.

The wind blowing against your face woke you up and you found out to your surprise that you were lying in the net and six of the men were holding it and flying with you. There were three on each side with a couple of them flying ahead and behind. You felt it was unwise to let them know you were awake as you could see that the ground was scattered with mountain peaks and the trees looked so little from the air. It would be a fall to certain death if they let you go, so you lay down and listened to them talk. From what you gathered, they were taking you to a place called Craggy Mountain to meet their master, Ishbatech.

They appeared to be descending as they approached a solitary mountain with an opening. The men flew in and joined hands to carry you into the depths of the caves. The walls of the caves had torches lined up to light the way. You observed that the walls had been smoothened and steps had been created on the floor of the cave to aid descent into the depths of the mountain. The dark, narrow cave passageway led to an open space and they flung you at the center of the space. You managed to get yourself out of the net and stood up, snarling. When you reached for your weapons stashed at your back pouch, you sadly realized that you had been disarmed when you passed out. The little men brought out their rods and started poking at you from all sides. As you made to attack them, you heard a calm, authoritative voice say, "stop."

You turned around to see a man you guessed was their master approaching from the other end of the large, empty space. Their master was a tall, slim man with a hard face. From the little information you were able to gather whilst in flight, you knew that he was a magician and had created all the flying creatures.

"Welcome to my abode," the magician addressed you.

"What do you want from me?" you yelled at him.

"I should rather ask, why you were at the Land of Beautiful Women. You aren't from there, right?"

"No. I am Princess Surefoot, searching for the healing stone on the Mountain of Lanogoza."

"Why did you attack my men?"

"Why were they killing helpless women?"

The magician laughed and his voice echoed against the walls of the hollow cave.

"It's no fault of theirs. They simply do my bidding. They are devout followers and listen to their master."

"I was fighting the wrong set of people, then."

He stared at you with an amused look on his face. "You want to fight me?"

"Yes, if only you will fight fair. It is easy to kill helpless women. Why do you not try someone that can fight back?"

"I could kill you with a snap of my fingers," he said dismissively.

"If you do not use your powers, I would not be that easy to kill," you replied coldly, watching his every step.

He stopped mid-stride and looked at you and smiled.

"You claim to be a warrior princess journeying to the Mountain of Lanogoza?" You nodded at him, wondering where the conversation was headed. "Prove it to me by fighting Arturech," he replied.

The flying dwarf men pushed someone towards you and you turned to look at a little blonde-haired boy, staring at you in alarm. You turned to look at Ishbatech in surprise.

"He is a mere child," you protested.

"Yes, I know," he said, staring at you with cold dark eyes, willing you to disobey him. You concluded that this magician must be heartless, sending his goons to kill innocent women and now directing you to fight a child who did not look older than ten years.

Will you fight the child? Turn to Chapter 25.

Or

Will you decide not to fight the innocent child? Turn to Chapter 81.

CHAPTER 12

The Left Door

✦✦✦✦✦✦✦ ✦✦✦✦✦✦✦

Looking at both doors left you very confused because they were exactly the same, from the chips on the wooden frames to the handles that looked rusted and rickety. Surely there was no reason for the old witch to lie to you. Besides, you intended to be very cautious when you went in. You decided to open the left door as she had advised. Turning the handle slowly, the door opened with a creak. Bright light almost blurred your vision since you were already used to the dimness of the cave and initially had to squint to get your bearing. Stepping through the door, you heard it slam shut and you turned around, but the door wasn't there anymore.

Instead, you saw a huge tree with broad leaves that stretched up to the blue sky. Turning around to observe your environment, you gasped in awe to see that you had stepped into a beautiful garden. There were roses, lilies and so many colors of flowers that you couldn't name and for a moment you were just enveloped in their beautiful flowery smells. The hag wasn't lying after all. This place was beautiful. You walked in the midst of blue, yellow and red daisies for a moment, distracted from your quest.

You saw a flower that looked like it was made of gold and ran to it and plucked it eagerly. You had never seen this plant before in all your journeys through the forests while on your quest.

"What sort of plant is this?" you wondered, as you held it in your hands. The golden, dusty pollen filtered through your palms and you watched it fall to the floor of the garden. Something caught your eyes. You saw a shoe poking out from the bed of the strange golden flower that you were holding. *What would anyone be doing here*, you wondered, as you dropped the flower and pulled out your knife, all the while moving cautiously in the direction of the shoe. On getting closer to the shoe, you saw it was still attached to a leg and your gaze travelled up to see a man sleeping with a sword held loosely in his palm. He was dressed in armored vest and his helmet lay on the floor beside him. *This has to be another adventurer*, you thought. *But he must be very lax as he was unaware of your presence.* You wondered how he had made it this far without dying, seeing that he was very uncaring about his safety. You held your knife in front of you in case he woke up startled and tried to attack. You gently kicked his leg but that didn't wake him up. Even when you became more vicious with your kicks, he still didn't wake up.

It was a very strange situation and you looked around, trying to understand what was happening. You noticed that there were many men and women, lying on the ground in different sleepWing positions. Suddenly, like a veil falling out of your eyes, you knew what had happened. You realized too late that you had been tricked. This was the famed Sleeping Garden. Tales had been told of a great place of beauty where adventure-loving men and women would rest for all eternity. No one knew the purpose for which it was created or who had created it. Up till that moment, the garden had been just a myth to you.

Turning around, you plotted your escape. But, with the door gone, you were trapped. You wandered around, confident that there had to be another way out of the garden. You were running through flowers unending, each step slower than the next, and you were finding it more and more difficult to move. Your senses were dulling and your breathing slowed down till you fell against a bed of pink flowers.

The last thing you saw was your mother's face and her voice urging you to wake up

You fell into a deep sleep.

Adventure Ends Here.

Sleep tight.

You can return to Chapter 65 or start the game again from Chapter 1.

~ SUREFOOT ~

CHAPTER 13

The Golden Door

⁂

The golden door was more attractive than the other one. The light shining from the door had an almost magnetic effect on you and you felt yourself impulsively swimming towards it. You placed your fishy-face on the door and it effortlessly swung open. As you swam in through the door, you observed the richness of the furniture, the plush cushions and lovely corals entwined across the chairs and tables, giving them a garden-rich beauty.

The singing was sounding closer but was different from the melancholic voice you heard earlier, whilst in the passageway. Approaching the sound, the face of the person behind the singing loomed closer and you watched a beautiful mermaid sitting, with her long, light greenish-blue scaly tail flapping, on a grey couch. She was combing her long, purple hair that fell over her slender shoulders, whilst singing and looking at a golden, hand-held mirror.

Her hair rolled and billowed in the water as she combed it and her voice was so sweet that you were quite enchanted. Soon the singing stopped when she noticed you through her mirror.

"How dare you?" she screamed, her face contorted in rage as she turned around to take a better look at you.

Startled by her anger and the fast change in her mood from singing to burning rage, you were unsure how to respond and tried to swim out of the room. You didn't want to bother her and had to continue on your quest. She screamed at you to stop and you ignored her and swam rapidly towards the door but found out that it refused to open, the way it did when you first came in. Turning around, you saw the mermaid floating towards you with a smile on her face.

"Who are you?' she asked.

You tried to explain, but she interrupted you with another question, 'How dare you intrude on my privacy?'

"I… I did not mean to impose," you said and she laughed mockingly.

"You don't mean to impose but here you are," she replied, using a fish tone to mimic your efforts to communicate with her.

"I think I should leave," you said and made to swim back to the door when you heard her shout.

"Stop."

For some reason you couldn't move around anymore, no matter how you tried to flex your tail muscles. The sound of her musical laughter came to you as she swam towards you, circled around for a while and suddenly stopped in front of you.

"Well…well…well, what do we have here?"

You didn't respond as you tried desperately to escape her hold. *What form of magic is this?* What was she using on you to prevent you from swimming?

"Oh my! This is interesting." She laughed, wringing her hands in delight. "I see you are not even from down here, are you? And not even truly a fish."

You stopped trying to escape as you wondered how she knew about your true form.

"Oh I see, you're wondering how I know? Well, I have powers here in this kingdom to see people for who they truly are. Besides, if you were truly from this parts you will know that it's not safe for you to come into my dwelling place." She snarled that last part, looking at you, her face almost dark in anger.

She snapped her finger and you could feel yourself stretching as the scales fell off your body. Your tail and fins stretched out and you could see your human self, legs and arms now appearing from what was previously a fish form.

"Oh, how delightful," she said laughing as you struggled to breath now that you were back to being yourself.

"It was nice to meet you but I must say goodbye now. I have other pressing matters to attend to," she said and with a swing of her tail, left the room.

You still couldn't leave that spot. Whatever magic she was using had transfixed you to that spot and you couldn't hold your breath for too long.

As your chest started to hurt and water rushed into your nostrils, the last thing you remembered was seeing the face of your mother. She had tears rolling down her face and her hands stretched out to you as she called your name.

"Surefoot," she whispered as you welcomed the cold blackness.

𝕬𝖉𝖛𝖊𝖓𝖙𝖚𝖗𝖊 𝕰𝖓𝖉𝖘 𝕳𝖊𝖗𝖊.

Try again, Game Player!

You can return to Chapter 41 or start the game again from Chapter 1.

CHAPTER 14

Pick the Stone

᭪᭪᭪᭪᭪᭪᭪ ᭪᭪᭪᭪᭪᭪

This was the purpose of your entire mission: You were here to get the healing stone back to Omahi Village in time to save your father. One of these stones had to be the healing stone and you had to find out which one. You walked to the stones and bent down to pull your small hunting knife from your boots, looking around cautiously, as you approached the silver carpet. The light from the opening in the cave shone on both stones and you studied them for a while. They both looked plain, dull and aged and you couldn't tell the difference just by looking at them.

You knelt down, reached out and picked one of them with your eyes closed. The stone felt cold to your touch. You secured the knife in your waist belt and felt the rough edges of the stone. Turning it around in your arms, you sighed with relief when nothing happened. You didn't know what you were expecting but the way you discovered the stone seemed too easy, in your opinion. You shrugged as you carefully placed the stone in your bag and turned towards the exit, to see the ancient dragon watching you.

Instinctively, your hand moved to the spear tied securely at your back. The dragon watched your move and shook his large head.

"There's no need for that. You have made a wise pick, brave princess."

You relaxed and your hand came back down. You listened as he continued to speak with his deep voice reverberating in the hollow cave.

"You're a brave warrior but are you wise? I need you to answer this question for me," the dragon said.

"What is your question, oh great ancient dragon?" you asked warily.

The dragon nodded and setting his steely gaze at you, began to speak.

"A young lad was placed before a hungry dragon that had starved for thousands of years. The lad was pitiable and cried to return to his parents but if the dragon spared him, he might not eat for the next thousands of years. What must the dragon do?"

This is indeed a dilemma, you thought. On one hand there was this child who was frightened and on the other hand, a very hungry dragon.

What will your answer be?

Will you advise the dragon to eat the lad? Turn to Chapter 97.

Will you advise the dragon not to eat the lad? Turn to Chapter 84.

CHAPTER 15

The Riddle

❧❧❧❧❧❧ ❧❧❧❧❧❧❧

On further prompting from the wizard, you walked towards the table and sat down reluctantly, quite worried about the riddle. You imagined the wizard smiling, since you saw the crinkle in his eyes. Looking around the cottage, you saw that it was clean and everything neatly in place. You were a bit curious about the life of this wizard and why his brother chose to live alone in the mountains. That thought soon faded from your mind when he cleared his throat as though to catch your attention and proceeded with his riddle.

To get to the Mountain of Lanogoza

One must do three things.

What are those things?

You pondered to yourself, *what is the answer?*

You looked at him and asked, "If I do not know the answer, what would happen?"

He smiled and you could see the amusement in his eyes as he said, "I will make sure that you don't get to the Mountain of Lanogoza, then."

This would require a lot of thought. What three things did you need to do to get to the mountain?

You would have to guess.

Turn to Chapter 29 or Chapter 43.

CHAPTER 16

Take It!

❀❀❀❀❀❀❀ ❀❀❀❀❀❀❀

The stone sat at the center of the empty room, plain and available for the taking and you gazed at it with longing. Right here within your grasp was the healing stone that would bring health to your father and good fortune to the Omahi tribe. The stone looked plain. How would you know if it was the magical stone?

The count had mentioned three magical stones and it was possible that the seer didn't know about the existence of the other two. You were excited and relieved that this opportunity had come to shorten your journey to the Mountain of Lanogoza and make you return home with the stone. You were also anxious to know why the count was rewarding you with this gift. You made up your mind. You would take the stone.

"Thank you, dear Count Dracula for this gift of the healing stone. You have been most kind," you said.

He nodded at you with a strange look in his eyes and indicated that you took the stone, which you eagerly did. Each step you took towards the stone, you moved more jubilantly than the next, as you thought of how many seas and mountains this singular act by the count had saved you from undertaking. At last, the stone was within your reach and you smiled as you reached out to pick it. As your finger touched the smooth surface of the stone, you felt something warm move up your arm and smiled.

Indeed this is the healing stone, you thought to yourself, still smiling as the warmth spread from your right arm to your shoulders and quickly with each moment, to every part of your body. A strange tingle started to spread from your fingers to all parts of your body and your hair started to rise up like you had static electricity running through you. Your smile faded into worry. Intense heat inflamed your hand and it started to move slowly, burning painfully across your hand that was still on the stone and you tried to let go but you couldn't.

"What is going on?" you screamed in alarm.

The heat was unbearable and you bit your lips to stop yourself from screaming. You struggled to move from the position you were in, while trying to get the stone, but you couldn't move an inch. The sound of dull footsteps made you turn to see Count Dracula walking towards you with both hands clasped behind his back and a look of disappointment on his face.

He paused in front of you as you struggled to free your hand that was pinned to the stone, while your body shook in spasms of pain. He raised his finger and touched your face, moving lazily and slowly to your neck.

"Poor princess, you're not ready for your quest, to be so deceived by me."

"I made a mistake…," you started, but he hushed you by putting his finger to your lips.

"Mistakes are costly in the game of life and death," he said with a smile and for the first time you noticed the sharp fangs at the sides of his mouth.

"No, please!" you screamed. The last thing you remembered was the cold look in his eyes, the feel of his sharp pangs biting down on your neck and your own deathly screams sounding down the hollow passageways of the empty castle

𝔄𝔡𝔳𝔢𝔫𝔱𝔲𝔯𝔢 𝔈𝔫𝔡𝔰 𝔥𝔢𝔯𝔢.

Sorry!!!

You can return to Chapter 94 or start the game again from Chapter 1.

~ SUREFOOT ~

CHAPTER 17

Fight the Skeletons

❧❧❧❧❧❧❧ ❧❧❧❧❧❧❧

There was no stopping now. The skeletons seemed hell bent on killing you. They were under the spell spun by their master, the wizard and there was no stopping them. You had to fight the skeletons, if you wanted to live. With that thought in mind, you went into the battle viciously, hacking away at the army of the undead that came at you. Soon, skulls and bony structures were flying in the air.

More and more of the skeleton armies attacked but you expertly avoided their swords, spinning around with your sword, jumping in flips to avoid their cuts, swiping them hard and breaking them apart. It was a long battle but soon all the skeletons were on the ground and you walked towards the wizard who had not moved from his sitting position, whilst the battle was on-going.

As you approached him with your spear ready in your hand, breathing hard with all the energy you had exerted in battle, a skeleton stood up behind you, raising a spear to stab you. You promptly turned around with a sharp swing of your spear, severing its skull from its body. You turned around

swiftly with your spear in your hand and pointed at the wizard.

The wizard stood up for the first time, acknowledging your presence by clapping his hand. He was old with sunken eyes and his long, white beard swayed with the wind blowing on the mountain.

"Well done, brave warrior. I tested your skills and you're worthy to pass. I'll help you cross the seven seas and mountains, but I need to change you into a form that will help you move easily through the seas or the mountains."

"What do you mean by changing me into a form, Wizard of Trasca?"

He smiled. "I'll simply change you into a form that will aid you in your journey. For example, a fish or a bird that can help you swim or fly easily."

"Why do you wish to help me?" you asked, skeptical of this wizard that had just tried to kill you, moments before.

"Brave warrior, you have passed my test. Not many adventurers have been able to do so, as you can see from the number of skeletons you just fought."

You looked around with sudden realization that all the skeletons were once adventurers like you and if you had been killed, you would have done the bidding of the wizard when the next adventurer came. A cold shudder passed through your frame as you felt sorry for the poor men and women that would never rest but keep on fighting, even in their death.

"You passed my test, so you have no need to be afraid," the wizard repeated, like he could read your mind.

"How do I change back to my real form?"

"Well, you can return to your form by simply wishing it, but be sure you don't wish it at a wrong time."

"When is a wrong time?"

"Enough questions, Warrior Princess. You need to pick a form."

You decided to give this a bit more thought. You needed a form that would help you travel easily.

What form will you change into?

Will you change into a bird? Turn to Chapter 50

Will you change into a fish? Turn to Chapter 30.

Will you change into a mountain wolf? Turn to Chapter 20.

~ SUREFOOT ~

CHAPTER 18

Into the Hole

⟿⟿⟿⟿ ⟵⟵⟵⟵

You have heard people say that to get the truth, then offer people no other choice but death and they will never lie. That saying hadn't failed you at any time as you were able to get the truth from enemy spies coming to raid Omahi Village. They always told the truth just before you eliminated them, so you could tell that the witch wasn't lying.

"Thank you, old witch," you said and made for the hole while the old hag counted her gold coins that you had traded with her. You cautiously stepped into the hole and saw a long stretch of passageway similar to where you had come from. The difference was that the walls had what seemed like molten lava sliding down them, giving the entire passage a reddish glow and the heat was oppressive. You had not gone far when you noticed the oppressive smell and wondered if it was magma floating down the walls and if that was the case then you were inhaling the distinct rotten-egg smell of sulphur.

You moved a step further and were suddenly spiraled into the air, screaming and kicking as you discovered that you were tied with ropes.

Hanging upside down, screaming and dangling from the ceiling, you realized too late that this was a trap. There was a niggling doubt at the back of your mind and you had pushed it behind you, having convinced yourself that the witch was telling the truth. You decided to cut the ropes off your legs but judging the distance to the ground, you knew you were going to land on your head. Whilst contemplating your escape options, you heard the sound of laughter and shuffling of feet and saw the old hag approaching with three other women. They all looked like the old witch, but you were able to identify her with the red boils sticking out of her large nose.

"You liar!" you screamed at her, making for her and the other women started giggling at your helpless state.

"I didn't lie," she shrieked.

"Let me down this minute. I paid you," you screamed in anger, wishing you had the opportunity to wring her neck until her eyeballs popped out.

"It wasn't enough. I want more," she replied, smiling evilly.

You decided to be smart about the situation, since she had the upper hand.

"Okay, I will give you whatever you want," you said,

The pressure from hanging upside down was beginning to have a negative impact on you as you felt the fluid draining from your legs to your head.

"Get me down from here," you managed to shout at her as your head felt heavy.

"I'm sorry, pretty one. But my sisters and I are hungry and you're going to be our food."

They came towards you, each holding a large club in her hands.

Adventure Ends Here.

I hope you taste good!!!

You can return to Chapter 33 or start the game again from Chapter 1.

~ SUREFOOT ~

CHAPTER 19

Don't Return the Key

❧❧❧❧❧❧❧ ❦❦❦❦❦❦❦

"Bring the key."

"We will help you."

"Yes, we will help you with your quest, so come on."

Something didn't seem right. You didn't trust those crafty witches and had no intention of giving them the key. What were the chances that they would keep to their end of the bargain and not kill you the minute they had a chance?

With that last thought, you promptly flew back into the hole, to depths where you could listen to them at a safe distance. They pleaded with you initially, their voices sounding very pleasant, making promises about gifts they would give you to aid your quest. When you stubbornly refused to budge, then the voices changed and became more demanding, more menacing and threatening to kill you.

You were not deterred by their threats as you felt that had been their plan all along. Somehow, you felt that this key would lead you somewhere.

"Come back here," they screamed.

"Give us our key, you wicked girl," another one snarled.

"Don't let her get away, Sister. Do something," one of them screamed.

You turned around just in time to see a flash of light and you swerved and it went past you, striking the inner side of the tree. Sparks and bark flew in every direction.

"Stop that, you imbecile."

"If you kill her, how do we get the key?"

"We will find someone else,' the one that tried to kill you screamed, as another flash went past you, this time ripping a large portion of the tree ahead of you and almost closing up the hole. The key flew out of your mouth as a result of the impact of the flash that had ripped into the side of the tree close to you. The key started rolling ahead of you and you snatched it up in your beak at the nick of time before it disappeared into a tiny hole.

You flapped your tiny wings even harder and kept on flying into the depths of the hole just as the opening collapsed. You could faintly hear the witch sisters shout in anger and start arguing amongst themselves. This act definitely sealed your fate, as there was no way you could go back the way you came. The only way out was to continue your descent into the dark underbelly of the tree and hope to find a way out. Flying deeper and deeper into the hole, you noticed to your surprise that the narrow tree passage had started widening and it led you to a wide, solid-looking oak door that appeared to be carved into the tree.

The door was shut, to your dismay and you hopped down and dropped the key from your beak in frustration, but in the course of lowering your head and looking up, **a** keyhole caught your eye. The shape of the keyhole looked eerily similar to that of the key you were carrying. You bent down to inspect the key and picked it up once again. You were right. This key in your beak was the right fit. There was just one problem: You couldn't open the door in your form as a bird. You remembered the conversation you had with the wizard.

"How do I turn back to my true form?" you had asked.

"By simply wishing it, but beware that you don't wish it at a wrong time," he warned.

You decided that there was no better time than now to change back to your true form.

You took a deep breath, as much as your little bird lungs could inhale and thought about changing to your true form. At first it seemed like nothing was happening but then your feathers stretched out and you stared in amazement as they started falling off and you could see your arms stretch out in front of you. You slammed against the wall of the tree with the force of the transformation and your bird body stretched in every direction as your legs, hair and human parts became what they used to be. Once again, you were yourself – Surefoot – a warrior princess and you lay down, spent and tired. There was no time to waste and although your arms were hurting from flying all that distance, progress had to be made. You had a quest that you intended to fulfill.

Standing up and flexing your muscles a bit, you turned the key in the lock and with a click, opened the door. It opened up to a massive, dark room, empty except for two wooden staircases, each leading up to what looked like a high mountain hidden by massive white clouds. A slight gush of cold wind blew against you, causing you to shudder, as it appeared that you had stepped into a gateway. This was the only explanation, indeed the very reason why the witches wanted the key. This was no ordinary key but a gateway into moving from one world to the next or taking you to the destination that you desired. The massive door swung shut behind you with a blast from that invisible heavy wind and you looked ahead, because there was certainly no going back now.

Shivering from the cold, you went to one of the stairs and started the long, winding climb up to the skies. The climb was long and tedious and you held on to the bamboo handles of the stairs as you were not certain how firm it was. Each step made you judge the safety of the stairs as they creaked and swayed slightly with each gust of the wind but you pressed on until it seemed like you could touch the sky. Finally, the stairs started winding down to a huge dark mountain with jagged peaks.

The stairs finally levelled off into a cave in the mountain and you moved quickly with renewed energy into the opening of the cave that had an ominous feel to it. The opening led into a dark, circular room and looking around, there was nothing in sight. Just as you had that thought, someone appeared at the far left of the room, startling you.

A pale-skinned old man, with long, white hair and long beards that rolled over his long, white robe, appeared before you. He held a cane in his left hand for support and beckoned at you.

With your experience in the course of this journey, you were very cautious and slowly bent down to feel the small blade tucked into your boots. You sighed with relief to find out that it was still there and cautiously made your way towards the old man.

"Who are you?" you asked, stopping just a few feet from the man.

"Welcome, Princess. You are at the base of the Mountain of Lanogoza. Pick a staircase to lead you to the healing stone. Your choice will seal your fate.

One staircase will lead you to the healing stone, the other to your doom."

"What staircase...?" you were going to ask but smiled as he pointed to your right and staircases appeared, leading up to the heights of the mountain. You could have sworn the staircases weren't there before. You had earlier just come into an empty room, then this man magically appeared and now the stairs.

"I see but you still have not told me who you are," you insisted.

He smiled and shook his head, leaning further into his stick as though he needed the support and said, "I'm Ludlum, keeper of the gateway to the mountains. I show myself only to those I favor. Not everyone gets to see me when they approach the base of the Mountain of Lanogoza."

"Why do you favor me, then?"
"You have a lot of questions that I'm afraid I can't answer."

"If I am favored, then why do you not show me the staircase that leads to the stone?"

"I'm afraid, you will have to figure that on your own," he replied, disappearing from sight and you turned back to look at both staircases.

You had to make your decision and continue with your quest.

You had to guess and pick the right staircase.

Turn to Chapter 45 or Chapter 56.

~ SUREFOOT ~

CHAPTER 20

A Mountain Wolf

﹡﹡﹡﹡﹡﹡ ﹡﹡﹡﹡﹡﹡

Your mind was already made up and you chose a mountain wolf. That was the only form you needed to navigate through this mountain and aid you easily on the journey to get the healing stone. He smiled at your choice and you expressed your concern about the transformation.

"How do I return to my true form?"

"Wise princess, indeed it is wise to ask such a question. You can return to your true form simply by wishing it," he said. He raised his hand and looked up at the sky, muttering strange incantations as the sky turned dark, then he pointed at you and you immediately transformed into a lithe, silvery grey wolf. Thanking the wizard, you set off on your journey, galloping down the mountain at top speed and navigating the sharp edges with expertise. You soon reached the other side of the mountain and continued slowly, this time down a rocky road.

You had reached a steep path when you saw a signboard, but your wolf eyes couldn't really read it that well. It seemed like it was the name of a nearby town and you felt that was a step in the right direction because you could seek help from the townspeople. Going in the direction the signboard indicated, you stumbled into a town, but you quickly observed that everywhere was deathly still.

A gust of wind went by, tossing a lone piece of paper across the street and it seemed like an ominous sign as the houses looked vacant and the streets were littered, like people suddenly abandoned their wares on the streets. There were no people moving around, no sounds of crying babies and your wolf senses detected danger. At the same time, with your keen sense of smell, you could smell fresh meat and your stomach rumbled as you realized that you were starving. The smell was coming from one of the houses ahead.

Will you get the fresh meat before looking around? Turn to Chapter 68.

Will you try to find out what the danger is? Turn to Chapter 49.

CHAPTER 21

Meet the Fairies

The soothing fairy music sailed through the air and you noticed about three of them singing to the tune. They danced and twirled with abandon and you almost wished you could join them in their celebration. They looked pretty harmless, like a friendly bunch of fairies and you decided to meet them. They could give you directions that would aid you in your quest. As you came out of your hiding place and gently advanced towards the clearing, their music slowly stopped with the singers *oohing* and *ahhing* in surprise. The abruptness of it all, bringing a sudden coldness to their festivity, made you want to assure them of your intention. They were probably afraid that you would eat them, since you were still in your wolf form.

"I am sorry, it is not my intention to alarm you all," you started out.

The fairies stopped chattering amongst themselves and kept on looking at you.

"I am Princess Surefoot, daughter of Chief Ziza and Queen Cohahi and I seek passage to the Mountain of Lanogoza."

One of them, a purple-haired fairy flew a little bit closer. "How is it that you're a wolf?" she inquired.

"A kind wizard transformed me to aid me in my quest. Can you please show me the way to the Mountain of Lanogoza?" you asked.

Her tiny wings glittered as she flew back to the others and they started talking in tiny, squeaky voices, chattering happily amongst themselves like chipmunks, turning to look at you whilst holding their animated conversation.

Your explanation must have reassured them as they all turned to you with a smile and the purple- haired fairy that had addressed you returned and said, "Yes, brave princess, indeed we shall show you the way."

She pointed at you and immediately the fur on your hands and entire body started to fold back in and you fell on the floor, transforming back to your true form.

You sat down on the floor of the soft grass, panting with the exertion of transformation.

"Thank you, but do I not need my wolf form for the rest of my journey?"

"No, you don't need that form for where you will be going, dear princess," she replied with a mischievous smile.

The others flew closer and you were suddenly aware of their huge numbers as they started to crowd around you in the clearing. You realized your mistake. These were no ordinary fairies. They were cannibal fairies and you could see their sharp teeth glittering in the daylight.

There was no need to run. You wouldn't get far without your wolf form.

Adventure Ends Here.

Don't be too trusting.

~ SUREFOOT ~

CHAPTER 22

Light the Fire

<figure>ornamental divider</figure>

It was dark in the cave, and you intended to light a fire, so you could see ahead. You didn't intend to hurt yourself by stumbling your way into a hole in the cave. The cave must have been inhabited by a human at some point, as you found a torch lying not far from its entrance. Also on the far left, you could see a small bowl that had oil, to light the torch with. You picked up the torch and placed it in the oily substance and with the help of a stone spark, you lit it up. Now with the benefit of the light, you made your way deeper into the cave.

The narrow passageway led into dark nothingness. You came across a bend in the cave and were just about to turn into it, when you heard a flying sound. Coming across the corner of the bend was a brood of flying cravuners. These birds had a putrid stench and all you could think of was pure evil. They were a group of blind vampire birds that could sense the heat that emanates from light and were heading straight for you. The heat your torch was emitting was like a beacon and they came at you from all sides. Screeching and pecking, their wings flapped in their thousands as they descended on you.

The smell was overwhelming and the cravuners descended in their numbers, pecking and biting you. You tried to use the torch to fight the birds but the wind generated by their flapping wings put the light off. The birds were pecking viciously at your head, pulling strands of hair and you screamed as you tried to get away, hitting at them in panic. You were trapped in the midst of a huge swirl of vampire birds that were biting huge chunks out of your body.

You couldn't fight back...

Adventures Ends Here, Game Player.

Be cautious next time!!!

CHAPTER 23

Fight the Snake

❧❧❧❧❧❧ ❧❧❧❧❧❧

The snake wrapped itself around your body and you could feel it tighten its grip as your wings fluttered helplessly in the air. Thoughts of your impending death raced through your head. This was not how it was supposed to end. You saw the face of your dying father, your mother's sad eyes and the smug look of Nadum, victoriously crowned the chief, because you didn't return with the healing stone.

No way! I will not allow this to happen, you thought to yourself, while the head of the snake inched closer as it wanted to start its meal. You started to peck at the snake's eyes which was something unexpected for a small bird to do and it threw the animal off balance. It tried to turn its head this way and that but you continued viscously pecking at it until it became blind and released you, falling from the high tree, to its death.

Immediately it let go, you soared into the sky, testing your wings to see if any of the bones in your feathers got broken as a result of the snake squeezing you. After gliding in the air a couple of times, you decided to continue on your journey. A lot of time had been wasted and you still had a long distance to go in your quest to find the healing stone. In your haste, you didn't notice the movement just by your side to the right. Something or someone was following you and had been tracking you for a while. A net covered you and as you fluttered around the net helplessly, you felt yourself being dragged fiercely and placed struggling, in a bag tied on a broomstick.

A loud crackling laugh sounded to your hearing as you hopped around in the bag, unable to get out and wondering where you were being taken to. Your abductor was one of the witches of the Western Sky and she had been pleasantly surprised to see you gliding in your bird form. She could, through her magic, see who you really were. She was excited to catch you and was in a hurry to take you home to her sisters. They definitely would have some use for you.

The sound of the rushing wind had stopped passing through your bird ears and you realized that you were no longer in the air. Someone snatched the bag, you could hear the dull thud of footsteps and the bag was set on the floor. You wondered what was going on and remained silent as you heard giggling and loud whispering from outside the bag.

A burst of light hit as the bag opened and your gaze fell on three female figures standing and regarding you while you stood in the cloth bag. You looked from the women to the surroundings and observed that you were in a dirty, old cottage. In the middle of the room stood a large cauldron and pots and pans were littered all over the house. Three brooms leaned against the side of the wall and your guess was confirmed that these women were witches.

The witches laughed in unison and you stopped inspecting your surroundings and looked at them. They were ugly with boils on their faces, long crooked noses and broken dirty teeth. They were dressed in long, black dresses, pointy shoes and a pointy black hat. One of them pointed a gnarly finger at you and you wondered what they planned to do with you.

'Brave warrior, we can tell that you have been transformed into this form by the Wizard of Trasca,' they chorused, laughing and revealing rotten teeth.

You had no idea what these witches intended to do with you and you looked around to see if there was a means of escape out of their den. At the same time the thought came to you to at least wait to find out what the witches wanted, but as their laughter built up and started resounding in the small cottage, all you could think of was how to escape. They started whispering amongst themselves again, nodding their heads vigorously in agreement. Somehow, you were certain that the conversation wasn't going to end well for you. They seemed so engrossed in their conversation and this seemed like a good opportunity to find your way out of the place.

Will you escape? Turn to Chapter 42.

Will you remain and find out what they want? Turn to Chapter 87.

~ SUREFOOT ~

CHAPTER 24

Go South

You decided to go south, accompanied by Nadum and the three warriors, to the outskirts of Omahi Village. The weight of the adventure began to dawn on you the more distance you put between yourselves and the land you had always called home. Your dark, long hair was blowing in the wind, while you were riding on Dusty who sailed effortlessly across the rocky paths along the way. Nadum drew closer on his horse and started conversation, to your irritation.

"You have to stop this madness," Nadum said.

"What madness?" you inquired, and the irritation could be heard in your voice.

"This quest is madness."

"I am on this quest to save my father, your chief."

Nadum was about to say something and you quickly interrupted him.

"I will not take advice from you at all, as I consider you a coward for not going on this quest."

Making that statement was dangerous. Nadum wasn't someone to be toyed with as the people and elders held him in great regard. It wouldn't do to make him an enemy, but you were very angry at his ambition to become chief at all costs.

The journey continued in strained silence after that last statement and you arrived at the outskirts of Omahi Village. You were to pass through Death Valley and this marked the point where the men were to return back home. You all stopped to say your final good byes. You avoided looking at Nadum's face after your argument and just nodded your thanks at the men who returned the nod and quietly headed back home.

After watching their receding images in the distance, you turned towards Death Valley. Somehow, you had to make it through there before nightfall. You had heard, while growing up, that it was unsafe to be at Death Valley at night. As you approached Death Valley, you noticed that the lush green buffalo grass gave way to dark, almost burnt earth. Even the soil appeared devoid of life. For as far as the eye could see, it was a large expanse of barren land. Dusty seemed reluctant to step into Death Valley, despite your prodding. He neighed and disobeyed your orders and didn't want to move forward. Eventually, you kicked him viciously and he lifted himself up and you fell off his back. It was a very strange action from your trusty horse and you quickly rolled, so he would not trample on you. He immediately trotted away, heading back in the direction you had just come from.

"Stupid horse," you muttered to yourself, picking up from the ground your bag of arrows and food that had fallen off the horse. You had no idea why he had behaved that way. Dusty had been a very reliable companion but it seemed this day was different.

As you made your way across it on foot, the ground seemed different. It wasn't hard and at the same time not soft. You felt a sensation of someone walking in the air. It appeared like your strength was being sucked away slowly. The air appeared to be still and there was nothing living moving around for miles, apart from a scattering of trees without leaves.

You looked up to see a gathering of dark clouds, as if it would rain any moment and you looked around for shelter. You uttered a sigh of relief when you saw what looked like a cave a short distance ahead. You reached the cave just in time, for the rain started falling in huge pellets with thunder and flashes of lightning. You dropped your bags and rubbed your aching shoulders slowly and turned around to examine the cave. You thought there was a hissing sound, but it could easily have been the sound of the rain. The sound appeared closer this time and something brushed past your head. You jumped, quickly bringing out your dagger that you had placed in your pouch. You looked around, straining your eyes in the dark cave and then you saw it hanging above the ceiling of the cave.

A huge snake descended, hissing and you struck it between the eyes. It recoiled and came back in anger. With your fast reflexes kicking in, your heart started to beat in anticipation of the fight that had begun. You side-stepped to the left just as the snake dived at you and simultaneously slashed at its neck with your right hand, making an upward to downward arc with your dagger, and watched as its head rolled out in front of you.

Something struck you from behind and hit the dagger from your hand. You fell face forward and tried to get up as more snakes slithered towards you. The whole place was filled with them.

You remembered the seer telling you to go east, west and north, but he never mentioned south. Your realization came too late, as a forked tongue was the last thing you saw.

𝕬𝖉𝖛𝖊𝖓𝖙𝖚𝖗𝖊 𝕰𝖓𝖉𝖘 𝕳𝖊𝖗𝖊.

Remember to follow instructions.

You can return to Chapter 109 or start the game again from Chapter 1.

CHAPTER 25

Fight the Child

The entire situation was sickening but there was something in Ishbatech's eyes that you couldn't place. Why was he asking you to fight this innocent child? Was it for sport or was he just a sick man?

You had the feeling that the magician wouldn't let you go if you decided not to fight the boy. You decided to go ahead and fight him, but with a plan not to hurt him in the process. You bent down and picked up your spear that the flying men had tossed in your direction, held it with a firm grip on the side and turned to look at the little boy who looked as though he was about to cry. Your resolve immediately faded and you turned once more to protest.

In the split second that you looked towards the magician, Arturech quickly picked up a sword from one of the winged men and ran in your direction. You swerved to your right by reflex and the sword went by your face with a fatal swoop. The brush of air from the movement of the sword on your face made the hairs on your hand to stand in fear. You would most certainly have been killed by this innocent child. You just turned around in time and lifted your spear to shield the blow from the boy who was attacking in fury. Again, and again, his sword made contact with your spear as you defended yourself from his attacks and stuck by your resolve not to hurt him. He turned and tried to cut your legs but you jumped in the air just as he swung his sword under you, narrowly missing your feet, whilst you simultaneously used the wooden end of your spear to hit him on the back. The winged men started laughing as Arturech stood up angrily, rubbing at the back where you had hit him. Ishbatech looked in their direction and they immediately became quiet.

Arturech stared at you angrily and lifted his sword, holding it in front of him expertly with both hands and you bent in an attack pose with your spear pointed at him. He screamed, his blue eyes blazing in fury and he seemed to fly in the air, bringing his sword down with force. Both weapons came in contact with the spear, breaking in two under the force. He smiled as he came at you with his sword in the air, but you immediately threw the sharp end of the broken spear at him and the spear struck him in the stomach. The winged men moaned in disappointment as the boy stopped mid-stride, held the side of the weapon protruding from his stomach and fell to the ground.

You turned back to the magician with tears on your face.

"I did not mean to do this. Why did you make me do this?" you screamed at him.

He chuckled at your sadness and nodded for you to look at the child.

You turned around but the innocent little boy wasn't there anymore. In fact, whatever you fought wasn't a human. The dead child had transformed into a long snake and you moved away in shock, when you realized the snake was dead.

Ishbatech smiled at you.

"I'm a magician, remember? You were not fighting an innocent child. Arturech most certainly would have killed you if you didn't fight back."

You were still trying to come to terms with what had just happened when he continued. "You are brave, young princess, but are you wise? I intend to test you by asking you a riddle. Make sure you don't give me the wrong answer."

Your heart beat in anticipation as he told you the riddle.

I destroy you.

No matter what you are.

Be you rich or poor.

Young or old.

What am I?

He smiled at you as you thought very hard. Three answers came to your mind while you pondered.

Is it success? Turn to Chapter 101.

Is it failure? Turn to Chapter 32.

Is it death? Turn to Chapter 86.

~ SUREFOOT ~

#

The women jostled their way across the field and you were pushed left and right as you stood rigid in the middle of the field. It seemed like you were frozen at the spot, confused about the pandemonium in the once beautiful and almost serene garden. There seemed to be no danger in sight but there was something causing the women to run, so you decided to follow them. You didn't know where danger was coming from and you were quite tired of fighting.

The women raced with fear etched on their faces, hair blowing in the wind and you followed a woman who was holding the hand of another younger lady. As they approached their door and pushed it open, you ran behind them and they turned to close it.

"No! Go away," the woman screamed at you.

"Please help me."

She shut the door in your face and you ran to the porch of the next house where you saw someone looking out of the window. Banging on the door, the lady's face peered through her window.

"Leave my porch this minute," she screamed in fright.

"Please let me in."

"No, you're a stranger. You will bring attention to us. Go away," the lady replied, closing her window.

You turned around, exasperated, felt a sharp pain on your abdomen and looked down to see an arrow sticking out of it.

You didn't see who fired the arrow and you toppled down the porch stairs of the house you just tried to enter.

Adventure Ends Here.

Please, what is chasing you?

You can return to Chapter 83 or start the game again from Chapter 1.

CHAPTER 27

Fight the Lions

The lions advanced slowly, ready to hunt, exposing large saliva-drooping fangs in a snarl. You were tired but had to survive, so you pulled out your knife and braced for the impact of the imminent attack by the ferocious-looking lions.

The attack came swiftly with one lion diving at you and you rolled out of the way, cutting it on the side in mid-air. The lion landed on the floor writhing and growling. Your blade had made contact with its jugular and it was bleeding out. The other one caught you off-guard in the short time you spent assessing your damage on the other lion and you both rolled on the floor of the dark cave, with the knife knocked out of your hand in the process.

It lunged at your head, its rancid breath on your face and fangs inches from the throbbing pulse on your neck. You held its face with both hands and struggled to keep it from snapping your face off. You pushed the beast that was on top of you with all your might, using your knees. With a scream, you exerted a lot of force and the beast was thrown off to a corner of the cave. But your joy was short-lived, as it came back immediately with a vicious growl. You reached out for your knife but it tore at your arm and you heard your voice screaming in pain. It sounded like someone else far away as the dull pain wracked through your body and you struggled not to lose consciousness.

The lion approached slowly, as you lay with a bleeding arm. It sprang at you and gave out a large wail in pain as your knife found its way to its heart. You had only one chance to hit the right spot and you did that with your other good arm. Then you lay back on the floor of the cave, panting in relief and exhaustion, as the animal shuddered and lay dead at your feet.

The iron bars leading to the dungeon opened. You stood up abruptly and steadied yourself, holding the knife with your uninjured arm. You were ready to fight whoever was coming in to attack you but instead, you heard the king's voice.

"Stop, Princess! We believe you. You passed our test. Now, you can pass through our kingdom."

You wondered why he suddenly believed you were a princess. Then you swooned, as you were losing blood. The next set of events happened very fast but you remember hearing the king say that he now believed your story about being a warrior princess from a faraway land. He added that only a highly-trained person with great fighting skills could have defeated his lions and who else but one of royal blood that had the best training in the art of self-defense.

The king ordered his servants to lead you out of the cave on account of the injuries you sustained during the fight. He ensured that they took care of you and nursed you back to health.

It would have taken a couple of weeks for your arm to be usable in any form of combat. Thankfully, the cut made by the lion was not as deep as you thought. Since it was treated immediately with a special healing balm, you healed pretty fast, which was surprising to the king, who kept coming to check on your progress. The healing balm was indeed magical but you also had very good genes that fast-tracked the process as well. Either that or the thoughts of your father lying in that feverish state kept coming to your mind, pushing you to get better and get on with your quest.

You wondered why the king suddenly started treating you with so much kindness. You found out why one night, when he came to the room that was assigned to you in the palace and finally stated his intentions.

He sat on a fancy-looking wooden chair just across your bed and looking at you somberly, said "Princess Surefoot, I'm glad you're getting better."

"Thank you, your highness," you whispered as you lay on a large cotton bed with your head elevated on two fluffy white pillows.

"Yet, I'm not happy that you're getting better, as it means you will leave me soon."

You were truly puzzled by that statement and responded cautiously "I would have thought that your highness will be in a hurry to see me leave his kingdom. I mean, you were initially skeptical about my presence here."

"Indeed, I was initially, because I didn't believe who you said you were, but you have proven yourself," he said, smiling.

He leaned closer and with a whisper, said, "I want you to stay and become my mistress. With your strength, wisdom and may I say beauty, we can win so many battles and kingdoms together."

His offer did not appeal to you but you had to be wise about your response as you couldn't tell what could trigger him into sending you back to the dungeon.

"That is a very generous offer, your highness, but I have to continue on my quest to save my father and my village."

He looked at you steadily for a while and then his eyes brightened as he responded, slapping his hands on his fat thighs and getting up with a laugh. "Alright then, Princess. My offer still stands, if you change your mind."

With that, he walked out of the room briskly without giving you time to respond and leaving you to wonder about his strange change of demeanor. A day after that strange conversation, you were ready to leave. The king was generous enough to give you a boat that he ensured was equipped with all the provisions you needed for the journey. At the king's orders, the soldiers had returned your pouch with the egg and feather the seer had given you, along with your weapons.

The king smiled at you as you both stood on the shore with his soldiers at a fair distance. He described you as a young, strong and beautiful warrior and went ahead to give you some advice.

With a solemn look, he turned to you and started, "In order for you to pass through this kingdom to get the healing stone, you have to cross the Sea of Illusion." You nodded and he continued, "This journey is fraught with danger. Are you sure you want to continue?"

"Thank you for your concern, but I have to continue on my quest and I will not be deterred by whatever dangers come my way."

He smiled and said, "Brave warrior, I hope you find what you are looking for." And with that, he waved his hand towards the boat. You nodded your thanks at him, walked towards the boat and entered it. With a final look back at the king, his soldiers and the view of the colorful roofs of the grand houses in the background, you turned and continued on your way.

The journey began with no surprises and the sea was unusually calm, until you made your way past some rocks jutting out in the middle of the sea. A fog appeared slowly, blinding your vision and you couldn't see ahead of you.

The boat started to rock as tumultuous waves arose, tossing your tiny boat, which seemed so tiny in the midst of the entire body of water that appeared to stretch out, unending. As the waves violently shook the boat back and forth, you held on to the side of the boat in fear. A huge wave started to build up and rose right in front of your boat. As the massive wave rose and the boat headed towards it, you knew the strength of this wave could completely wreck your boat when it eventually fell.

What will be your next move?

Will you jump into the sea and swim to save your life? Turn to Chapter 2.

Will you stay on the boat and defy the waves? Turn to Chapter 47.

~ SUREFOOT ~

CHAPTER 28

The Glowing Hole

⁂

The witches and their request could wait. You had to find out what was glowing in that section of the hole, leading away from the dark hole that appeared to descend even further into the huge oak tree. The witches were awaiting your return outside the hole, and had no idea you were going to take a detour. There could be gold there and if you were lucky to find it, then not only would you fulfil your quest, but you could become very rich in the process. The hole glowed even more as you approached it and you flew even faster with growing anticipation of what you hoped to find. The hole continued to narrow as you approached it and it started getting hotter, but you didn't want to turn back. Eventually, you approached the hole and noticed that the glow was like a flame.

It looked like liquid flames were pouring from the sides of the hole and dripping down. It seemed like a fire was about to start from within the tree, but mysteriously it just circulated around the hole. You stared at the flames in wonder, then you noticed that you were staring at two yellow eyes, glinting evilly in the dark.

You had just come face to face with a Gesanti. They were glowing demons that lived deep in the bellies of huge, old trees. They fed on the sap of the trees and melted everything else that they came across, except the trees that they lived in. You realized your mistake and tried to turn back, but the demon snarled at you, stopping you in midflight.

"You dare come into my kingdom?"

"No, I was just passing through," you squeaked.

"You're a traveler in bird form?" the Gesanti hissed angrily.

"Yes, I am an innocent traveler who means no harm. I was just passing by," you repeated, but it laughed, with fire pouring out of its mouth.

"You were not just passing by. What did you think you would find in this hole?"

Your silence made it laugh even louder and more fire poured out of its mouth but surprisingly, like the ones burning in the hole, it didn't burn the tree from within.

"I am sorry. I will return to where I came from." You turned to fly away, but its next words chilled you.

"You're greedy. You expected to find gold. You're not worthy to be here," it snarled and you turned around as it opened its mouth and directed fire towards you.

Flying out of the way, the flames rushed past you, the heat almost setting you on fire. You turned around and started flying away but the demon gave chase, spewing fire towards you. Screaming for the witches to help, you flew towards the hole, narrowly avoiding the fire that was aimed at you. You were getting close to the entrance and you could see the witches peering in as they heard you scream.

"Help… help," you yelled. You were relieved to see that the witches had noticed you coming up.

"Do you have the key?" one of them asked.

"No! Help…," you screamed as you started to emerge from the cave.

The witches looked disappointed. They watched coldly and did not attempt to intervene as the demon emerged behind you, giving chase. Its last fiery discharge caught you this time and you burst into flames.

Adventure Ends Here.

Curiosity kills the cat.

You can return to Chapter 52 or start the game again from Chapter 1.

~ SUREFOOT ~

CHAPTER 29

The Wizard

To get to the Mountain of Lanogoza,

One must do three things.

What are the things?

What did you do to get ready for this journey, you thought for a while and nothing came to your mind. As time passed, the wizard's patience began to wane and he slowly stood up.

"Wait…wait," you pleaded.

"I have been waiting."

"I need more time," you pleaded.

"If you have waited this long to give me an answer, then…"

"Please just give me more time," you pleaded again, staring at his deep, dark eyes peering at you through bushy brows.

As more minutes ticked by, the wizard could see that you were struggling and his countenance changed. Darkness spread from behind him, heading towards you, hands like shadows reaching out to you.

'I'm sorry, Princess, but you can't continue your journey,' he said in an angry voice.

You turned to run, but you barely made it out of the door before he turned you into a frog. Walking towards you, he picked you up and promptly put you in a large, glass jar.

𝔄𝔡𝔳𝔢𝔫𝔱𝔲𝔯𝔢 𝔈𝔫𝔡𝔰 𝔥𝔢𝔯𝔢.

Sorry!!

You can return to Chapter 15 or start the game again from Chapter 1.

CHAPTER 30

A Fish

The Wizard of Trasca waited patiently for your decision. You thought really hard and decided you would change into a fish. He nodded and said, 'You will be able to swim through the seas, but you will have to walk on the mountains.'

You agreed and he indicated for you to follow him. He walked you to the edge of the mountain, where he pushed you off the edge. The wind rushed through your ears as you fell, tumbling in the air with your hands and legs flailing helplessly. You knew that you shouldn't have trusted that wizard, as he had tricked you into certain death.

You screamed as you looked up at his form fading slowly away, like smoke in the distance. Just as you were about to crash to the ground, you appeared on a shore overlooking a large sea.

The wizard appeared again, floating over the water while you looked up at him.

"I thought..."

"You thought I was going to kill you?" he asked, amused.

You nodded your head, confused about what had just happened. One moment you were falling to your death and now you were standing in front of a sea.

"It's magic, difficult to understand and I keep my word," the wizard said, reading your mind easily. Having said that, he continued, 'This is the Sea of Eternity. Beware of the dangers, Princess,' he cautioned, waving his hand at you. You were immediately transformed into a fish, flopping helplessly on the sea shore until he picked you up and placed you in the sea

You were gasping for breath while flopping on the shore and the minute you got into the water, oxygen flooded through your gills and you started swimming around excitedly. The wizard appeared in the water and you turned to him.

"Be careful, brave warrior. I wish you the best in your quest."

You mouthed a *thank you* and bubbles of water escaped from your mouth in the process, to your amusement. The wizard disappeared, this time for good.

You swarm about, excited about your new form and glanced down at your colorful orange fins flapping them and testing the speed with which you cut through the sea floor. The beauty underwater captivated you – from the crystal-clear light blue color to the colorful school of fishes and the green plant life that gave it an underwater forest feel. The beauty of your environment almost made you forget your quest but as you continued on your way, a school of fierce warrior fishes spotted you and soon, they had you surrounded. They had never seen your kind before and tasked themselves with knowing every single fish in the area.

'Who are you?' they asked.

"Why do you ask?" you answered boldly.

~ A FISH ~

"This is our territory, and you must give us reason to let you pass," they replied, swimming around you and spoiling for a fight. There was no need to aggravate them further, so you replied.

"I am just a fish journeying through the sea."

They looked at you and laughed.

"Of course, you are just a fish, we can see that. So are we all, just fishes," they said, laughing and you joined them because indeed your response was hilarious, but they stopped abruptly, causing you to stop laughing as well.

The leader, called Sunta, said, "I need to be sure you are what you claim to be. What do we fishes fear the most in the Sea of Eternity?

You had to give them an answer or else they would know you were an impostor.

Will you say a shark? Turn to Chapter 60.

Will you say that you don't know, and decide to fight to pass? Turn to Chapter 75.

~ SUREFOOT ~

CHAPTER 31

Her Request

The cloud fairy was evidently angry and it showed when the clouds began to gather and turn dark. Small flashes of lightning coursed through the sky with a small rumble of thunder and the horse neighed nervously.

'You can either kill the hydra and pass through my domain or go round and encounter the three witches of the Western Sky. Believe me, they are more cunning and wicked than I am,' she said, flaunting her bluish pink hair and floating away.

The witches of the Western Sky didn't sound like people you wanted to encounter and you decided to call her back.

'Come back, I…I will fight the hydra."

She stopped and turned around slowly on her cloud and smiled and the sky started to brighten up.

"I knew you will change your mind."

"Do I have a choice?" you asked, a little bit angry at this interference in your plans, which seemed to be going on well after leaving Ishbatech.

She twirled a strand of her hair in her fingers and smiled. "No, you don't have any other choice except you have plans to meet the witch sisters."

"I do not know about the witches …," you began to say and she interrupted quickly.

"You definitely don't want to meet them, I assure you," she said quietly.

Where do I find the hydra?' you asked.

'Come with me,' she said, turning around and floating ahead of you into the clouds. You nudged the horse and followed the mischievous fairy. The clouds parted ways as you approached them and you marveled at this small cloud fairy's power and ability to control them.

After a couple of hours of flying through the clouds, you approached a solitary house deep in the sky. The rectangular shaped house with a butterfly roof was all pink and made up of clouds. You were astounded and wondered if someone actually lived in it. That question in your mind was soon answered when she urged you to go in and you approached the door and alighted from your horse, stepping on the cloud steps leading to the large, circular door. As your legs touched the cloud step, you winced a bit in fear thinking you would fall through the clouds to your death, but to your surprise the cloud was solid.

You stretched your hand and turned the handle of the round knob on the door and it turned easily, opening up to a quaint cottage. Inside the room was cozy and there was a fireplace in a corner. The entire cottage as well as the furnishing were all pink. The large sofas had blankets thrown lazily on them. A cat was lying down on one of the couches and it looked at you in a disinterested manner as you approached. It jumped off the couch and sauntered away with its tail in the air, towards an old, pink woman with pink long hair that fell to the ground of the cloud house.

She had a kind smile on her face and stopped to give the cat a loving pat. Then she approached you and the cloud fairy that was no longer floating on a cloud but was now flying beside you with her silvery wings.

"Welcome back, Mira. I see you brought a guest this time."

"Yes, Mother Cloud," Mira, the cloud fairy responded. Two of you had not exchanged pleasantries before this time, so you were just getting to know her name.

Mother Cloud walked towards the fireplace and collected a large, black kettle that was boiling over the fire. Walking to a large table covered with a check pink and white silk table cloth laden with delicious-looking cakes on a large plate, she promptly started making tea. She slowly started cutting pieces of the cake into a large pink plate set up on the table. You all waited and watched her humming and setting up the tea and cakes on the table.

"So, who might our guest be?" Mother Cloud asked after a while and just as Mira was going to explain, you interrupted.

"I am Princess Surefoot, daughter and only child of Chief Ziza, leader of the Omahi tribe of warriors who control the Great Plains."

Mother Cloud paused while pouring out tea into three small, white teacups.

"I see, we are dealing with royalty here." She turned around, offering hot cups of tea to both of you. The cloud fairy promptly collected hers, warming her tiny fairy arms with the hot cup safely nestled in her fingers. The weather outside was cold, with all the storm that Mira had been summoning in anger.

You shook your head and rejected the steaming hot cup of tea that she had stretched out to you with a smile.

"You're sure, you don't need a hot cup to warm yourself?"

"No thank you very much," you replied.

"So, to what do I owe this visit?" Mother Cloud asked, looking pointedly at Mira who smiled mischievously, shrugging and sipping her tea. She floated to the large, well-laid table, set down her cup and promptly picked a slice of cake and placed into a large plate. After biting into it and chewing for a while, she turned to both of you.

"She's going to help me kill that hydra."

Mother Cloud looked at you in alarm and back at Mira.

"Did you tell her what the hydra is capable of doing?"

"I might have left out some details," Mira replied, turning around and picking her cup of tea.

Mother Cloud looked back at you resignedly and said, "Well that explains why she brought you to me in the first place. Here I was thinking you were both here for a friendly chat. It gets pretty lonely here in the clouds, with just my cat."

"That's not fair, Mother Cloud. I visit you often," Mira managed to say through a mouth full of cake.

"Yes, you do, when you're not on one of your naughty adventures. Half the time, I'm afraid that the hydra has gotten you, too."

Mira turned to her and smiled. "I know you're scared it will get me but I'm smarter than my brothers and sisters and now we have a warrior that can kill it."

"I wish her better luck than the others before her," Mother Cloud said quickly before Mira shot her a warning glance.

"Wait! There were others before me?" you asked, alarmed but they both ignored you.

Mother Cloud addressed you like she was just seeing you for the first time. "Welcome, brave warrior. In order to destroy the hydra, you need one of these weapons. Pick the most suitable one. Think wisely, because the hydra has seven fiery heads and hundreds of hands. If you pick the wrong weapon, you shall die at its hands. Only one of these weapons will defeat the beast and unfortunately, I can't choose the correct weapon for you, as I have no idea what weapon will actually kill the beast."

"Where are the weapons?" you calmly asked and she pointed at an empty corner. "I cannot see any weapons."

She smiled and nodded at the space and you looked back at the corner that was initially empty but now had three items lying by the wall. You moved closer to inspect them and turned back to her in surprise.

"Am I to select from only these items?"

"Yes," they both chorused, smiling at you.

The weapons lying by the wall were a bow and arrow, a spear and a discus. After their description of the hydra, it was amazing that they wanted you to use these weapons to defeat it.

"So, am I to pick only one weapon here and not to use my own weapon?"

"Yes, and if you use your own weapon, you will surely be killed by the hydra," Mother Cloud replied.

What will you do?

Will you choose the spear? Turn to Chapter 100.

~ SUREFOOT ~

Will you choose the discus? Turn to Chapter 7.

Will you choose the bow and arrow? Turn to Chapter 90.

CHAPTER 32

Failure

I destroy you.

No matter who you are.

Be you rich or poor.

Young or old.

What am I?

The answer seemed pretty obvious to you. What else could anyone, no matter the age or status, be afraid of, apart from failure? You had a victorious smile on your face as you said, "No matter someone's status, failure can affect you," you replied.

Ishbatech smiled at you.

"I'm sorry, pretty one, but you are wrong. I guess you're not as wise as you are brave," he said indicating to his winged men to come for you.

As the men approached you with their rods in hand, you were determined not to let them take you away easily. The first person reached out for you and you slammed your foot in his chest and he flew back, hitting three of the men and they toppled to the floor. The others rushed at you and started hitting you, but this time you fought back. You had no weapon in hand but you were using your hands and feet deftly, hitting until you got one of the winged creatures and wrested his rod from his hand. With that weapon, you started hitting them and warding off their attacks but they were coming in droves. You held up the rod in the air, as one of the men had fallen under your blows. Just as you were about to hit him with it, you felt a presence right behind you.

You swerved around in a hurry to find Ishbatech looking at you intensely and all of a sudden you were unable to move. The rod fell off your arms, you lost the ability to move and speak and fell on the floor. The magician smiled and asked his men to carry you away.

"Throw her into the heart of the mountain," he commanded, walking away.

They happily seized you as you had killed a lot of them already and they marched away, lifting you high in the air. You were unable to resist, due to some magic that Ishbatech must have used on you, but observed that they carried you even deeper into the depths of the mountain. As the passages got narrower and darker, the entire place appeared to be hotter.

Even the little men were muttering about the heat and talking amongst themselves that they couldn't wait to get out of there.

The heat was now very intense, the environment appeared smoky and the place exuded a sulphur-like smell. Your eyes widened in fear as they approached an open hole in the center of the cave where sparks of light flew up from the red-hot volcano bubbling underneath.

You tried unsuccessfully to move or plead with them. They tossed you into the fiery flames.

Adventure Ends Here.

Sorry, that must have hurt!

You can return to Chapter 25 or start the game again from Chapter 1.

~ SUREFOOT ~

CHAPTER 33

Hide and See

❧❧❧❧❧❧ ❧❧❧❧❧❧

You hid behind a rock just as a giant, ugly-looking ogre passed by and you let out a sigh of relief. Thank goodness, you were fast, because ogres usually ate humans. Making sure that there was no one coming up ahead, you made your way down the underground passage. The walls of the passageway got narrower and darker as you went down. After a while, your eyes got used to the dim light of the passageway. You casually glanced at the walls and noticed some strange markings on it.

Stopping to observe the markings, you saw that the figures were images of adventurers who were sprawled in different throes of death. You felt a chill go through your body and decided not to look at the walls again as you went down. The chill you felt earlier disappeared and you went deeper into the hole which got warmer.

The passage opened up to a smaller cavern and you observed a figure, dressed in a grey shapeless robe and bent over a large, black pot, cooking. You approached the person and pressed your knife against the person's back. The figure, a toothless, aging woman, turned round, smiling. She had a large nose with two large, red boils on it and immediately you could tell that she was a witch. She confirmed that with her next words.

"Brave warrior, I was expecting you," she said.

"How come?" you asked.

"I saw you in my pot," she said, stirring the contents of the large, bubbling black pot and the bubbles floated to the top of the pot, releasing thick smoke that rose up to the ceiling. You wrinkled your nose at the offensive smell that came out from the pot. Somehow, you didn't want to know what she was cooking in that pot.

"You seek to find the Mountain of Lanogoza?' she asked coming closer, releasing **a** toothless grin.

"Yes. Can you show me the way?" you asked, taking down your knife. She didn't seem harmful, at least from your initial assessment of her.

"Of course, I can, for that chain around your neck," she said, reaching for your neck.

"No! Ask for something else, old witch," you replied, avoiding her touch. There was no way you intended to hand over the necklace that was a gift from your mother. It was a family heirloom that had been passed down through several generations and no old hag was going to take it away without a fight.

"Okay, if you won't give me the necklace, then let me have the feather the seer gave you," she said in her raspy voice.

You were surprised at first that she knew about the feather, then you remembered that she was a witch.

"Ask for something else."

"I want the feather," she insisted.

"Well, you will not have it," you replied. The seer never told you what the items were for but you were sure that handing them over to a witch in the depths of a cave was not wise.

"How do you intend to pay me, then?" she asked, looking disappointed.

"I will give you two gold coins."

"Four," she interrupted.

"Three," you insisted

"Deal," she replied, smiling and stretching out her hand for the gold coins.

She eyed you as you brought out your pouch, counted the coins and placed them in her wrinkled, hard, palms. Excited, she examined the coins, turning them in her gnarly hands and holding them up to the light.

"Show me the way, old woman," you interrupted. She looked up at you with a glint in her eyes and pointed at a large hole on the left side of the cavern. Interestingly, you had not noticed the hole and it looked narrower and darker than the passage you had just emerged from.

"That's the way," she said interrupting your thoughts and you turned back to look at her.

"Are you sure?" you asked.

"Yes." She nodded, still looking at her coins. You quickly pulled out your knife and held it against her wrinkly neck.

"You had better not lead me down a wrong track and waste my time, because if you do, I would come back and slit your throat."

The old hag's eyes widened in fear. She raised both hands in the air and whispered in her raspy voice, "I swear on my dead mother, that's the way."

You let her go and sheathed your knife into the pouch and turned towards the hole.

Will you go? Turn to Chapter 18.

Will you refuse to go? Turn to Chapter 65.

CHAPTER 34

The Snake

⋙⋙⋙ ⋘⋘⋘

The snake's sharp fangs were exposed and descending to your feathery skin. There was no way that you were going to come to this horrible end. There had to be something that you could do to avoid being eaten by the snake. As its large head swung in your direction and its forked tongue slid out, you could see the face of your father as he lay in his hut.

In your mind's eye, your father looked just the way he had the day you left him. His lips looked parched and dry as he mumbled incoherent words.

There was no way your quest would come to such a tragic end. You could imagine what elder Maraba and the rest of the elders would do to your mother. If you did not return with the healing stone to save your father, she would be unceremoniously removed as acting leader of the Omahi tribe. You imagined the favored Nadum crowned the new chief of Omahi and the smug expression on his face as he sat on your father's throne.

"Nooooo," you screamed and your wings flapped in anger. Not only did you despise Nadum as a potential lover, you also despised him as the leader of the tribe. In your opinion, he wasn't fit to rule the brave tribe of warriors as he was a coward with no loyalty to his previous chief. He bore the marks of a traitor and you feared for the life of your mother after you were gone. You urged yourself to calm down and think of how you would survive this. Maybe the snake would understand if you tried speaking to it and you proceeded to do just that.

You spoke to the snake, trying to reason with it by explaining your mission and begging it to let you go. It didn't understand the gibberish you were speaking, and probably mistook the sounds you made as signs of fear.

The snake started wrapping itself around you and you knew that there was no way to make it understand that it had to let you go. Its tongue flitted out as it imagined feasting on you, which caused you to start pecking it angrily but you were a small bird and your actions incomparable to the snake that was bigger than you.

Your wings flapped in panic as its head lowered and it bit you, waiting for the poison to spread, numbing your senses before swallowing you.

Adventure Ends Here.

What's a healing stone to a hungry snake?

You can return to Chapter 44 or start the game again from Chapter 1.

CHAPTER 35

Help the Merman

⚘⚘⚘⚘⚘⚘⚘ ⚘⚘⚘⚘⚘⚘⚘

The merman looked so sad and his story was so heartbreaking that you immediately decided to help him. As the door opened, for an instant you wondered what you would do and quickly darted into a large wardrobe by the corner of the room. The mermaid queen burst into the room in a fury and from your hiding spot, you observed the altercation going on in the room. Her purple hair moved with each wave of the undercurrent and her blue eyes narrowed in an angry slit as she surveyed her husband and the room with her bluish- green tail splashing around angrily.

"Where is she?"

"Who are you looking for, dear?"

She laughed wickedly and continued, "Don't act all innocent with me. I'm looking for that princess who came in here in fish form." The king looked at his wife in surprise and she smiled wickedly, "You seem to forget that I have powers and I see and hear everything."

He put his head down and she continued "I thought you would have learnt your lesson by now after I got rid of that stupid, blonde ..." She didn't finish her comment as the king snarled and dove at her, pushing aside the furniture to grab her. For a moment it seemed that he might succeed in harming the queen who looked surprised at his attack. He probably had not done this before but she turned aside and he crashed past her. He looked enraged and charged at her with an infuriated look in his eyes. She smiled and pointed at him with her long, blue fingers and his eyes started to bulge as he remained transfixed on a spot, holding his neck. His face was turning blue and you knew that you had to do something, but couldn't in your fish form.

You remembered the conversation that you had with the Wizard of Trasca.

You can change back to your true form by simply wishing it but be careful you don't wish it at a wrong time.

There seems to be no better time than now, you thought to yourself as you wished to revert to your true form. You immediately started vibrating, your fins stretched out to your hands, the tail split into two and your legs emerged. Immediately, you realized that you couldn't breathe so you had to act fast. You pulled out the dagger from your boot and burst out of the wardrobe, distracting the queen that was focused on killing her husband. She turned her attention to you and pointed her long fingers at you. In that moment, the merman fell to the ground, trying to catch his breath. You swam away, not letting her point her fingers at you and she screamed in frustration, trailing your movements with her hands.

"Stay in one spot, you cowardly princess."

The merman had recovered and held her from behind. You, noticing the opportunity swam up to them as she struggled against the brute strength of her husband's grasp. Her eyes widened in fear as you approached. Finally, you were in front of the struggling couple and she opened her mouth to mutter spells that would have destroyed you in an instant. You were faster and sliced her neck with the knife in your hand and she died instantly, falling limply to the ocean floor without so much as a gasp. At that point, you started to gasp, having held your breath for long. The merman rushed to you, opened his mouth wide and a ball of water came out of it. He held it in his hand and placed it over your face. You were surprised to find that you could breathe in that ball of water that King Octan had made and you whispered your thanks to him.

"No, I should be the one thanking you for ridding me of that wicked Queen Ivrie. I guess you would want to be on your way now?' he asked and you nodded. He opened his right palm and in it shone a diamond ring. He walked up to you, the ring still in his palm. "Thank you so much. I'll restore my kingdom to the way it used to be before Queen Ivrie filled it with death and sadness. I believe the death of my love has been avenged now and I offer you this gift." You raised your hand to say you didn't need any gift from him and you were just helping, but he continued, "This is no ordinary ring. It will take you the place where you need to be."

With that, you allowed him place the ring on one of your fingers. He held your finger with the ring on it and asked you to close your eyes and imagine where you wanted to be at that time. You did just as he asked. *To the Mountain of Lanogoza, to reach the end of my quest and get the healing stone and save my father,* were the thoughts rolling in your head. You started to feel lighter as you saw the images of your father and mother float through your mind and you no longer felt the touch of the kind merman king.

A huge mountain almost reaching the clouds was right in front of you, on opening your eyes. The smell of fresh mountain air filled your nostrils and your gaze travelled up the imposing angles of the mountain side to the snow-covered peaks and you smiled to yourself. The ring given to you by King Octan had brought you where you needed to be – at the foot of the Mountain of Lanogoza.

Checking to be sure that you had your pouch with your weapons and your dagger firmly strapped in your boot, you made your way to a large opening shaped like a skull in the cave. On entering the cave, a damp, putrid smell assailed your nostrils and you saw the decomposing corpses of cravuners, which are vampire birds, littered along the mouth of the cave. You decided to move cautiously so as not to run into them. The good thing was that they had a terrible stench and you would be forewarned by their smell before you actually saw them.

As you made your way into the depths of the cave with your knife held in front of you, the passage in the cave got narrower and narrower. The temperature inside the narrow passageway began to rise and you started to choke and cough. That didn't stop you from going ahead and you soon got to the end of the hallway which had two passageways. One was a dark passageway with shards of ice dripping from the ceiling and the other looked like an extremely hot passageway lined with fiery charcoal.

Which of these passages will you take, since there seems to be no other way forward?

Will you pass through the cold passage? Turn to Chapter 80.

Will you pass through the hot passage? Turn to Chapter 91.

CHAPTER 36

The Gold Stone

✦✦✦✦✦✦✦ ✦✦✦✦✦✦✦

The gold stone continued to shimmer and you just couldn't take your eyes off it. This had to be the healing stone. None of the others seemed to wield as much power as it. The golden shimmers reflected by the light fell like soft petals on the floor around the stone. The beauty of the stone held you in a magical trance and you started gravitating towards this enchanting stone.

This has to be the one, the healing stone I have been searching for all this while, you thought to yourself. At last, this marked the end of your journey, and you intended to return home at once and in time to save your father, you hoped. Stretching your finger towards the stone, you turned back to the ancient dragon and said, "The healing stone has to be as elegant and beautiful as the gold stone. This is the one I will pick."

The dragon was in the shadows all this while but you could feel his gaze on you. He moved out in the open and regarded you with cold eyes that were filled with something else you couldn't place a finger on.

"This is your choice, Princess?"

"Yes, it is my choice," you whispered in confusion, trying to understand why the dragon was staring at you in this manner.

The dragon nodded at you and said, "Well done, Princess. I don't understand how you were able to impress the count, but you have just proven to me that you are beautiful on the outside, but within, you have no depth of wisdom."

Then you understood the look on his ancient face. It was a mixture of disappointment and contempt.

"I made a mistake, let me choose another," you cried in desperation.

"There are no second chances," the dragon screamed, his eyes narrowing in anger as he opened his mouth.

The dragon opened his mouth wide and breathed a ball of fire at you. You tried to dive out of the way but you were not fast enough and went up in flames.

Your screams were echoing down the hollow end of the passageways.

Adventure Ends Here!!!

Wrong choice. Try again.

You can return to Chapter 67 or start the game again from Chapter 1.

~ SUREFOOT ~

CHAPTER 37

Go North

You decided to go north on your horse, Dusty, accompanied by the four warriors that had waited patiently whilst you said your goodbyes to your mother and the villagers that had gathered around. Nadum and the other men were to accompany you to the outskirts of Omahi Village.

Nadum drove alongside your horse, while the other two men were on both sides of you. It seemed like he wanted to say something, but you didn't want to give him a chance. You were still upset at his cowardice, for refusing to go on this quest and with a kick to its sides, urged your horse to go faster.

He caught up with you easily and shouted over the sounds made by the noise of the horses' hooves as they galloped on their way. "Stop this madness, woman."

"What madness?" you shouted back.

"This quest is madness. It is certain death."

"I need to save my father."

"Your father cannot be saved. I am sure you know that, Princess."

"He can be saved. The people need my father at this time,"

"I am aware they need him but you do not have to take this risk."

"Why do you care?"

"I care, because this quest is not meant for you. Come home, marry me, and let us start a life together."

"I see, you finally have said what your plan was all along. You want to be chief, and marrying a princess is another feather to your headdress." .

"Do not be stupid, Princess. You need to be at home, taking care of children."

At that statement, you turned around to look at him in anger and shouted, "I have hunted, fought beside you and other warriors. Why did you not send me home, then?'

"Princess…"

"Not another word from you. I will not heed the advice of a coward."

At that, Nadum sighed and went quiet, focusing on his riding but you could see his face set hard and angry as you all continued the journey in silence. As you approached the outskirts of Omahi Village, everyone stopped and quietly bade you farewell and watched as you navigated your way down the grassy plain. You knew that this journey you were undertaking was a dangerous one but you were quite determined to get the healing stone on time, to save your father. You rode some distance down a long stretch of buffalo grass and found the grass dying off, to reveal a large desert.

The ground was hot and the sun beat both you and Dusty until you were thirsty. Soon, you had finished all the water in your pouch and lay down on the hot sand. Dusty was standing beside you, panting and you were worried that if you didn't get water soon, both of you would not be able to make it out of this desert alive.

With that thought in mind, you stood up and whispered soothingly to your tired horse.

"We have to continue, Dusty, or else we die." You spoke without knowing if he understood what you said, but were glad that he followed you faithfully as you led him, still thirsty, on the journey.

In the distance, you noticed something large approaching. It spotted both of you and started coming really fast. There was nowhere to hide in this huge desert and you waited and observed that a big tyrannosaurus, also called a T-rex, was coming towards you. It seemed to consider you a lavish lunch.

As it sprang at you, its teeth flashing in the light, your trusty horse, Dusty ran in the way, knocking it with his hind feet in the face. The T-rex shook its massive, ugly head and snapped at Dusty, promptly dividing him in two.

Everything had happened so fast and you just barely dived out of the way as the massive animal charged at you. You somersaulted in the air, bringing out your knife in flight and landed on the back of the monster. The death of your horse was more than you could bear and you kept on stabbing the beast while it tried to get you off its back. You held on viciously, stabbing at the beast's neck until you probably hit an artery. It shuddered, screaming in pain and fell down with a massive thud.

You slid off its back, partially covered with its blood and made sure the animal was dead by cutting its neck wide open. Exhausted and tired, you staggered to your horse with as much strength as you could muster. You dug a small hole and managed to bury Dusty. Dusty was not just an animal but a friend and you didn't want his corpse to be eaten by the vultures circling lazily up in the sky. After what would seem like a long while, tired and demotivated by the death of your companion, you continued on your way. *The quest is more important and bigger than any losses that I have experienced,* you thought to yourself and the thought gave you the strength to carry on.

You saw something glittering ahead and were initially afraid that it was a mirage, but as you got closer, you saw a pool of water. You were so thirsty from your long trek and fight with the tyrannosaurus that you ran and knelt by the pool.

Will you drink from the pool, since you are very thirsty? Turn to Chapter 82.

Will you wait for a while? Turn to Chapter 62.

CHAPTER 38

Find Your Way Out

The girl moved ahead and you backed away slowly. From what she had said, Count Dracula didn't seem like someone that you wanted to encounter. Also, there had been stories told about a strange count that lived in a lonely castle and sucked the blood of his victims. You definitely had no intention of meeting him. Somehow, you had to find the way out of this castle. There had to be a passage to the other side of the road. It was clear that there was a road ahead. The view of the winding road went sloping up the hill but the castle was just right in the middle and there was no way you could climb over it. You got an idea to find another staircase so you could get a better view.

She noticed you weren't coming behind her and turned around, halfway up the castle.

"No, come back!" she screamed, hurriedly coming down the stairs and you turned around and started to run.

Running in the opposite direction, away from the staircase, you went through a long, dark passageway. The passage was dimly lit by lanterns placed strategically at various sections.

You could hear the high-pitched voice of the girl begging you to stop and come back but you ignored her and kept running, trying to find a way out of this dreadful castle and its owner. The girl seemed determined to stop you but you were fast and after running through a maze of doors, as this castle was much bigger inside than it looked on the outside, you soon lost her. You no longer heard the desperate stamp of her feet as she made to catch up with you or the sound of her shrill voice as you followed passages that led you deeper and deeper into the castle. The lanterns were no longer strategically placed in this section of the castle and a damp smell hit your nostrils as you got into even darker passages. You stopped to look around you and get your bearing. The passageway looked long, dark and uninviting and was heading even deeper into the castle.

There was a disturbing sound that kept building and initially was like a small vibration. It started to sound closer and you turned around to see a colony of bats coming after you and you started running down the passageway. The screeching sound was overwhelming and soon the bats were flying all over you, screeching in high-pitched sounds and pecking at you. They were so many and the place was so dark that you leaned against the wall and tried to roll into a ball to avoid their attacks. The swarming continued with the bats. You lay still until after a while, there was silence. Looking up, you noticed the bats were swirling around just across you and wondered what was going on. Bats hardly behaved in that manner. They continued swirling in the air and started descending to the ground, still going in a circular motion. To your surprise, the swarm of bats were morphing into a human form, the arms, legs and face coming into view. After a while, the bats disappeared completely and, in their place, stood a pale, white man with blood-red eyes, wearing a black cloak.

He didn't look happy. "You come into my home uninvited and move around my hallowed grounds without permission."

You tried to say something, but he moved very fast and was at your side in seconds, holding you to himself almost in an embrace. Then he opened his mouth and exposed his fangs.

Adventure Ends Here.

Always take permission.

You can return to Chapter 77 or start the game again from Chapter 1.

~ SUREFOOT ~

CHAPTER 39

Walk through Him

The man was old but looked cunning and his eyes twinkled through his long, shaggy white eyebrows and you studied him a bit more. He stood tall, with his white robe blowing in the wind. His long, white hair and beard swayed slightly as he studied you, awaiting your response. You didn't think he meant you harm by fighting you physically, so you made your decision.

"I will pass through you," you said calmly, approaching him.

He smiled at you and nodded and his body started melting away like smoke, slowly evaporating into the atmosphere. You stopped in your tracks as you wondered what sort of trickery this was, but you heard his deep voice saying, "Wise princess, you may enter."

You approached the huge, stone lions that all of a sudden took a life of their own and opened their mouths, snarling at you. You jumped back in surprise, pulling out your knife as the lions growled once more and looked up, immediately freezing once again into their stone-like trance. The massive gate opened up slowly with a low creak, to reveal a magnificent city of tall towers with pink, yellow and blue-arched roofs. You looked around in surprise, amazed at the uncommon sights. The streets were lined up in what looked like gold and filled with men dressed in long tail coats and top hats and women in ball gowns and wide-feathered glamorous hats.

The streets were busy and everyone went around their business, chatting and exchanging pleasantries until you walked by. The silence was deafening and you could feel their curious stares bore into your back, as you walked past. You didn't dress as glamorously as their women and the blood splatters from your recent battle with the zepenter must have been the reason why your presence was quickly reported to the king of the land.

In no time, the palace soldiers, smartly dressed in their blue and red uniforms with gleaming silver buttons and long, black boots surrounded you, with swords in their hands. They tried to take you by force to their king. You couldn't allow that as it would derail your quest and you didn't have time to waste. You pulled out your dagger and with a flying leap, attacked the first soldier in front of you and slit his throat. As another soldier made to hold you, you turned quickly, flipping him to the ground.

The crowd watched in horror and at the same time amazement, at your skills in fighting. The other soldiers rushed at you and you fought them all but they were too many. Soon, they had you cornered and you fought back like a wild beast. They increased in their numbers, subdued you, despite your kicking and screaming, tied your hands behind your back and led you to the palace.

They led you down a winding road and you could see ahead, to your amazement, a large palace made out of glass. The windows were gleaming like diamonds and trees lined up the walkways. You entered the broad, arched door which led to a magnificent staircase made up entirely of glass, spiraling up to the second and third floors. There was no time to admire the glass staircase and chandeliers hanging at the entrance of the large hallway, since you were led to the royal throne room.

The king and queen sat on high, golden chairs, with the armrests shaped like eagles. They both wore long robes that trailed down the length of the chair. The king's golden crown sat on his round head. He had ruby red cheeks and looked so chubby, like he might explode into a billion pieces of sweets. He was chewing on a cake that he held on his left hand, the icing dripping from his hand to his impeccable white shirt. The queen was the exact opposite of her husband. She was slender and her blonde hair fell down her shoulders, underneath her golden crown like a golden wave. She looked at you with blue, questioning eyes and pouted her ruby-red lips in thought. They both looked at you in suspicion and then started a barrage of questions about your presence in their kingdom.

"Who are you?" the king asked, still chomping on his cake that was making a mess on his shirt.

"I am Princess Surefoot, daughter of Chief Ziza of Omahi Village."

The queen eyed your blood-stained clothes and said with a look of distrust, "You certainly don't look royal to me."

"Why are you here?" the king replied more seriously now, wiping his cake-filled hand on a napkin that a young servant had just given him. He threw the napkin at the young lad who ran off with the plate of half-eaten cake.

"I am on a quest and I simply wish to pass through your land," you replied calmly.

Your quiet responses as opposed to the fight you had put up earlier when the soldiers tried to capture you, seemed to make them distrust you even more.

"We don't believe that you don't wish us any harm. It was reported that you have killed ten of my men. Take her to the dungeon," the king roared at the soldiers.

At their pronouncement, the soldiers dragged you off and threw you into a dungeon. The place was dark and smelled of dampness and death. You looked around for a way out and as you moved forward, your feet stepped on something. The sound your feet made on the ground was crunching and you looked down to see bones that appeared to be parts of human skeletons littered in a trail leading to a dark opening in the dungeon. Whatever it was that killed and feasted on the people that were now skeletons, was definitely in that opening. Your suspicion was confirmed when you heard a growling sound coming from that direction.

You sensed impending danger and bent down to check for your dagger that you had safely stashed in the waist band of your trousers. Thankfully, the soldiers didn't find it when they had taken all your other weapons. A streak of daylight shone through a small window that was at the top of the cave wall. The window was just small enough to let in air and not big enough for someone to escape. With a growing sense of trepidation, you sensed the growling getting closer and looked around to observe another opening just across the cave. A sense of dread enveloped you. You had no idea what was in that dark interior, but definitely the growling was coming from there. You started to back away, with your arm unconsciously resting on your waist-band, ready to pull out your dagger and defend yourself.

Your heart was racing as you anticipated what might emerge from the dark hole. You heard the slow padding of feet and an increase in the intensity of the growls, as whatever it was sensed your presence. Maybe it could hear the beating of your heart or sense your fear. You had no idea what was going to emerge from the darkness and you carefully pulled out your knife and set yourself in a fighting stance, in anticipation of what was coming your way.

Two huge lions emerged from the darkness of the hole with such force that they initially hit each other in their bid to come out. They snarled at each other and turned around in unison, staring at you, baring huge, carved teeth and growling at you, drooling in anticipation of a tasty meal.

What will be your next move?

Will you fight the lions? Turn to Chapter 27.

Will you try to avoid the lions by trying to climb up the walls of the dungeon? Turn to Chapter 66.

~ SUREFOOT ~

CHAPTER 40

Flee!

There were just too many of them. It seemed like the more you killed, the more they appeared. There was no way you could possibly kill all of them. You turned around to run. All you wanted was permission to go past the mountain. You wondered why the wizard was sending his army of skeletons to attack you.

Wielding your spear that you unhinged from the strap on your back, you dived at the skeletons that had formed a line in front of you. They were coming at you, wielding their weapons but with one swift move you swiped at the line, sending bones flying in the air.

You continued swiping at them viciously with your spear, driving them back. Realizing that you couldn't destroy all of them, you quickly ran back the same way you had come, to the side of the mountain. You hefted your spear on your back and started to descend the mountain as fast as you could. There was no way they were going to climb down with you, since the wizard didn't want you on the mountain and now you were getting off it. At least, that was what you thought.

The skeletons followed after you, very fast in their movements, climbing down the side of the mountain. A couple of them came close and started stepping on your hands. You held the leg of one of the skeletons and pulled it when it was trying to grab at you. The others seemed more enraged and were climbing down very fast. You continued your descent, trying to avoid them but they were soon on both sides of you. They were trying to pry your fingers off the mountain but you tried to hold on tight until one of them used its knife to pierce your left hand. You screamed, letting go whilst the skeleton beside you pushed you off the mountain. As you fell screaming, you could see the wizard, a man bent with age, his white beard waving in the wind, staring down at you from the top of the mountain.

Adventure Ends Here.

I hope you landed safely without a parachute.

You can return to Chapter 55 or start the game again from Chapter 1.

CHAPTER 41

Two Massive Doors

⋙⋙⋙ ⋘⋘⋘

The shark was right behind you as you swam with all your might. Waves of water propelled you forward, caused by the actions of the shark snapping at you. You started maneuvering through the water, avoiding its attacks and ducked into an opening in the sunken ship just before the shark hit the side with a loud bang. Fortunately, the space you went through was too small for it and you could imagine it ramming its large tail at the side of the ship in anger, as you swam faster into the recesses of the abandoned ship.

The shark might be lurking outside the ship waiting for you to come out, so you decided to stay inside, moving very fast within the rooms of the ship. You didn't stop in case the shark had made its way inside. Surprisingly, the sunken ship looked neat inside, as though someone lived in it. You continued, amazed at the cleanliness of this abandoned ship, when you heard a deep voice singing a melancholic song.

Someone was definitely living on this boat and you became very curious and followed the sound of the voice down a clean passageway with several doors on both sides. Swimming slowly across the neat passageway, you came to two massive doors ahead of you.

One was a golden door marked with diamond arrows, and the other was a pale, dark door, shining with blue, glittering stars.

Will you try to open the golden door with diamond arrows? Turn to Chapter 13.

Will you try to open the dark door with blue, glittering stars? Turn to Chapter 71.

CHAPTER 42

Escape

They kept on laughing continuously and to your bird ears, the sound of their voices was like a tempest. You flew up into the air and fluttered around the cave where they lived, hoping to find a way of escape. The cottage walls loomed large to your bird senses and you fluttered around, eagerly, searching for an exit.

There appeared to be no exit out of the cave, as it had no windows and the only entrance was a huge, bolted metal door. You were chirping in desperation and this alerted the witch sisters. They came after you, grabbing their brooms as they tried to swat you down. You flew around expertly, avoiding the brooms that came in your direction and flew towards the left side of a dusty ceiling, looking for a corner to hide. A cat sprang from a dark corner there and you narrowly avoided being snatched by its sharp claws. You chirped desperately and turned, just as a net flew over you and once more you were captured to face the laughing faces of the ugly witches. They looked at you with disappointment, shaking their long-crooked noses at you. The cat came back and tried to get you out of the net and they shooed it away. It gave you a grudging look, whilst licking its chops.

"You tried to run away, brave princess?" one of them asked.

"That wasn't very nice," the other added.

The third was silent and she came closer, looking at you struggling in the net.

'I'm sorry, warrior. You can't run away,' she said, pointing at you and laughing. You tried to scream but your throat seemed to have closed up. The witches appeared larger than usual, the boils on their noses becoming larger and filling up with pus. It appeared you were melting into the ground and into nothingness.

𝔄𝔡𝔳𝔢𝔫𝔱𝔲𝔯𝔢 𝔈𝔫𝔡𝔰 𝔥𝔢𝔯𝔢.

Foolish decision!!!

You can return to Chapter 23 or start the game again from Chapter 1.

CHAPTER 43

Three Things

꧁꧂

Time seemed to stand still as the words of the riddle replayed in your mind.

To get to the Mountain of Lanogoza,

One must do three things.

What are those things?

Your hands subconsciously came to the chain around your neck and you closed your eyes to see the smiling face of your mother. It seemed that the events of the journey from the time she gave you the chain to when you said your goodbyes started playing in your mind. You saw again the battle with the skeletons and the discussion with the Wizard of Trasca, where he asked what form you wanted to change into. He had asked if you wanted to be a bird, mountain wolf or a fish and immediately the answer came to you. You opened your eyes to see the wizard watching you closely and you gave an answer to the riddle.

"To get to the Mountain of Lanogoza, I must walk over mountains, swim across the seas, fly above the mountain and the seas, if I have wings."

"Wise princess, you may go," he said, nodding, his eyes once more crinkling into a smile.

"I do not understand. How do I continue on my quest?"

"Let me worry about that," he replied, raising his staff as his face slowly started to fade, dissolving into smoke. You looked around in alarm to find that the entire cottage was slowly disappearing before your eyes. You were suddenly lifted in the air and felt yourself transported with such great speed that there was no time to react. The wind was rushing through your face and you were hurled in the air, turning around in semi-circles and eventually landing on a soft bed of grass. You tumbled out of the grass that you had been so graciously deposited in, to see the opening of a cave. It seemed like a face with the open mouth marking the entrance to the cave.

Making your way through the entrance of the cave, you marched on with determination but with a sense of caution. You had no idea what awaited you inside the cave and you had to be careful. The long, dark passageway was winding into the belly of the mountain and it led you to a small, open space. Looking around, you saw no other path leading away from this space, so you went into the cave.

A slight movement caught your eye as a large tail headed your way and by reflex, you jumped away just in time before it crashed into the wall behind you, shattering it into tiny blocks of stone. Rolling to a kneeling position, you raised your knife to attack and your eyes met the eyes of the ancient dragon. He was huge and stared at you with large, red eyes, breathing smoke from his mouth.

"Why are you here?" he snarled at you.

"I am Princess Surefoot, daughter of Chief Ziza and Queen Cohahi from the Omahi tribe and I seek the healing stone to save my father."

~ THREE THINGS ~

The dragon regarded you quietly and lowered his wings as the smoke in his breath slowly started disappearing.

"You seek the healing stone to save a life?"

"Yes." You nodded, still holding your knife ahead of you in defense.

"If indeed you seek the stone to save a life and not for wealth, then I'll not attack you anymore, so stand down."

You were uncertain but the gentle look in this magnificent beast's eyes made you drop the knife to the side and tuck it into your boot for safe keeping.

The dragon regarded you and continued, "Well done, brave princess, but in order to get the healing stone, you must go through one of those doors." You looked in the direction he indicated. The wall caved in with a huge crash and in its place two large oak doors stood solidly, both of them identical to each other.

You both walked to the two massive oak doors and stared at them, unsure, as the ancient dragon stared at you.

"One of them will lead you the healing stone."

"Where does the other one lead?"

The dragon regarded you with wise eyes and turned away to stare at the huge doors. "Only one that is pure in heart is fit to get the stone. So, choose a door, Princess," he replied, his face expressionless.

Which of the doors will lead you to the healing stone?

Turn to Chapter 53 or Chapter 69.

~ SUREFOOT ~

CHAPTER 44

Observe

It wasn't yet dark, so why was the sky darkening? You flew close to the ground and dropped on a tree. This appeared to be a safe location as the green leaves from the trees offered you protection and covered you from what you saw next.

You discovered that the darkening sky was caused by a brood of vampire birds called cravuners, flying across the sky. Your bird senses were unable to detect their pungent smell. Humans are able to smell these birds from far and quickly avoid them as they can easily rip anything living to shreds, down to their bones.

They soon faded out of sight. It was a good thing that you stopped flying as you didn't stand a chance against the vampire birds, no matter what form the wizard had turned you into. The main advantage cravuners had was in their numbers and they could easily swarm around their prey from all sides, giving little room for self-defense.

While you were watching the cravuners fly across the sky, you did not notice that a small snake had slithered towards you and encircled your legs. You felt some pressure against your legs, fluttered your wings and noticed something was holding you back. You looked down and then saw the snake as it opened its mouth, exposing its fangs and ready to bite you. What could you do?

Will you speak to it and explain your quest? Turn to Chapter 34.

Will you fight it? Turn to Chapter 23.

CHAPTER 45

The Magical Staircase

✦✦✦✦✦✦✦✦ ✦✦✦✦✦✦✦✦

As you stared at both stairs in mild confusion, you wondered, "*Which of these staircases will lead me to my quest?*" Closing your eyes and taking a deep breath, you calmed the beating of your heart and decided to let fate decide which path you were to take that would ultimately lead you to the end of your quest.

Eyes still closed, you placed one foot ahead of the other, allowing Mother Fate to lead you on. In your mind, you could see and smell the beautiful flowers that flourished only in the vast grasslands of the Omahi fields. You could hear the innocent voices of children singing and the sound of women welcoming the men back from the hunt. All of a sudden, your feet landed on a step and it held firm. You heaved a sigh of relief, opened your eyes and kept on climbing. The staircase was grand and it widened, leading through the dark cave up to an opening in the sky.

Curiosity got the best of you and looking down, you observed you were a long distance from the depths below, which was no longer the floor of the cave but a raging sea beneath you. The damp darkness of the cave wall had disappeared and in its place the walls of the cave were crumbling and giving way to a dark, cloudy atmosphere. The stairs now appeared to be leading up into a soulless sky. Looking back down again, you noticed that the movement in the sea below was caused by something large and dark stirring the water with long, black tentacles that stretched out for miles, causing waves which crashed against the rocks. You looked up again as perspiration flooded your forehead. It would be a disaster to lose balance and fall. You had no intention of being food for that creature in the sea, whatever it was. Your hand unconsciously moved to the chain that your mother had placed on your neck and you continued the ascent with no intentions of being distracted further by the happenings below.

Treading with caution, as the staircase had no railings on either side, you were about to put a foot ahead of you when the step in front of you disintegrated into a cloud of dust. Subconsciously, you jumped up in the air and did a mid-somersault and landed three steps ahead, just as the next step crumbled. You started skipping from one step to the other, making sure that you didn't put your full weight on any of them. Each step you landed on disappeared in a cloud of dust, so your movements had to be fast and deliberate. One pause or false move and you were sure to plummet to your death. Eventually, your antics paid off and with one final jump, you succeeded in ascending up this magical stairway to the Mountain of Lanogoza. The stairs completely crumbled behind you, falling with a loud crash into the sea, while you stood at the summit of the mountain. *That could have been me falling along with the stairs*, you thought. You stilled your panting and looked ahead, for the journey wasn't over yet.

After walking some distance away from the edge of the mountain, you approached a huge, black door carved into the mountain. Taking time to study the door, you observed it didn't have a key hole so probably it wasn't locked. There was no harm in finding out. Heaving a sigh of relief after surviving the staircase of doom, as you named it in your mind, you turned the door knob.

Just one twist of the knob and the door slid open easily, like it had been recently oiled. Immediately, you were almost blinded by a bright light engulfing you. The door opened up to a room full of gold heaped on the floor and against the walls – all kinds of golden swords, jewelries, necklaces, chains and amulets. You smiled in disbelief, walking around, admiring ancient golden amulets, helmets, swords and heaps of gold coins in chests. The room had more riches than one could ever dream of. What if you took some home with you?

Not only would you return with the healing stone, but you could get rich in the process of doing so. After all you had been through, you deserved it.

Will you pick one? Turn to Chapter 10.

Will you continue on your quest? Turn to Chapter 72.

~ SUREFOOT ~

CHAPTER 46

Into the Dark Cave

⊷⊷⊷⊷ ⊷⊷⊷⊷

This might be the Mountain of Lanogoza where the famed healing stone was situated and you intended to continue with your quest and get the stone in time to save your father and ultimately the entire village. You stepped cautiously into the dark cave, and looked around, until your eyes got accustomed to the dim light. The cave narrowed out into a passageway which you intended to explore. Thoughts of getting a light to aid you on your passage down the dark caverns came to mind but something warned you against it.

You had come to trust the instinct that had saved you many times in battle. A warning to bend and narrowly miss a flying arrow or the charge of a maddened animal during a hunt, came to mind. That thought still lingered as you stepped forward, one foot after the other, walking slowly down the stony passageway winding down into deep nothingness. You stretched out your left hand to feel the cool smooth sides of the cave, with your knife firmly grasped on the right.

Then the smell hit your nostrils, before you had a chance to move even further into the depths of the cave. A dank, putrid smell. You knew that smell and it meant danger. The thought of danger came before you heard the sound of their wings flapping from the depths of the cave and coming in your direction.

Cravuners were approaching, in their numbers. They were a flock of evil, vampire birds with a stench that could make anyone reek. The good thing was that they were blind, so you leaned against the wall as they flew past in their numbers, screeching in high-pitched tones. Cravuners were attracted to light despite their blindness as they could sense the heat and you were relieved that you didn't light a fire. You pressed yourself into a hollow of the cave, as they flew past, to avoid one of them hitting you. If one of them became aware of your presence, the entire group would be on you in a matter of minutes. They were so many of them flying past and the smell was overwhelmingly horrendous. You held your hand to your mouth to prevent yourself from retching, and continued to watch them sail past in their numbers.

The screeching and the numbers of cravuners started to reduce after a while and you made sure the coast was clear, before you continued on your way. The passageway still had the lingering, putrid smell of the vampire birds and with time you got used to the smell. The passageway down the cave was dark and winding. You saw drawings of adventurers in different throes of death, on the cave walls. You wondered who did the markings, and reasoned that maybe they were warnings for people not to venture beyond this point. The images were so gruesome. You refused to look at the walls and focused on the quest ahead. After walking some distance down the dark cave, you heard a rushing sound like so many waters, gurgling and splashing in the distance, and at the same time, you heard a melancholic voice singing.

The voice was so sweet and tender and the words of the song gave a message of joy and deep sorrow at the same time. The voice was almost lulling your senses and transfixed you on the spot. Whoever was singing sounded closer and you could hear footsteps approaching.

Will you wait to see the person? Turn to Chapter 74.

Will you hide in another section of the cave? Turn to Chapter 57.

~ SUREFOOT ~

CHAPTER 47

Defy the Waves

The waves started taking a life of their own, tossing and crashing about and you watched in fear as a huge wave started building right in front of the boat. The monstrous wave rose and the boat was helplessly forced by the unrelenting sea towards the wall of water that was ready to crash into the tiny boat. Thoughts kept racing through your head and you wondered what to do. The waves looked ready to crash into the boat and you knew for sure that the massive wave would destroy the boat.

It seemed that the world stood still at that point in time as you held on to the boat which tossed you about, almost unseating you and throwing you into the sea. The wind blew viciously against your face and your long, curly black hair moved back and forth. It seemed as if everything slowed down. You could hear your breath coming out fast and a face materialized in your mind.

Her gentle smile, kind, dark eyes, full, black hair and strong look. It was your mother. She stretched her hand towards you lovingly.

"Breathe, child..."

"Mother!" you exclaimed, stretching one hand towards the vision in your mind, whilst holding on to the side of the boat so as not to get thrown out.

"Stay…. Stay in the boat!" she said and with a smile, her image disappeared.

"Mother!" you screamed again as the wind tossed you like a rag doll and the sea water poured into the boat. You held on to the side of the boat and took a deep breath, closing your eyes just as another wave descended.

You expected the wave to crash with all its fury, pulling you and the boat into the depths of the sea, but after what seemed like a long time, you realized to your surprise that nothing happened. It appeared that the wind had ceased. The mad howling of the wind had ceased and you opened your eyes and wondered at how calm the sea was. One moment, there was a maddening storm and a monstrous wave that threatened to drown you, but now everything was just like when you ventured into the sea at the beginning.

For one moment, you almost felt that you had imagined everything, and looked around, unsure. Then, it slowly came to you as you remembered the name of the sea. You guessed that the waves and the wind were all an illusion. No wonder it was called the Sea of Illusion. Everything you had experienced was not real. You sighed with relief and were just about to relax when all of a sudden, water rose up right in front of you as a huge water demon erupted in a watery burst. It was a creature you had never laid your eyes on. It had seven heads and what appeared to be twenty hands attached on its huge barrel of a chest. The beast had fourteen eyes, and they were all trained on you as you sat in the boat. With a scream, it lifted its huge tail out of the sea and slammed it back on the water, creating waves that forced the boat backwards.

You held on to the boat in alarm, trying to access the situation and wondering if this creature was real. The water demon snarled at you and its numerous hands thrashed about in the sea, causing major ripples that kept the boat in a state of continuous circular motion and you were beginning to get dizzy.

What was happening seemed to be very real as you were experiencing it now, but so was the storm that just ended moments ago. This was a creature that you had never encountered or fought before in your life. As the boat turned to face the water monster, it opened its mouth wide and fire proceeded out of it, setting the boat on fire. As the front part of the boat went up in flames, the heat scorched the hair on your head and burnt your finger as you moved backwards in the boat. The realization that this might be real dawned on you, despite the Sea of Illusion situation. Surely everything happening now was as real as it could be. The soaring flames that threatened to engulf you was enough reason to abandon the boat.

This most certainly isn't an illusion, you thought, as the fire raced through the boat. The water demon confirmed your thoughts by smashing the boat with several of its numerous arms and you narrowly avoided being pummeled to death, by diving into the sea.

What's your next move?

Will you go under water and try to swim away from it? Turn to Chapter 96.

Will you fight it? Turn to Chapter 6.

~ SUREFOOT ~

CHAPTER 48

The Ugly, White Stone

❧❧❧❧❧❧❧ ❦❦❦❦❦❦❦

The golden stone glittered before your eyes and the blue stone had balls floating in its transparent depths and you were mesmerized by their beauty. It was a very hard decision selecting between these varieties of stones and you thought of what your answer would be.

What did you expect the healing stone to look like? Made of gold or so transparent that you could see through it? What did either of them mean, in the true sense of the word? Flashing or transparent didn't give you a sense of stability, unlike the rock that was sitting beside them. It paled in comparison to their beauty and appeared ugly. Yet, as you thought about it, you realized that the seer didn't prepare you to expect anything more than a common stone. Looking at the ugly stone again, you felt a sense of peace that flooded your being as you moved away from the other attractive stones.

True healing usually comes from a place of ugliness, a thought came to your head as your hand stretched towards the pale rock. As your hand made contact with the stone, it felt cold to touch and when you picked it up, a soft glow appeared in your palm and went all over your body, filling you with so much peace and calm. You stood there for a while, unable to move, not wanting to stop this relaxed sensation that the stone was making you feel. A movement to your right made you turn to see the dragon regarding you with a look of pride and happiness. He was impressed!

He bent his head low and spoke to you, "Worthy princess, it isn't what is outside but what's inside that really counts. You are worthy of the stone, so take it."

You held the stone to your chest and with a relieved smile on your face, said, "Thank you."

The dragon looked deep into your eyes, his eyes glowing but you could see no evil in them "Now, I'll help you home."

"How?" you asked.

"Just close your eyes and hold the stone to your chest," he replied.

With a smile on your face and still feeling the beautiful warmth of the stone all round your body, calming you and loosening any tension from your muscles, you held the stone to your chest.

You could hear the dragon speaking in his deep voice, "Think of your home."

You closed your eyes and imagined your mother's hut, the children playing outside, the wind moving on the tall grass in the field, the smell of the flowers and all of a sudden, the dragon's voice seemed to fade with each passing moment. Your hair fluttered across your face as you felt a rush of wind and your body started to feel warm, like the sunlight was caressing your skin. Opening your eyes, you found that you were standing on a field of grass with the stone pressed possessively against your chest.

The huts were all arranged in a circular pattern across the field and you could see children running around at the center. Women were sitting in front of wooden fire pits as they made their evening meal, and the men would be returning anytime soon from hunting game in the forest. You couldn't believe it. You were home now and for a moment just stood there in disbelief. One of the children spotted you and pointed. The chatting women stopped and stood up to observe the solitary figure standing across the field.

Soon enough, your mother disengaged from the group and looked in your direction.

"Surefoot!" she screamed in excitement and started running towards you.

This sparked excitement amongst the other villagers and they followed after her, all screaming your name.

For a moment, you still stood there in shock, but watching your mother running towards you with her arms outstretched broke something inside of you.

"Mother," you screamed and made towards her. It seemed like the world stood still as mother and daughter ran towards each other across a field of dancing, tall grass.

Both of you stopped for a while, regarding each other with joy and happiness. Queen Cohahi, with a look of joy and relief, smiled at you and stretched her hands and you ran into her embrace. At that time, you were no longer the strong warrior that you had grown up to be. You were your mother's daughter and she was holding you and muttering sweet words in your ears.

Congratulations!

Adventure Ends Here.

You have so much to tell them.

CHAPTER 49

Look Around

There was something not quite right about this town and although you were starving, you needed to know what the danger was. Your wolf senses were tingling and that feeling was greater than your rumbling stomach. For some reason, a voice in your head wanted you to remain in hiding and observe the environment. After waiting for some time, you decided to come out from behind the rock where you were hiding. Just then, there was movement at the side of a huge building just across the street and you observed werewolves coming out from the building. One of them had a hand in its huge fangs and they were splattered with blood. That explained why the entire town was empty. Werewolves were dangerous and ate anything flesh and the people in this town were unfortunately their victims.

You were right to have remained in hiding as there were a lot of them in the pack and you wouldn't have survived a fight with them. Watching them closely as they sauntered from the building and spilled out into the streets, you saw that they were a formidable number that would have been difficult to subdue. Your attention was taken by one of the werewolves that had its nose in the air and was sniffing away like it could smell something. You went further behind the rock, as it kept on sniffing and slowly started making its way towards the rock where you were hiding. Your heart started to race as you thought of your chances of survival and the possibility of outrunning an entire pack of werewolves. As you leaned closer to the rock, unsure of your next move, the werewolf stood right in front of the rock and this time, you could hear the sniffing sounds it made, as it was just about to come face to face with you. A loud howl interrupted its progress and it turned to see the other werewolves chasing after someone. It howled in glee, forgetting the strange smell from behind the rock and followed the pack in their chase.

You could hear the gurgling sounds of pain as the victim was being torn to shreds by the werewolves and quietly used the opportunity to escape from this strange town. It was sad that someone had to die, but you would have been discovered and killed if that diversion had not occurred.

After you had put some safe distance between yourself and the werewolves, you started off at a faster pace, no longer afraid that they could hear the sound of your pattering feet. The pangs of hunger were long forgotten as you ensured your safety from the monsters that you had just encountered. As you continued on your journey down the mountain, you heard the faint howling sound of the wind. A mighty breeze started blowing and the sky started darkening. A flash of lightning confirmed your fears. It was going to rain soon and you wondered what to do. Looking around for some form of shelter, the lightning flashed and you saw an opening like a hole by the side of the mountain that you could just squeeze into. The wind started picking up and more flashes with a resounding crack of thunder announced the start of the rain. What did you intend to do?

Will you get into a hole? Turn to Chapter 63.

Will you continue on your journey, so as not to waste time? Turn to Chapter 95.

CHAPTER 50

A Bird

You looked at the Wizard of Trasca, quite unsure and he could read the doubt in your eyes. How were you sure you could trust this old wizard who had just sent an army of the undead to attack you?

"Do you doubt my intentions, Princess? You mustn't. The dangers are real and you have passed my test. I only wish to help you, as I've helped others."

"How do I turn back to my true form?" you asked.

"By simply wishing it, but beware that you do not wish it at a wrong time," he warned.

You thought about the different options and it appeared that a bird was the best option, since you could fly over mountains and seas in that form. It seemed like he could read your mind, as he started smiling and you noticed he appeared larger, while you shrunk in size. Your hair shrunk into your skull, feathers started appearing on your body and you started chirping and hopping around.

~ SUREFOOT ~

The old man had disappeared from his position on the mountain and the only evidence of his presence were the scattered skeletons and the fire burning idly at the side of the mountain. You spread your wings and soared into the sky. You were not so used to your wings yet and found it a little bit difficult to fly but after a while, you mastered the rudiments of flying and started gliding in the air.

You soon got to enjoy flying so close to the clouds, with the wind whistling through your feathers, that you almost forgot your quest.

Turn to Chapter 107.

CHAPTER 51

Give them
the Key

The witches were peering in through the hole with a look of concern and fear in their eyes and they urged you on with kind words.

"Come on then, brave warrior."

"You have our word."

"Give us the key and we will help you in your quest to the mountain."

"Remember the clock is ticking and you have a long journey ahead of you."

There was really no point wasting more time as they had just reminded you of your quest. Well, what did you stand to lose? You had finally found the key they wanted. You placed the key once more on your beak, flew out of the hole and gently placed it in the outstretched hand of the first witch that you saw outside the tree. They patted your back gratefully.

"Brave warrior, we never could have done this without you," the first witch croaked.

"You are indeed very kind," the second one said.

The third one chuckled. "You keep to your word as well."

"Now you have to keep yours, too," you reminded them, as you couldn't wait to get on with your quest.

They started laughing hysterically and you wondered what was so amusing about them keeping their part of the promise. They began to speak and you understood what was happening.

"You must have heard of us, brave warrior princess."

"We are the Witches of the Western Sky."

"We don't ever keep our promises," they said, as their laughter echoed in the sky, like thunder.

They started laughing once more, and you realized you made a mistake by giving them the key. The witches definitely planned to do you harm. You flew up in the air and tried to make it back into the hole, but it was too late as a hand held firmly to your feather and that was the last thing you remembered.

Adventure Ends Here.

Don't trust everyone, Game Player.

You can return to Chapter 99 or start the game again from Chapter 1.

~ SUREFOOT ~

CHAPTER 52

The Hole In the Tree

⸙⸙⸙⸙⸙⸙ ⸙⸙⸙⸙⸙⸙

The witches kept on screaming at you when they noticed your hesitancy and you hopped around the edge of the hole, quietly contemplating your decision.

"Get in the hole."

"Get in."

"Come on, what are you waiting for?"

There was no need to put it off any longer. Your chances of escape were slim, as you were dealing with witches. *There is no other option than going on their quest*, you thought to yourself as you flew into the hole in a bid to help the witches retrieve the key as they had requested. As you flew into the dark hole and began your descent, you noticed that the passage through the hole got narrower and realized that the witches were right. In your human form, you couldn't get into the hole. That explained why the witches couldn't get in, with all their magic.

You kept on flying into the hole and observed that the further into the dark hole you went, the narrower the passage in the tree became. Eventually, you came to the end of the passage in the tree that was branching off into two different parts. One was descending into the lower depths of the tree and. The other was leading up the tree and glowing like gold. This aroused your curiosity as you wondered what was causing the glow in that other opening.

Would it lead you to the witches' lost key or would it lead you to gold left in the tree? This could be a distraction, but what did you have to lose, if you decided to check it out?

Will you go to the glowing part of the hole? Turn to Chapter 28.

Will you continue your descent into the earth? Turn to Chapter 99.

CHAPTER 53

Door One

The dragon's gaze was expressionless and you both regarded each other quietly. Turning back to look at both doors, you willed your heart to decide which of the doors to take. Although you were tired as you neared the end of your quest.

Which of these doors would lead you to your destination? you wondered and subconsciously touched the chain around your neck that your mother had given to you. Your fingers caressed it, bringing memories from home — the sound of the children playing, the women chattering as they prepared food and the smell of the forest when you were involved in a hunt. A faint breeze teased your temples, brushing a single strand of hair across your face. Your hand extended and you turned the handle of the door on the left, which rolled open with a loud groan.

The door opened up to a large, stone-grey room that was empty, except for a massive stone slab at the center. A glass casing with a plain, grey stone was placed at the center of the table and you cautiously walked towards it. *This has to be the healing stone*, you said to yourself, smiling as you gently opened up the glass casing and brought out the stone. It felt cool to touch.

A warm sensation of peace enveloped you and spread across your entire body, lighting you with a strange fire from the tips of your fingers to the soles of your feet. Indeed, this was the healing stone and you turned to smile at the dragon, but just then, the ground started shaking. The stone slab shattered into pieces and crumbled at your feet and you jumped back in alarm as the walls started to shake as well. You spun around to see the dragon watching you. You were going to say something, but a loud crash behind you made you turn around.

The ground where the stone slab used to be had disappeared into a huge, gaping hole which had suddenly appeared in the ground and was starting to widen in your direction. Turning around, your eyes met the dragon's just as the door slammed shut, trapping you in the room. The hole in the ground was advancing towards you at a fast pace and you had to react.

You placed the stone in your pouch, jumped in the air and lifted yourself up on the wall, holding on as you watched the entire ground fall away. The gaping hole stared at you ominously and you started nimbly climbing up the wall, holding on to sharp edges to avoid falling to your death. A loud cracking sound made you look down and you watched the ground close back again. You remained on the wall, unsure if this was a test. The huge oak door opened up and the ancient dragon walked in and looked at you with amusement in his eyes.

"You may come down now, Princess.'

"How can I be sure that the ground won't give way?" you asked, feeling suspicious.

"You have my word," he replied with a finality in his tone that made you let go of the wall. You let yourself land with a bow and stood up immediately, dusting the sand from your fingers.

"Brave warrior, the stone has found you worthy and now you can return home."

"Thank you, but how do I get home?"

"Close your eyes, brave warrior and think of your home."

You closed your eyes and touched your chain and a faint smile appeared on your lips as you thought of home. The air started to spin around and you opened up your eyes to see the dragon watching you with a smile, as his deep voice boomed. "Goodbye, brave warrior princess."

A mass of cold air swept you off your feet and you found yourself sailing through the clouds at a remarkable speed. Time seemed to have frozen in place, then you were moved in different directions before everything stood still and you saw yourself standing in the familiar Omahi fields. You touched the side to feel your pouch with the stone safely in it. Sighing with relief, you looked up to see women and children coming out of their huts and staring at you.

"Surefoot!" A familiar voice cried and you recognized your mother who exclaimed in surprise and happiness as she ran across the field to embrace you.

Congratulations,

Wise Game Player.

CHAPTER 54

Fight the Old Man

"**P**ass *through me must mean fighting the old man,*" you thought to yourself with a smile on your face. That was a very easy choice for you to make. This definitely had to be what he meant by passing through him, and you reminded yourself that you were Princess Surefoot. You remembered the sound of battle as you fought invaders coming into your homeland. Fighting was something that you were not afraid to engage in. You had not only killed men but hunted down, fought and killed lions, bears, and more recently a zepenter. Definitely, you were not new in the act of battle and this particular situation was just too easy in your opinion.

What harm could this old man do to you? You smiled and pulled out your knife from the pouch slung on your back.

"I will pass the gate by killing you," you sneered, as you started circling the old man who was still watching you closely.

He smiled at you. "I know you are brave, Princess. But here in the Land of Magic, your strength is nothing."

"Let us see if that is the case," you screamed and made for him with your knife in the air.

He raised his staff and pointed it at you and a blast of invisible air slammed against you, throwing you on the floor. You immediately did a back flip and stood up. He was clearly using magic and you had to strategize. There was no time to think, as you saw him open his hand and a ball of flame came hurtling towards you.

You dove out of the way and the flame hit the spot you had just vacated, setting the grass there on fire. You gasped and turned to look back at the man who was smiling at you with an evil glint in his eyes.

You tried to stand up, but he was pointing at you with his staff and you found your feet rooted firmly to the ground as if invisible hands held you firmly in place. You struggled to move but couldn't and raised your arm to aim the knife at the old man from that distance. He opened his hand again, letting go of another ball of fire that was hurtling slowly towards you. You felt the impact of the heat, burning flesh and the sound of your screams as you burst into flames.

𝔄𝔡𝔳𝔢𝔫𝔱𝔲𝔯𝔢 𝔈𝔫𝔡𝔰 𝔥𝔢𝔯𝔢.

Wrong Decision!!!

You can return to Chapter 9 or start the game again from Chapter 1.

~ SUREFOOT ~

CHAPTER 55

Go West

⁕⁖⁖⁖⁖⁖⁖⁖⁖⁖⁖⁖

You decided to go west with Dusty, accompanied by the four warriors, to the outskirts of Omahi Village. As you rode together, your thoughts were on the journey ahead and you noticed that Nadum was trying to start a conversation with you, but you ignored him.

You were disappointed at his decision not to go on the quest and knew that he had an ambition to be chief when your father died. From the conversation in your father's hut, it was very obvious that the elders seemed to be in support of his leadership and it was only a matter of time before they asked Queen Cohahi to step down from her temporary leadership.

Nadum tried unsuccessfully to keep up with you to force you on a gentle trot but you kept galloping with Dusty and he soon gave up. As you all approached a mass of rocks signifying the boundaries of Omahi Village, the group slowed down and the horses went on a gentle trot.

A huge mountain towered in front of you. The sides of it that you could see, appeared steep and you managed to see the jagged snowy peaks far ahead. This was the mountain where the famed Wizard of Trasca lived and the men could not go beyond this point. The wizard was a very cunning old man, but there was no other way to pass through, except you climbed this mountain. At this point, you had no need for a horse, so you alighted from Dusty and handed him over to Nadum.

He used the opportunity to grab your hand and you were forced to look at him.

"You can stop this madness and come back home with me."

"What about my father?"

Nadum shrugged and said, "He is an old man and old people die."

"I see. Is there any other reason why you do not want my father to stay alive?"

Nadum's face hardened as he said, "I do not know what you are implying, but I am just concerned for your safety."

"Well, you can stop being concerned about me. I have a quest I need to embark on," you replied coldly, turning around and slapping Dusty on the rear as a signal for it to return back to the village. The faithful horse neighed in response and turned, heading back to the village on its own. You watched the horse galloping away, its hooves making a dust cloud in the distance. You turned to see that Nadum and the other men were watching you quietly. Nadum leaned forward and said, "You are as stubborn as your mother. I hope your stubbornness does not get you killed."

He turned around and rode away with the other three warriors. After watching them for a while, you hung your bag on your shoulder and started climbing nimbly up the steep sides of the mountain. It took a lot of hours of grueling effort, groans and near misses, but eventually you got to the peak.

After lifting yourself up on the mountain, you were immediately struck by the fact that it was very windy at the peak. It seemed like a storm was brewing. You noticed an old man sitting with his back to you at the other end of the mountain. You could see his long, grey hair falling on his back and he wore a long, straw-colored robe. He seemed to be looking at a fire that he had kindled at his feet for warmth. As you cautiously approached, you stepped on something that crunched at your feet. You looked down and saw skeletons on the floor. The number of dead bodies was startling and it made you pause in your tracks. You decided to approach the wizard and as you got closer, you noticed the light of the flames burning in his eyes as he stared at it with so much intensity.

This definitely must be the famed Wizard of Trasca. You were sure of that with each step you took as you got closer to the old man sitting by the flames. You didn't want to startle him but you wanted him to grant you permission to cross his mountain. You shuddered to see the different piles of skeletons all over the floor of the mountain and you wondered what could have killed them. Looking around, you noticed pieces of armor and weapons on the ground and then you guessed that these were dead adventurers. Your questioning thoughts came to an end when the wizard raised his hands up slowly without turning around, indicating that you stopped.

Still without turning around or looking at you, he stood up slowly, raised his hand to the sky and with a loud voice, he said, "Arise!"

You wondered what he meant by that but not for long. The ground began to shake as the skeletons of all the dead adventurers littered on the mountain floor started rising up. You watched, alarmed, as their joints came together. You could hear the creaking sounds as the bones came together, and suddenly a large army of skeleton warriors stood before the wizard. He pointed in your direction and they looked at you with their sunken holes for eyes.

They picked up their fallen swords and moved very fast towards you. You pulled out your spear strapped to your back and jumped in the air, slicing downwards at the same time, scattering bones left and right.

You fought hard, breaking their bones into pieces as they surged towards you, but that didn't hinder them as more came after you.

Will you continue to fight? Turn to Chapter 17.

Will you run for your life? Turn to Chapter 40.

CHAPTER 56

Staircase Two

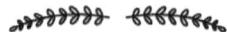

Which of these staircases will lead me to my quest?

This silent question flowed through your mind as you gazed at both staircases, unsure. You decided to let fate decide for you as you closed your eyes and walked towards a direction. You let your feet guide you to what Mother Fate had decided for you. Each step, with a niggling doubt, brought you closer to the end of your quest. Finally, your feet landed on a step and it held firm. You heaved a sigh of relief, opened your eyes and kept on climbing. The staircase was grand and it widened, leading through the dark cave up to an opening in the sky. Out of curiosity, you decided to look down and observed you were a long distance from the depth below, which was no longer the floor of the cave but a raging sea.

What is going on? Where is the cave? you thought to yourself in a panic.

All through your ascent up the staircase, your mind didn't register the change in the environment around you – the walls of the cave crumbling away and giving way to a dark, cloudy atmosphere with the stairs leading up into an overcast sky. Your mind had been focused on the end game, which

was securing the healing stone in time to save your father. Right now, you were very aware of your environment and the staircase with no railings to support you was now giving you cause to worry. Deciding to tread with caution going forward, you put a foot ahead of you just as the step in front of you disintegrated into a cloud of dust, causing you to lose your balance. You started tumbling to your doom, screaming. The wind was rushing past your ears fast, as you fell, legs and hands flailing helplessly in every direction. Your mind tried to think of a way to save yourself. You remembered the Wizard of Trasca and tried to imagine yourself back in bird form, but a blast of cold wind hit you and a scream erupted from you, breaking your focus.

The sound of the tumultuous waves of the sea was louder now and you looked down to see that you were closer to hitting the water with a force that could most certainly kill you, judging by the height and speed of your descent. You saw something in the water, as you got closer. It was a large creature that had lots of tentacles spread out, causing the water to move violently, thrashing against the rocks. It had seen you and was raising its slimy tentacles towards you.

Adventure Ends Here.

You are quite unlucky, Game Player!!!

You can return to Chapter 19 or start the game again from Chapter 1.

~ SUREFOOT ~

CHAPTER 57

Hide!

The voice was really beautiful, and you still felt the dulling sensation as you listened to it. You noticed that your feet started dragging a bit and you had this strange desire to just let go of everything and lie down and sleep. You were unable to move, or at least it was a lot of effort to do so and you leaned against the wall, feeling drowsy. It seemed like you were transported to the grassy plains of Omahi Village and you watched the children playing in the grass smiling and chasing a rabbit.

As you sat on the grass, watching the sky and feeling the evening breeze on your hair, a hand touched your shoulder, shaking you. You turned to see the worried face of your mother, screaming at you in panic.

"Wake up…wake up, daughter."

Snapping out of your reverie, you pushed yourself away from the wall and decided to find somewhere to hide and observe the source of the singing. You discovered a hollow along the wall of the cave and crawled into it just in time before a fast-moving body of water passed by, taking everything along its path.

You held your breath in mild panic as you realized that you could have been torn into bits, as the raging water passed you by just inches, roaring away down the dark corridor of the cave. Following the deadly body of water was a beautiful lady wearing a white silk gown, her long, white hair flowing to the ground and almost transparent, like water.

She passed by slowly, still singing in her melodious voice, unaware of your presence in the crook of the cave just to her left. The sound of her singing started to dull your senses again, but you shook your head and closed your ears as you realized that she was the famed Mimanto. She sang to attract unsuspecting adventurers who would stand, enchanted by her voice, only to be swept away by a flood of water at her command. You heaved a sigh of relief and came out of the crook of the cave that had just saved you from this devious being.

It appeared the cave had a lot more in store for you, after your near-encounter with the cravuners and now Mimanto. You marched more cautiously, wondering what next you would see in the Mountain of Deception. You saw a bright light peeking into the cave up ahead and as you approached it, you realized that it was an opening at the back of the cave. The opening was evidently leading you to a larger room and you intended to find out where it led. As you were about to pass through the opening, a dwarf came out.

He had huge, bulging eyes and sharp teeth that showed as he gave you a shrewd smile.

"I'm Hippo, guardian of the Mountain of Deception. You can't pass until you tell me what is long and short, what is fat and slim and what is short and tall."

There seemed to be barriers and tests at every step that you took in this quest and it was obvious that Hippo didn't intend to let you pass until you gave him a response.

~ HIDE! ~

You thought hard about this strange riddle.

Will you say a form changer? Turn to Chapter 98.

Will you say that you don't know and fight to pass? Turn to Chapter 70.

Will you say he is the one? Turn to Chapter 3.

~ SUREFOOT ~

CHAPTER 58

Politely Decline

'I am sorry, I cannot accept your kind offer, dear Ishbatech. It is a very tempting and generous offer but I need to find the healing stone in time to save my father,' you replied.

He smiled at you. It appeared he was just testing you with that offer and your answer must have been what he expected you to say.

"Wise answer, Princess. Now, I shall help you. Follow me," he said, walking across the field.

He led you through the field of flowers to a wooden stable which had magnificent horses and singled out a white horse. He snapped his fingers and the horse developed beautiful wings. The transformation was a surprise to you and you gasped as the beautiful horse walked towards you and placed its face in your hands. The horse was so beautiful. You patted its face and let your hands run through its back and lovely white wings that it immediately spread out for your admiration. This horse reminded you of Dusty and you smiled, looking back at Ishbatech.

~ SUREFOOT ~

"It is so beautiful. Thank you so much."

"You're welcome, dear princess. I believe you need to be on your way," he said, pointing to one of his winged men who came towards you with all your possessions, which included your weapons and pouches.

You collected the items, securing the pouch around your back, the spear tied to your side and nodded thanks at the magician as you nimbly climbed on the back of the horse. The beautiful horse spread its wings and started its ascent, while the magician and his creatures waved at you until they looked like specks of dust from your elevated position in the sky.

The flying horse soared across the sky with you on its back and you admired the beautiful clouds as you rode through them. Below you, the mountains lined up with streams of sparkling oceans spread out as far as the eye could see. The view was so beautiful that you didn't immediately notice someone ahead of you, until your horse neighed as it noticed her standing there.

A small, pink fairy stood in the midst of the clouds, her pretty, transparent wings fluttering in the air as she flew around with an angry look on her face. She shot an arrow into the sky and it rained heavily with great thunder and lightning, impeding your progress.

The pink cloud fairy stood up in the clouds, feet spread apart with hands on her waist, smiling at you, happy that she had hindered your progress, as your horse was acting nervous with the lightning flashing dangerously around both of you. You had heard of cloud fairies before and they were supposed to be friendly. Why was this one being intentionally malicious and preventing you from moving ahead?

What will you do?

Will you bring out your sword and attack her? Turn to Chapter 64.

Will you ask what her grievance is? Turn to Chapter 79.

CHAPTER 59

Find Your Way

The sound of fairy music filled the air and you watched them dancing away with their tiny wings, looking like lots of beautiful fireflies in the field. The scene looked very beautiful and the fairies appeared friendly, but something prevented you from getting their attention. You couldn't explain why you didn't shout out for help but somehow you felt there was no need to bother those merry bunch of fairies. Watching them one last time, you turned away and continued your trek through the forest full of lush foliage and prancing animals, until you stumbled upon an old cottage at the center of the forest.

The cottage was small and made up of wood, with a chimney and had a neat, little garden at its side. The smoke coming out of the chimney was an indication that someone was inside. The two large windows didn't give anything away when you peered in and so you decided to nudge the front door with your snout. It surprisingly swung open and you were face to face with a hooded figure sitting on a wooden chair facing the door.

He wore a cloak made up of animal skin, with rough, dark hair and bushy white brows and a part of his face was covered with a hood, such that you couldn't see his facial expression. You paused from going in and he said in a deep voice, **"Welcome, brave princess. You may transform now."**

"How do you know that I am not really a wolf?"

"I can tell you're not in your true form, because I'm a wizard."

His revelation made you even more reluctant, as you didn't know his intentions.

"There is no need to be afraid of me, Princess. I see your true nature even though you're in wolf form and I can change you myself, but I won't."

"I need this form to continue my quest."

"You needed it on the mountain, brave princess. I believe you met my brother, the Wizard of Trasca?"

"Yes indeed, he changed me to this form."

The old wizard nodded and continued, "You must have impressed him to get a gift like that. I'm his brother, the Wizard of The Enchanted Forest. Now you may transform," he commanded quietly.

You closed your eyes and spoke the desire to transform to your true self and watched in amazement as the fur shrunk into your body and you started to stretch back into your human self. After a few minutes, you lay panting on the floor with the exertion of the transformation and stood up slowly under the watchful eyes of the hooded wizard of The Enchanted Forest.

"Now I have transformed as you requested. I would like to continue my quest."

"And so you will, but you must solve my riddle first. Your answer will determine whether or not you'll get to the Mountain of Lanogoza," he replied quietly.

You stared at him for a while, wondering what he wanted to ask. He remained seated on his wooden chair. You noticed his long staff in his hand that he dropped on the table and adjusted his hood. His face was still hidden from you and he stared at you from his very bushy eyebrows that almost covered his beady eyes.

He smiled and asked you to sit down.

Turn to Chapter 15.

~ SUREFOOT ~

CHAPTER 60

A Shark

You thought to yourself, *the shark is the ruler of the seas.* What else could possibly frighten all the fishes in the Sea of Eternity?

"A shark," you replied confidently. That had to be the right answer but you were surprised when they started to laugh again in their gurgling, "fishy" voices.

"Wrong," Sunta declared.

"You're not worthy to pass The Sea of Eternity."

"I cannot be wrong. What else is scarier in the sea?" you reasoned, trying to back away.

Sunta had a smug, fishy expression on its face and refused to answer as they all crowded you. You tried to show some sense of false bravado and demanded an answer.

"Tell me what the right answer is," you asked

"You will never know, impostor," Sunta replied

They advanced towards you, baring their sharp teeth and you realized that this wasn't going to end well if you didn't act fast.

"Stop, we can just talk about this." You reasoned, all the while backing away as they followed your movements with their eyes.

"There is nothing to talk about impostor." Sunta screamed and in unison they all came after you and you darted into nearby corrals. You tried to swim in between the colorful corrals hoping the fishes will get distracted but they were hot on your tail and everywhere you turned was a vicious looking fish in the way

"Why?" you asked, backing away as they all crowded around you with their teeth bared.

"Why? We are hungry," Sunta declared and they all made for you, biting and ripping out chunks of flesh.

Adventure Ends Here.

Wrong Answer!!!

You can return to Chapter 30 or start the game again from Chapter 1.

CHAPTER 61

The Feather

T here were so many of them and they laughed at you, praising their leader, whom they addressed as King Acrylic. He looked at you admiringly and he laughed with his fellow horsemen as you studied him. You had heard of him. He was the legendary king of half horsemen and he killed people without pity.

Luckily for you, he wanted to marry you. You felt in your pouch as the horsemen made to grab you and your hands brushed against the feather that the seer had given you.

You held it in front of you and immediately became invisible. They looked for you in confusion and began to argue and fight.

You avoided making contacts with their bodies as punches flew between them, wings, tails and muscles all involved in the brawl of the heavens. You headed for your final destination – the Mountain of Lanogoza.

From a distance, you could already make out the white, glistening snow on the mountain's peaks. You descended gradually to the mouth of a cave and like Hippo predicted, the wings disappeared. The mountain loomed threateningly ahead of you, reaching out towards the skies. You brought

out your knife and moved cautiously into the cave. The walls glistened of some silvery mineral that you couldn't identify, making the walls shimmer in the dark and you heard the sound of footsteps coming down the dark passageway. You noticed a movement up ahead and paused as you saw the shadow of a creature coming towards you. The creature appeared to have things crawling on its head.

What will be your next move?

Will you stop and fight it? Turn to Chapter 102.

Will you avoid it by jumping behind the rock just beside you? Turn to Chapter 8.

CHAPTER 62

Wait

You were very thirsty after the intense battle with the T-rex, but decided to wait for a while before drinking the water. It was quite puzzling to find this pool of water in a desert. Despite the nudge of thirst from your parched mouth and throat, you tiredly sat by the pool of water, looking at it and trying to make up your mind. You didn't have to think for long when you noticed a green ball of light in the depths of the water. It was getting larger as it came to the surface and what looked like a woman with several tentacles jutting out of her head, came out of the water.

Her emerald green eyes gleamed as she smiled at the look of surprise on your face. The long, red tentacles made up her hair and they had a life of their own. Each one of them was springing out in different directions from her head. You sprang up in alarm and continued to stare at her without saying anything as she remained in the water, observing you.

"My name is Vanotica, the Queen of Zenoisa and this pool of water is the entrance to my kingdom," she said and nodded at you, expecting you to also introduce yourself.

You had overcome your initial shock and looked at her, trying to decipher her intentions, but her green eyes were difficult to read. Apart from the smile on her face, she didn't give away any emotion, so you decided to introduce yourself as well.

"I am Princess Surefoot, daughter of Chief Ziza and Queen Cohahi, rulers of the Omahi tribe that controls the Great Plains."

Queen Vanotica's smile broadened as she said, "You're far from your home in the Great Plains." She indicated the bare desert, looking around and back to you. "What brings you here...alone?" she hissed, looking very serious all of a sudden, her smile disappearing.

You didn't yet know her intentions and could not trust her with the details of your quest, so you gave a vague response. "I am on a quest and do not wish to trouble you. I was only thirsty and stopped by your pool."

"As you should be, seeing that you're in a desert. If you had drunk from my pool, without asking, I would have slain you immediately."

You heaved a sigh of relief and relaxed a bit. It seemed she had no bad intentions after all.

"You can drink from my pool," she said, her smile coming back to her face.

The desert was indeed a dry and unfriendly place and you didn't think you could get water anywhere else for a long time, so you thanked her and made for the pool.

"Not so fast, Princess," she hissed, with a mischievous gleam in her green eyes.

You looked at her questioningly and she said, "You can drink water from my pool, only if you win me in battle."

You were very thirsty and tired, but you needed to drink the water. The rolling desert sands stretched for miles on end. You looked back at Vanotica, who now had an evil-looking smile on her face. What was the guarantee that she would let you walk away from her without engaging you in a battle? She seemed to be spoiling for a fight and although tired, you intended to give her just that.

You pulled out your spear and held it firmly, feeling the comfort of the wooden weapon against your hands, reminding you of battles that you had fought and won with it. Pointing the sharp spear towards Vanotica, you charged at her with a loud battle scream.

The spear narrowly missed Vanotica's face by inches as she dodged the blow by swerving left real fast. One of the tentacles on her head was sliced in the process, falling with a thump into the water. She looked at it in anger and with a screech of pain, stretched out her hands towards you. She shot out of the water and you saw that she had seven tails, violently thrashing about and ready to hit you.

You promptly dived out of the way as one of the tails came at you, and you rolled to the side and inserted your spear, pinning that tail to the ground. She screamed in pain as the other tails lunged at you, one of them knocking the spear off the tail. One of the tails tied up your leg and started to pull you towards the pool, while the others hit you from all sides. You were fast losing strength, having just fought a dinosaur and trekked a long distance through the desert.

To win her, you needed to be lucky.

Choose a chapter that will determine your fate.

Turn to Chapter 5 or Chapter 83.

Good luck!!

~ SUREFOOT ~

CHAPTER 63

The Thick Forest

⊱⊰

The wind was getting very intense and blew up stones, twigs around, with the few scattered trees on the mountain bowing to its merciless savagery. Lightning flashed even more now, accompanied by a loud crack of thunder. A few spatters of raindrops were sufficient to make you look around for shelter to avoid the storm. There was no way you could continue on this quest in this weather and as the rain started to intensify, soaking up your thick, grey fur, it was hard to see your way through the darkness. A flash of lightning showed you what looked like an opening on the side of the cave and you quickly made for it as the raindrops felt like tiny blows on your back. The clouds looked dark and unforgiving and it seemed like they were opening up to release a deluge of rain.

Crawling into the hole was the best thing to do. You shook off the water that had drenched through your fur and curled up to sleep. You were still a bit hungry but soon fell into a dreamless sleep and only stirred when the heavy rainfall had withered away to just drizzles. Venturing out of your hiding spot, you continued on your journey, anxious to make up for lost time.

The mountain was muddy from the heavy rains. In your hurry, you slipped and started rolling down the mountain and were unable to arrest your fall. You bumped against rocks that prevented you from falling over the mountain, but still continued to roll downhill, until a huge rock cut your fall. The impact almost knocked you out, so you took some time to catch your breath and then stood up. Shaking off the dust, you found out that you were at the base of the mountain, overlooking a vast expanse of thick forest.

The thickets at the edge of the forest seemed to act as a barrier to keep people away. They were entangled with prickly points that gave you sharp, painful cuts as you went through them. Eventually, you broke through the other side of the thickets and the forest trees were standing tall in straight lines, towering up to the sky like a gigantic army.

Going into the forest, as your feet crunched against the fallen dry, brown leaves, you were immediately enchanted by the beauty of this green foliage paradise. The forest floor had little squirrels and other animals scampering around, gathering nuts and climbing back up the tree. They were not scared of you, despite your wolf form.

You could see tiny dots of light on the forest floor. The movement of the trees with the wind caused the sunlight to penetrate through the thick roof of broad leaves. The blend of colors and sound of animals gave a magical feel to the forest atmosphere. You began to feel at home and almost forgot your quest, until you heard someone singing.

The sound seemed to be coming from the left of where you were standing and you set off running towards the sound. As the singing got louder, you slowed down and peeped through the bushes to see a large clearing. The clearing was filled with magical little creatures that you identified as fairies, dancing away into the evening. They wore colorful dresses and had flowers on their hair and were fluttering around with little silver wings. The scene was so beautiful and you realized it was the first time you were encountering fairies. You had only heard about them in folklore, that they didn't relate with humans and had magical powers. As they pranced about, twirling in midair, they looked like beautiful fireflies.

You wondered if they could give you directions on how to get to the Mountain of Lanogoza.

Will you meet the fairies? Turn to Chapter 21.

Will you try to find your way on your own? Turn to Chapter 59.

~ SUREFOOT ~

CHAPTER 64

Attack the Cloud Fairy

⊰⊱⊰⊱⊰⊱⊰⊱

The sky darkened as the clouds gathered and lightning started flashing dangerously around you, spooking your horse. The horse started to neigh and fly about in fright and you tried to calm it down, while getting very upset with this annoying cloud fairy. What trouble did she have with you trying to pass through the clouds? Cloud fairies were known to be friendly creatures but this one was having a good laugh at your expense, as you struggled to control the horse that was spooked with the flash of lightning and the jarring sound of thunder. You held on to the horse and forced it to take a dive as a flash of lightning went past you.

That was dangerously close as you could have been burnt to a crisp. You could hear the high-pitched voice of the cloud fairy laughing mockingly and it got on your nerves. The malicious fairy made you lose precious time and you intended to teach her a lesson. You were the last traveler that she would ever have a chance to impede their progress and have fun at their expense.

You kicked your flying horse and spurred it towards the cloud fairy. The horse responded faithfully, despite the fact that it was spooked, and began its ascent towards the fairy that was perched on a cloud above, looking at you in amusement. The horse's wings stretched out as the lightning reflected against the broad whiteness, giving it an unnatural beauty and it flapped effortlessly as you came closer to the fairy. Pulling out your spear that you had secured on your back, you placed it on your right hand, whilst holding the neck of the horse with your left hand to maintain your balance.

She observed your sudden hand movement of taking your spear and you saw her smile disappear and her small, pink face contort in rage. She lifted her tiny hand in the air, pointed at you and the horse and immediately the clouds ahead of you started to come together. You halted the horse in alarm but the clouds formed into a ball and hurtled straight at you, covering you and your horse.

The ball of clouds felt like a warm, thick blanket enveloping both you and the horse with no way of escape. The cloud formed a thick barrier between you and the environment, cutting off your view and air supply. Not only could you not see ahead of you, you started choking because it was getting more difficult for you to breathe with each passing minute. Your horse started to panic and prance around uncontrollably and you lost control and fell off its back, toppling to Earth.

Adventure Ends Here.

Foolish decision!!!

You can return to Chapter 58 or start the game again from Chapter 1.

~ SUREFOOT ~

CHAPTER 65

Refuse to Go

⬩⬩⬩⬩⬩⬩⬩ ⬩⬩⬩⬩⬩⬩⬩

There was something about the gleam in her beady eyes that made you doubt the old witch. Swearing on the life of her already dead mother was also not at all convincing.

"You swear on the life of your dead mother?" you asked the old hag, smiling and moving closer.

"I … I swear on that poor woman's life. She was a good woman," the old woman whispered, moving backwards.

You snatched her by her long, rough white hair and pulled her towards the open hole. She was about to scream but you quickly covered her mouth with your palm to stop her from doing so and pushed her into the hole that she had indicated. Standing at the entrance of the dark cave, you watched the old hag stumble and turn around. She started walking pretty fast for her age, towards you. She was mumbling something to herself and didn't want to go even further into the dark cavern. You wondered what she was afraid of. You wondered what she was so willing to send you to encounter.

You moved forward and with both feet wide apart, pushed her with all your might. She screamed with fright as the force of your push propelled her forward into the narrow cave and she fell face first on the cave floor. Then it happened very fast – ropes appearing from the dark, latching on to her legs and arms as she screamed. The ropes lifted her up and she was left dangling face down from the top of the cave.

It was a trap, as you had suspected and you quickly brought out your knife and waited as she screamed in the dark, begging to be let down. From the corner of your eye, you could see three shadowy figures appear from both walls of the dark cavern, holding what looked like clubs in their hands.

"Help me down, sisters," the old hag screeched.

"What are you doing there?" another raspy voice asked, as the figures stood peering at the old hag.

This was your cue to approach the group and you ran towards them with your knife in the air.

"Watch out, look behind you!" the hag screamed as they turned but you quickly slashed one of them on the throat. The figure grasped her throat and fell as blood gurgled from her open throat. The other two seemed to have awakened from their slumber and charged at you, screaming like banshees. They looked just like the old hag, but were surprisingly fast.

One of them swung the club and you bent down, sliding under it as it passed across your head in seconds. Swinging around, you stabbed her on her back and she screamed, falling to the ground. The other hag screamed and swung at you left and right, with you guessing her mood each time and stepping in the opposite direction. She decided to stop the left, right attacks and struck at your chest with the club, but you held it abruptly, surprising her and pulled it towards you, at the same time delivering a blow to her face. She staggered back in shock, a hand to her mouth and you followed after her, kicking her until she fell unconscious on the floor. The other hag that you had stabbed was crawling away. You walked up to her and with a twist, snapped her neck in two.

The old witch hanging from the ropes screamed. "Nooooo... You killed all my sisters!"

You walked to her swinging frame slowly, wiping the blood off your knife on your leg.

"You all got what you deserve," you said pushing her. That action caused her to swing from side to side, screaming all the way.

"Get me down," she yelled.

You viciously cut her ropes and she fell down with a hard thud on her back and started howling in pain. Ignoring her cries of pain, you knelt down beside her, bringing the knife to her neck. You felt she deserved to die, since she had planned to kill you. She stopped her whimpering as she felt the cold, sharp blade against her rumpled neck and she smiled.

"I...I'm sorry, we were just hungry, that's all. It is hard to find food here."

"So, you eat unsuspecting adventurers?"

"Only the ones that are foolish enough to fall in the trap. No harm done, right? You killed my sisters and now we are even," she said, giving a big smile and exhibiting her almost toothless gums.

'Show me the right path to the Mountain of Lanogoza," you insisted and pressed the knife even further, causing the sharp blade to nick her neck, drawing a bit of blood.

'You must go back to the passage and you'll see two doors. Take the left one, which will lead you to the mountain, but before that...Ha!'

'Before that, what will happen?' you asked.

The old witch kept on laughing and you slit her throat quickly and cleaned the blood from your knife. Without looking back, you made your way out of the hole and went back to the passage that she had described. Truly in front of you, as clear as day, were two doors. They were both strong, wooden doors that stretched out in height to about eight feet. They looked very similar and you wondered which one would lead you to your destination. The old hag had asked you to take the left door.

Will you take her advice? What if the witch had lied to you, again?

Will you take the left door? Turn to Chapter 12.

Will you take the right door? Turn to Chapter 77.

CHAPTER 66

Avoid Fighting the Lions

The two ferocious-looking lions snarled at you and bared their sharp teeth and you looked at them this time with a mixture of fear and exasperation. You were already exhausted from all the fighting you had done earlier with the soldiers and the zepenter. You were definitely not in the mood to fight two hungry-looking lions.

There has to be another way, you thought to yourself and looked around in desperation, as the lions started slowly advancing. Obviously, they were stalking you from across the cave and would soon advance in an attack. You had to be quick in finding a way of escape. You had to create some form of distraction and fast. The lions were making their way towards you as you picked up a big stone and quickly hurled it in their direction. The stone made impact, crushing one of the lion's paws, stopping it in its tracks as it roared in pain.

This action aggravated the uninjured lion and it made for you in anger, its long mane standing up frightfully as the light flashed against its sharp, curved teeth when it flew at you.

You jumped into the air, just missing the sharp claws of the beast as it dived at you and landed on the spot you just left.

It turned back immediately and started after you, but you landed on one side of the wall and were holding on tight to it. You were relived to feel the roughness of the dungeon walls and used the protruding stony edges as a leverage to climb up steadily on the walls. Progress was slow and steady and your plan was to get close to the window and find a way to open the hole so you could climb out of the cave. There was no way you were going to survive fighting the lions, especially when you had upset them. You were almost getting close to your target and started grinning in victory as you could hear the lions growling and scratching at the sides of the walls in anger.

You were gaining some traction and with excitement started advancing faster up on the wall when the rock where you just placed your right leg broke away.

"No *way! This is not happening,*" you thought to yourself, but you lost your hold on the wall and fell down screaming, into the hungry mouth of one of the waiting lions.

Adventure Ends Here.

You're supposed to be brave, Game Player.

Start again, if you dare!!!

You can return to Chapter 39 or start the game again from Chapter 1.

~ SUREFOOT ~

CHAPTER 67

Reject It!

Y ou could feel his cold, watchful gaze as he studied the maze of
emotions running through your face. This could be it, the end of
your journey with the price of the healing stone just within reach.
You had faced so many obstacles and finally this was the end. There was
no need to put your life at risk continuing this journey across the remaining
seas and mountains, when the count was gracious enough to offer you the
healing stone.

Your smile faded as you looked up at the count's smug expression and you
wondered why he was kind enough to just let you have the stone. He was
the same person that you heard usually drained the blood of his victims and
was responsible for killing that girl's parents and keeping her here to serve
him. There had to be a reason why he was offering this gift so freely. *Maybe
it is just a test,* you reasoned to yourself, whilst watching his cold, bloodshot
gaze fixed on you. The seer had not told you this version of Count Dracula'
story. He had asked you to go to the Mountain of Lanogoza and there,
you intended to go. The count seemed to have read your mind as his smile
slowly faded before you spoke.

"Thank you, dear count, for this gift. You are truly kind. However, I cannot take this healing stone."

"Why?" he asked quietly, still watching your every move, which made you quite uneasy.

"I am glad you offered me this gift. However, I was asked to journey to the Mountain of Lanogoza to get the healing stone and I intend to go there."

"This takes away the rest of the journey, Princess. Are you sure you won't reconsider?"

Indeed, that question was very tempting, as you were already feeling weary thinking about the journey ahead, but you once more politely declined his offer. The count moved so fast, like a flash of lightning and he was in front of you, caressing your hand, once more with that smile on his face.

"I was very hungry," he said, leaning closer and you raised your hand to push him but he held on tight, almost locking you in a romantic embrace and gazing at you with a mesmerizing look.

"What are you doing?" you asked in a whisper.

"Reconsidering killing you," he said, letting go and stepping away. He walked with his back facing you to the other end of the room, almost like he was intentionally keeping some distance between two of you.

'You're very wise, Princess. No traveler has ever resisted taking the stone. What gave me away?" he turned around, amusement and curiosity in his eyes.

You were still confused about his strange behavior and wondered the best way to protect yourself if he planned to attack you. You chose to remain silent whilst watching him closely.

"No need to answer," he said, brushing his own question aside with a flick of his hand and turning back to look at you, holding out his hand. He quickly offered an explanation for your unspoken question as you stared at the closed palm that he held out to you.

"For giving me the right answer, I shall give you a gift."

You raised your eyebrows, wondering what this mischievous count had up his sleeves again. He opened his palm and a soft glitter caught your eye.

"Come closer, I don't bite," he said with a broad smile, revealing the sharp fangs on both sides of his mouth. You paused and stood facing him defensively, but with a tired sigh he was once more in front of you. Once again, you saw how fast he moved. He held your hand and you tried to resist, but he calmly smiled at you.

"Please stop trying to fight me all the time. We both know I have the upper hand here," he said, smiling.

"Don't be too sure of that," you replied angrily. He raised his eyes to look at you and quickly held your neck, pushing you against the cold wall. Then he raised his lips to yours and you turned your face away.

"You find me repulsive, my dear princess? You know I can make you stay here with me, forever?" he asked. Then he held your hand gently and you could feel him pushing something down your middle finger.

"What are you doing?" you asked, looking down at the glittering ring that he placed on the middle finger of your right hand. He backed up with his hands in the air, as a sign of surrender.

"My gift to you."

"You intend to keep me here?"

"I would have loved to do so, but you passed my test and now you can leave."

"Then why did you give me the ring?" you asked, confused.

"I've given you a present to help you find your way to the Mountain of Lanogoza."

"But why?" you said, still looking at the sparkling ring on your finger. You moved away from the wall where he had pushed you earlier, looking around for the fastest exit. He was right that you couldn't fight him, but you could try to get away.

"Don't bother trying to run," he said, easily reading your mind once again. You looked back at him, exasperated.

"I have no intentions of harming you. If you rub the ring on your finger, it will take you to the Mountain of Lanogoza."

You were very reluctant to rub the ring and wondered if he was telling the truth this time around. His eyes became cold as he gazed at you.

He took a deep breath and started walking towards you with determination in his steps. You wondered why he didn't come at you like a flurry of wind, as he was used to doing.

"Princess, I have given you a gift, a free pass to leave my castle. I don't intend to offer it to you again. If you don't rub on that ring and leave, then you will remain here with me."

His steps sounded heavily on the floor of the castle as he marched towards you with an expression on your face you couldn't read and immediately you started rubbing the ring in panic. It didn't seem like it was working and he was almost close to you. You looked up to see him smiling and with a wave of his hand, your weapons were in your hands. You looked at your

weapons and back at him as he started to dissolve before your eyes, with the mischievous smile still on his face. You managed to croak, *thank you*, before disappearing from his castle forever.

The next few minutes were like a blur. You were rapidly sailing through the clouds and your hair flew all over your face as you were transported at lightning speed. Your eyes were hit with sensations of different colors flying around you – golden, blue and red lights skimming through your vision. You closed your eyes as it seemed like you were going crazy and began to fall to the ground from a great height. You screamed as your body rotated in circular motion and you could see that you were headed for a dark mountain that suddenly appeared in front of you. You narrowly missed a sharp peak of ice that was jutting out of the mountain, as you kept falling. Just as you were about to hit the ground, everything slowed down and you were suspended just above the front of a cave that led into the mountain.

You raised both hands, holding the spear and knife and it seemed like a magical force held you and gently dropped you on the ground. The ring on your finger disappeared and you wondered if it had returned back to its master, after fulfilling its task of transporting you to the Mountain of Lanogoza. There was no time to dwell on such thoughts as you still had the task of finding the real healing stone inside the mountain. Quickly, you secured your spear in place at your back. Holding your knife in front of you as a means of defense, you cautiously made your way into the cave.

The cave was dark within and you walked in cautiously and noticed broken pieces of skeletons littered all over the cave. You guessed they were other adventurers who had come to an untimely end and you hoped you would have a better outcome than them.

You smelled them before you could hear them and quickly leaped to a section of the cave and leaned down, just as you heard the sound of flapping wings. You were repulsed by the overwhelming rotten smell of cravuners. They flew past in their numbers, making high-pitched screeching sounds as they passed, each flap of their wings sending the most revolting smell your way and you struggled not to gag. The vampire birds were attracted to light and luckily for you, you had not lit any torch and were wise enough to duck on time. They were known to rip the flesh off the bones of their prey until there was nothing left.

After what seemed like a while, the last of the vampire birds filtered out of the cave and you came out of hiding, making your way even further down the cave. The passageway narrowed even further and although your eyes had gotten used to the dimness of the cave, it seemed to be getting darker. A small ray of light shone ahead and you hastened towards it and found yourself in an open, circular space in the heart of the cave. The ray of light came from the sunlight shining through a hole at the top of the cave and as you turned to assess the environment, a movement caught your eye. A large tail made for you and you jumped away in time to avoid getting crushed. Rolling to a kneeling position, you raised your knife to attack and your eyes met the eyes of the ancient dragon. He was huge and stared at you with large, red eyes, breathing smoke from his mouth.

The eyes held no animosity. If anything, you saw some amusement in them. The dragon walked towards you, unafraid, though you looked fierce, like you were about to attack him.

"Put down your weapon, Princess," he hissed at you.

"You attacked me first," you said defiantly, not willing to let down your guard.

"As I should. I'm the guardian of the Mountain of Lanogoza and you entered my territory without permission," he said with pride and stopped some meters away from you.

Indeed, the dragon had spoken a wise thing and you lowered your knife reluctantly and stood up to face this huge beast. He nodded, swinging his tail to the left and slowly to the right, then turned around and asked, "You seek the healing stone within this sacred mountain, right?"

"Yes, I seek the healing stone."

"Why? Is it for fame or fortune?"

"No." You wanted him to believe your true intentions. "I seek the stone to heal my father."

He regarded you with cold eyes narrowing into slits, almost like he was trying to read your soul.

"I see. Well, you impressed the count, let's see if you will impress me as well. I have before me three stones. Which of them is the healing stone?'

You wondered what stones he was talking about. You remembered entering an empty room. Following his gaze, you saw three stones at the center of the room, sitting on a rock that appeared to have been hewn from the body of the cave. You could have sworn that they were not there before.

The light from an opening at the top of the cave shone on the three stones and you stared at each of them, whilst the dragon patiently waited for your selection. The stones you saw were all different, and your attention was immediately drawn to the beautiful golden stone. The light shone directly on it, reflecting golden shimmers all around the magnificent stone and on to the surrounding floor.

Just beside it was a blue stone that looked transparent. You knelt down to inspect it and discovered that you could see right through it to the wall across the other side of the room.

The last was an ugly, pale, white stone. One of them had to be the healing stone. You were finally here at the Mountain of Lanogoza, being watched by the cold eyes of the ancient dragon, its guardian. Which one of them was the healing stone?

Will you pick the gold stone? Turn to Chapter 36.

Will you pick the blue stone? Turn to Chapter 104.

Will you pick the ugly, white stone? Turn to Chapter 48.

CHAPTER 68

Get the Fresh Meat

꙳꙳꙳꙳꙳꙳꙳ ꙳꙳꙳꙳꙳꙳꙳

There was certainly something very wrong with this town, but right now you were starving and decided to go find the fresh meat. Your keen sense of smell drew you to the place where the smell of fresh meat was the strongest. Your stomach grumbled even more as you got closer. There had to be a butcher shop somewhere where they killed animals and you wondered how you intended to explain to them that you wanted to feed on their wares. You got to a small, delicate house with the door slightly ajar and you paused, a bit concerned as you expected to be at a barn with live animals being ushered in by humans. There was still no sign of life and your keen wolf senses didn't detect any movement close by. Stepping into the house through the open door, immediately your human alarm bells started ringing. There was blood everywhere.

The blood was from humans that had been torn apart, whose remains lay all over the floor. You no longer felt hungry and were quite nauseous as you wondered what could have happened to the people who occupied that house.

You didn't want to wait to find out. As you made to turn away, you heard a howl just behind you and found your exit barred.

Werewolves were staring at you with red eyes, baring their sharp teeth.

There was no point running. You couldn't outrun them, as they made for you with saliva dropping from their exposed fangs.

Adventure Ends Here.

Learn to heed warning signs.

You can return to Chapter 20 or start the game again from Chapter 1.

CHAPTER 69

The Stone Pillar

⁂

The dragon's gaze was expressionless and you both quietly regarded each other. Turning back to look at both doors, you willed your heart to decide which of the doors to take. You were tired as you neared the end of your quest.

Which of these doors will lead me to the healing stone? you wondered. You promptly stepped forward and turned the handle to the door on the right and the door rolled open with a loud groan.

In the center of a massive stone-grey room rose a stone pillar and sitting on that pillar was a plain stone encased in glass. *This has to be the healing stone*, you said to yourself, smiling as you ran to it. You picked up the glass and opened it gently and brought out the stone. It felt cool to touch and a prickly sensation went up your arm.

Holding the stone victoriously, you turned around to see the dragon watching you. He had not moved from the position and he stared at you

with that expressionless gaze.

"I got the stone," you screamed in delight, raising the stone in the air, but the dragon remained silent. The walls of the room started to shake and stone from the walls started crumbling and falling all around, filling the room with dust. You looked up at the dragon that still watched you and screamed for help. "What is happening?" you asked, confused.

"The stone doesn't find you worthy," he replied quietly.

"Why?" you screamed, running towards the door but it slammed shut, separating you from the dragon as you began to pound the door, asking him to let you out.

The room continued to shake as the stone table broke into pieces and crashed into the floor. Looking around desperately for a way of escape, you watched in horror as the ground dissolved underneath you, sending you hurtling into the dark depths of the unknown. The last thing you heard were your screams of terror.

Adventure Ends Here.

Sorry, Game Player!!!

You can return to Chapter 43 or start the game again from Chapter 1.

~ SUREFOOT ~

CHAPTER 70

Fight Hippo

Y ou thought about the riddle for a while and couldn't think of any answer that could possibly fit that description.

What is long and short?

What is fat and slim?

What is short and tall?

What right did this dwarf have to ask you such a tricky question? You were sure that there was no answer to this ridiculous riddle. You pulled out your knife and looking at him squarely you said, "I do not know the answer to your riddle but I demand the right to pass through this cave."

"You demand?" Hippo asked, with a glint of amusement on his face.

Hippo was playing games with you and wasting your time in the process and you were not having it.

You quickly lunged at Hippo, who moved away very nimbly. He was quite fast for such a stout figure and you found yourself chasing after him, as he avoided your attack at every turn.

Suddenly, Hippo started replicating and you looked around in confusion at different little hippos that were all around you, jumping and stabbing you into submission with sharp, little sticks.

They were too many and you could not fight them. Together they overwhelmed you and tied your arms and legs with ropes.

Hippo reappeared and advanced towards you with a short spear.

"It's foolish to pass by force," he said coldly.

He drove the spear into your heaving bosom.

Adventure Ends Here.

That wasn't wise.

You can return to Chapter 57 or start the game again from Chapter 1

CHAPTER 71

The Dark
Door

There were glittering stars on the dark door which shimmered, as your fish nose touched it, opening inwards easily and you swam into a room you could describe as gorgeous. That deep voice sailed towards you, confirming the source of the singing that you heard a few moments ago from the long passageway. The sound was getting closer as you swam into the surprisingly clean and well-maintained room in this wreckage of a ship in the depths of the sea. Different colored plant life crawled from the floor into the wooden chairs and tables that gave the room a beauty that was indescribable. You paused as you saw someone sitting in what would have once been a stone fountain. His large, blue tail was flapping out of the tub as he sat, looking quite subdued by a garden made up of sea plants and corals, within the ship. He was a merman.

He looked very sad and his voice was enchanting, but you were not sure if he was harmless so you lingered, a bit unsure until he turned and saw you and smiled. He waved at you invitingly and you swam up to him. When you got closer, you were struck by how handsome he was. His dark, blue eyes were the color of the ocean and his blue hair billowed with each movement of the underwater current.

"Why are you sad?" you asked, as you got closer, truly curious as to why he sat all alone singing a sad song that almost broke your heart.

"It's a long story, dear little fish but first I must ask who you are. I assume you are new to these parts."

You felt you could trust him, so you began, "I am Princess Surefoot and I am on a quest to get the healing stone. I have been transformed by a wizard to this form, to aid my passage through the sea."

He shook his head sadly and looked at you, "I knew you were not from around here because you would have known that all who live in the sea, fear to come in here."

"Why is that?"

"I don't know if there is time to tell you, as your life could already be in danger as it is."

"I want to know," you insisted. There was something about this kind-looking merman that made you want to help him.

"I'm King Octan, ruler of all in the Sea of Eternity. One day, I met this beautiful mermaid, Ivrie with eyes as blue as the ocean and purple long hair that flowed for miles. I fell in love and married her and thought that was the happiest day of my life. I was wrong. She only tricked me with her beauty and is actually cold and evil. She has changed what was once a happy kingdom to a dark and sad one. She kills anyone that dares to disobey her and people flee once she appears. No one is allowed to see me or interact with me."

"You are the king. Why can't you do something about it?'

He smiled sadly and continued, "I am king that's true but she has great powers and I'm afraid I can do nothing about that." He paused and he looked like he was struggling with a lot of thoughts on his mind. After a short while, he continued. "A month ago, I met a young mermaid that ventured to the garden at the back of this ship because she had lost her way. Like you, she was not from around these parts and I explained to her the danger she was in. She was truly beautiful and I was mesmerized by her eyes that glowed like the sun and her long, beautiful blonde hair. I was afraid for her life and guided her away, but she came back the next day to talk to me. I believe that we fell in love that same day."

Our love and friendship grew from that day on and we had a secret location where we met. I thought our love for each other was a secret, until that fateful day. We were supposed to meet at the secret location, but she wasn't there. I searched everywhere and I couldn't ask anyone for help so as not to put her in danger and also because no one is allowed to speak to me. All those who live here swim away when they see me approaching. I wondered every day where she was. I lost my appetite and will to even live. One day, when I returned from my search, the evil Queen Ivrie swam to me holding my love's beautiful hair band that I had given her and suddenly I knew what had happened."

He started to wail and you tried to comfort him as best as you could, when the door to the room suddenly opened. He looked at you with alarm and fear clearly etched on his face and back at the door.

What will be your next move?

Will you find a place to hide? Turn to Chapter 105.

Will you try to help the merman? Turn to Chapter 35.

~ SUREFOOT ~

CHAPTER 72

Continue on Your Quest

❧❧❧❧❧❧❧ ❦❦❦❦❦❦❦

Gold filled the entire floor of the room, piled from the walls to the floor and glittered invitingly. You thought of the end of your quest, returning with the healing stone and riches that would make the entire tribe celebrate for a long time to come. Looking at the amulets and trinkets lavishly spread on the chests, you wondered how they would look on your mother. She was a strong and yet simple woman but she deserved it more than anyone else.

Take the gold, a voice said in your head.

No one is here and no one will care, repeated that same voice in your mind.

This is just a distraction, you thought to yourself and decided to continue on your quest. Picking an item may be something you could consider, after you got the stone. As you moved away from the gleaming gold pieces spilled all over the room, you looked around for an exit.

Your eyes darted back and forth as you walked away from the gold, looking for a hidden door when you noticed it. Someone or something was watching you. The gold reflected on two large slits of eyes. Jumping back in surprise, your hand fell on your knife at your side, ready to defend yourself.

The eyes watched you with a hint of amusement and at the same time they were scrutinizing you, almost as though they were seeing into your soul. You soon saw the owner of the eyes as he stepped away from a large chest of gold and the light reflected on the scales on his huge body, sending out a silvery sheen of halo around his face. He looked regal as he quietly moved across the gold littered around the room. For such a large creature, he moved swiftly across the room, without toppling anything in its wake. It almost seemed like he was gliding in air. His presence was so majestic that for a moment, you were unable to speak as you watched him move with intent towards you.

Suddenly, you knew. This was no ordinary creature. This was the ancient dragon, the keeper of the healing stone in the Mountain of Lanogoza.

Your hands nervously felt for the knife at your waist and his eyes narrowed when he noticed that movement and stopped a few feet from you. The dragon spoke with a deep voice that reverberated around the room, causing the gold cups and objects hanging by the side to fall. One rolled and lay by your feet. You looked at it casually and raised your gaze back to the dragon.

"Wise princess, you're not greedy like most adventurers. I'm indeed proud to hand over the stone to your worthy hands." You sighed in relief, not relishing the idea of fighting this massive creature. As though he read your mind, he said, "Believe me, you wouldn't have stood a chance against me in battle."

"Thank you." You sighed, all of a sudden, weary with the task of the entire journey weighing on your shoulders.

"Come with me," he said, and led the way from the golden room. You followed respectfully behind, giving some distance as you didn't want to get squashed by the massive tail gently moving back and forth. The dragon stopped in front of the entrance of a cave and indicated that you go ahead. Stepping aside for you to pass as his massive frame almost blocked the entrance, you moved past him to see an open space with nothing in the bare room but a stone table. On top of the table was a plain stone in a glass encasing. You turned back to look at the dragon that nodded at you and you went slowly towards the table. All kinds of thoughts went through your mind. *Is this the end of the quest? Can I trust the dragon?*

You approached the table, gently opened the glass case and stretched out your hand to touch the stone. The minute you touched the stone, a warm feeling went through your fingertips, spreading across your body and all the way to your toes. All the pain and weakness that you felt in the course of the journey seemed to flow out of your body and you turned, startled, to the dragon that looked at you, smiling.

"You feel that?"

"Yes," you whispered as tears of joy filled your eyes.

"That is the healing stone and it has chosen you. Now hold it to your heart and it will take you home," the dragon said in a loud voice.

You collected the stone carefully and holding it with both hands, placed it against your chest. The room started to spin. You could see the face of the ancient dragon spinning around you as his voice resonated, "Go well, brave warrior princess."

The ground seemed to split into two and you felt yourself falling, as you held on to the stone. It seemed you were falling from a long distance. The wind hammered against your body and your long, black hair wrapped itself against your face with the force of the wind.

Eventually, everything became silent and you found yourself standing in a field. You felt the stone against your chest and smiled, but your pouch felt very heavy. Pulling out your pouch that was hanging at your side, you opened it to see gold coins, chains and amulets. The dragon must have given you the gold in the course of parting with you. You smiled, overjoyed and looked up to see that the field you were in was the Omahi field. You could see the brightly-colored huts with smoke from cooking, rising in the air. Children and women were sitting outside their houses and they had noticed you. A lone figure separated from the rest of them and was calling your name and running towards you. It was your mother and you made for her, both of you running across the field into each other's arms.

As the wind fanned your hair while you slowly ran towards your mother, you were happy that you were home and had fulfilled your promise to return with the healing stone from the Mountain of Lanogoza.

Congratulations.

Adventure Ends Here.

CHAPTER 73

Pick a Stone

❧✦✦✦✦✦✦ ✦✦✦✦✦✦✦❧

This was the purpose of your entire mission. You were here to get the healing stone back to Omahi Village, in time to save your father. One of these stones had to be the healing stone and you would have to find out which one. You walked towards the stones, bending down to pull your small hunting knife from your boots, looking around cautiously as you approached the silver carpet. The light from the opening in the cave shone on both stones and you studied them for a while. They both looked plain, dull and aged and you couldn't tell the difference just by looking at them.

You knelt down and reached out and picked one of them with your eyes closed. The stone felt cold to touch and as you lifted it, you ensured that your knife was safely secured in your belt. You turned the stone around in your hands, feeling the rough edges of the stone and sighed with relief that nothing had happened so far. You didn't know what you were expecting, but it all seemed too easy in your opinion. You shrugged as you carefully placed the stone in your bag and turned towards the exit.

The floor started to rumble, the walls of the cave caving in with huge chunks of rock falling inwards into the opening like a mighty earthquake. With a scream, you realized you had selected the wrong stone and ran towards the other stones.

The last thing you saw was the ancient dragon, shaking his huge head at you.

Adventure Ends Here.

Tough luck!!!

You can return to Chapter 7 or start the game again from Chapter 1.

CHAPTER 74

The Voice

❖

You had to wait to see the person who owned such a lovely voice. The person could help you on your quest. The voice sounded closer, and you turned around, smiling in anticipation. Whoever had that lovely voice definitely had no intentions to harm anyone. The voice was so sweet and calm. As you listened to it, you were almost in a trance, as you felt your senses dulling. You turned around sluggishly, with both hands hanging limp at your sides. You were incapable of thinking or feeling anything at this time. All you felt was this increasing desire to let go of all your worries and fall asleep.

All of a sudden, a fast-moving body of water came from around the bend and hit you, pushing you along the dark corridor and slamming you against the rough walls of the cave in the process. As the water got into your mouth, nose and eventually your lungs, you realized that the voice you heard was that of the ancient Mimanto, who always sang with an alluring voice to entice people.

Mimanto had great powers and could command the water. She distracted people with her voice, whilst she sent a body of fast-moving water to drown unsuspecting adventurers.

That realization was the last thing you remembered as the water slammed you against a sharp bend in the cave.

Adventure Ends Here.

Curiosity kills the cat.

You can return to Chapter 46 or start the game again from Chapter 1.

CHAPTER 75

Fight to Pass

＊＊＊＊＊＊＊ ＊＊＊＊＊＊＊

There was something about the way Sunta and his school of fishes regarded you and you realized that there was no right answer to their trick question. They intended to kill you, no matter what answer you gave them. Something in their *fishy* side glances and snickering made you realize that. Although they had the upper hand in experience, since you had just become a fish for some hours, you intended to fight your way through.

"Well, it so happens that I do not know the answer and I intend to pass," you said, and swam towards them with determination. You were a much smaller fish compared to them and were outnumbered but you didn't intend to let them kill you without a fight. Sunta and his school of fishes made for you as you swam furiously towards them and just as you were about to hit each other headlong, the fishes darted away, leaving you alone.

All the warrior fishes had taken flight and you were puzzled. It wasn't you who drove them away. You were very sure of that fact. You looked around and saw yourself in a deep and dark section of the Sea of Eternity. Suddenly, your fish senses alerted you of danger, but you had no idea what direction the danger was coming from. A shadow fell across you as a huge beast rose behind you, casting a shadow on the sea floor. You turned around to see a shark, and it opened its mouth to bite you, but you were fast and darted away quickly. It came after you with speed.

You fled, along with other tiny fishes that were running away from the shark that was tailing you closely. You were getting quite tired, unaccustomed to swimming with fins, but the closeness of the monster just behind you made you push yourself even further.

An object rose ahead of you, and you could make out a small, sunken boat in the depths of the water. You had just a few moments to get in there.

Will you be able to make it?

Pick a chapter and decide your fate.

Turn to Chapter 41 or Chapter 93.

CHAPTER 76

Fight the Lead Centaur

You had no more time to waste with the laughing centaurs and decided to fight their leader.

"I have the right to pass!" you yelled at him. The other half-horsemen laughed at you.

"Do you know who you are talking to? You should be happy he likes you. He is Acrylic, the king of flying horsemen, and he kills people like flies," a blonde-haired centaur said, looking at you in anger.

You told them that you didn't care about who their leader was and reached for your knife. That action erased the smile from Acrylic's handsome face and he flew closer, while his men circled both of you, watching to see how the battle would end.

The battle was grim as you both faced each other and you attacked first, swinging at Acrylic with your knife. The blade narrowly missed the centaur's handsome face, now filled with rage as he screamed, flying to you in fury. His muscled arms stretched to the sides as he swung out at you with a whip in his right hand. You held the rope and pulled at him and he flapped his

wings, angrily backing away. You suddenly let go of him and he flew back, losing his balance with the unexpectedness of your action. You came back at him with your knife straight ahead, pointing at his neck. You struck at him but he countered your attack and you went at each other, blow for blow. The fight was intense but you were beginning to get the upper hand. When the others saw that you had almost defeated their king, they all combined forces and started attacking you. They overpowered you and about four of them held you mid-air while Acrylic flew up to you with his long blade swiping in rage, cutting off your wings.

You watched in horror as the beautiful wings fluttered in the air, falling slowly to the ground. The other horsemen laughed while Acrylic waved his sword in victory. His tail swung from side to side as he flew around you and the men, with a smile on his face.

Although you protested, they gagged you to stop your screams. With the help of the other centaurs that provided ropes, they tied your hands and feet, placed you on Acrylic's back and took you away by force.

Your protests were mere mumbles. No one could hear you because of the gag they had placed in your mouth and the sound of their laughter as they flew across the skies back to their home.

𝔄𝔡𝔳𝔢𝔫𝔱𝔲𝔯𝔢 𝔈𝔫𝔡𝔰 𝔥𝔢𝔯𝔢.

I hope you make a good bride!!!

You can return to Chapter 3 or start the game again from Chapter 1.

~ SUREFOOT ~

CHAPTER 77

The Right Door

⚜⚜⚜⚜⚜⚜⚜ ⚜⚜⚜⚜⚜⚜⚜

The two doors looked similar, with no distinguishing feature that you could base your selection on. From the wooden frames, your eyes went over the rusty handles and you could have sworn that even the rust markings were the same. That old witch had lied the first time and with that evil laugh she gave just before you slit her throat, you knew she definitely had something up her sleeve. You decided to choose the right door, the exact opposite of her advice, turning the handle slowly and it opened with a creak.

You were surprised to see that the door led outside. As you stepped through the door, you heard it slam shut and you turned around but the door had disappeared. There was no way for you to return back to the cave and it was okay for you. If this way led you on to your quest, you were more than willing to face whatever came your way. Looking ahead, all you saw was a grey sky, no plant life or birds in the air, just a long, dark and lonely road. Adjusting your pouch, you went down the road, looking around the strange environment. On the left and right of this road, the land looked dark and bare for miles until it seemed like the clouds met with the Earth on the far horizons on both sides. You wondered where the road was leading to, since there was nothing else up ahead as far as you could see. There wasn't any sign of wind and you wiped off the sweat that was gathering on your brow and sliding down into your eyes. Looking up, you noticed a large castle looming ahead of you. There was no way to bypass it, because it stood in the center of the road. It had a gothic look and cast a sinister shadow on the barren land surrounding it. The entrance door was made out of metal and was shaped like a large V.

You felt a sense of foreboding standing in front of its rocky entrance. Cautiously climbing the three steps carved out of the rocky hard sand, you approached the door. The door opened up easily with a slight touch but made a low, creaky sound, like it would need some oiling soon enough. It opened up to a barren hallway, with no furniture and the walls looked plain, with peeling, yellowish wallpaper. You wondered how you could get to the opposite side of the road, as this castle was impeding movement across it. A flurry of movement made you look up to see a woman coming down the stairs that led up the castle. Her long, white, flowing gown gently brushed the old, creaking steps. Her skin was as white as snow and she had long, black hair flowing down to her back.

You waited patiently and studied her as she came down but somehow you didn't feel threatened by her. All the same, your hand slid to your side, you felt the knife hidden away from view in your belt and watched her steps as she approached you. She was staring at you with her large, dark eyes. There was a long, awkward silence, with both of you assessing each other before she spoke. "Welcome, brave warrior to Count Dracula's castle."

You nodded at her and asked, "I wish to go to the other side of the road. Can you tell me how to get across?"

She turned away. "I'm afraid I can't help you with that."

"Why?" you asked.

She turned around with a sad look on her face, "Only Count Dracula knows the way out of this castle and most adventurers after meeting him, don't ever leave the castle alive."

She searched your face for any sign of fear, as she wrung her hands in worry.

"Who are you to the count? you asked, more curious about this pleasant girl than the count that she had just described.

"It's a long story. The count killed my parents when they stumbled into his castle. I was just six years old at the time and they had gotten lost searching for a way out of this barren land. He kept me and wouldn't let me leave."

You looked at her with compassion.

"So why have you never tried to run away?"

"Where do I run to? This is the only life I know," she replied sadly.

You looked around the dreary castle, at its bleak walls with no furnishings and she interrupted your thoughts, "I'll take you to the count. He probably knows you're here already. Follow me."

She turned around, her long hair whipping gracefully as she moved towards the stairs.

Will you follow her? Turn to Chapter 94.

Will you try to find a way out on your own? Turn to Chapter 38.

~ SUREFOOT ~

CHAPTER 78

Get the Stone

✦⊱⊱⊱⊱ ⊰⊰⊰⊰✦

There was no time to waste. You had to complete your mission. Enough time had been wasted already with the fight you just had with Medusa. The healing stone was just within your grasp and you could feel it deep inside your heart. There was another feeling of dread that you couldn't place a finger on but you ignored it and went through the opening. You were immediately struck by a sense of wonder as you stepped into a room of crystals. The temperature in the room was cool and you wondered where the cold breeze that you felt came from. Your feet crunched against particles of crystals that might have fallen from the ceilings and the sides of the walls of the caves and you stared at the play of colors just ahead of you.

Your gaze went from the light coming in from the top of the ceiling to a beautiful display of blue and golden colors, reflecting off a glass case on a stone slab in the center of the room. Somehow, the lights were being reflected and bouncing off the crystals jutting down the ceiling above it and on the walls of the cave. For a moment, you basked in the overwhelming sense of wonder and peace that you felt. This had to be the healing stone and you had to hurry up and get it. What was the chance that your father was still alive? You approached the stone slab with a sense of excitement and near disbelief that you had come to the end of your quest. The stone was right there within your reach and you had worked so hard to get here. Hastily, you reached for the glass case and a sharp sensation like electricity jolted through your hands. This definitely had to be the healing stone, you smiled to yourself and tried to reach out again. As your hand reached towards it again, you felt something hard hit you across the face and chest, knocking the breath out of you and tossing you like a limp rag half across the room.

A sharp pain went through your back as you were impaled by a sharp crystal jutting out of the cave where you were slammed against. You bit back a scream of pain and looked at the protruding crystal, with its sharp edge tinged with blood from the left side of your chest.

What just happened? you wondered, looking from the protrusion on your chest that narrowly missed your heart and your gaze wandered across the room. In your haste, you must have forgotten and you turned your head left and right to shake the wave of dizziness that threatened to overwhelm you. The stone was guarded by the ancient dragon. How could you have forgotten about that and assumed you could walk out with the stone, without encountering the dragon?

The dragon had been watching you from some dark corner of the cave with big red eyes full of hate and anger. You could almost feel the hatred across the room as he approached slowly, with his huge tail switching left and right, pushing the crystals across the floor and making grating sounds. *I have to get out of here*, you thought. You tried to get yourself out of the wall but you were stuck firmly there. Each movement you made caused blood to spurt out of your chest and you screamed out loud as you tried unsuccessfully to free yourself.

You noticed that the grating sounds of his movement had stopped and he towered over you, casting a huge shadow on the wall of the cave where you were. The ancient dragon raised his huge wings, covering the entire room. You observed him raising his head, watching the sides of his neck bulge as flames moved to the long snout. The last thing you remembered was big red eyes and flames heading your way.

There was no time to react. You heard your voice and you were screaming. The voice you heard was bloodcurdling and full of pain as you got burnt to a crisp.

Adventure Ends Here.

Beware of the dragon!

You can return to Chapter 103 or start the game again from Chapter 1.

~ SUREFOOT ~

CHAPTER 79

What is her Grievance?

The entire sky lit up as lightening flashed about dangerously close and the sound of thunder made your horse panic. As you struggled to control and soothe it at the same time you tried to remember what you had heard about cloud fairies. They were known to be very kind to people that had seen them fly close to Earth, as they lived only up in the clouds. It is possible that they behaved differently when you were in their territory in the sky. There certainly must a reason for this malicious display by the cloud fairy and you decided to ask her what her grievance was. The sound of the thunder was deafening, but you could hear the cloud fairy laughing. She was enjoying the state you were in, struggling to control the horse that was prancing about in the sky and also afraid of the noise. It was hard, but you let your voice be heard above the noise of the thunder.

"What have I done to offend you that you impede my progress in such a manner?" you yelled, trying to level your gaze at the cloud fairy.

Her mocking laughter stopped suddenly and her expression revealed that she looked surprised that you chose to talk. She had been standing on a large, dark cloud, but she skipped to a smaller ball of cloud. With her legs spread apart and her hands on her waist, she floated down to your level.

"You came to my domain without seeking entrance," she said, when she had come to your level.

"If that is so, I am truly sorry. Could I pass through the clouds, please?" you asked.

You went ahead to explain to her your mission to the Mountain of Lanogoza. You told her how you got the flying horse and were now continuing with your journey, but you feared that so much time had been lost, with the delays.

She quietly listened to you and you noticed that her facial expression went from angry to calm and then excitement. With a wave of her tiny hands, the lightning suddenly stopped, the noise of the thunder waned into eerie quietness and she smiled at you mischievously. The horse stopped prancing about and calmed down with you patting it gently on the side, all the while watching the cloud fairy, surprised at her change of mood.

"You may, on one condition," she finally said, still excited.

'What condition?' you asked, suddenly suspicious of her change of mood.

She gave you a solemn look and started to explain, "Long ago, the cloud fairies lived happily in the clouds in their thousands, but the clouds were invaded by a hideous beast called the hydra that started to kill us. The cloud fairies that survived have fled this area and now dwell in the hidden mountains by the Lost Sea. I fear the hydra might kill me too, being the only cloud fairy left. You have to destroy it or else, you won't pass."

'What is a hydra?' you asked, confused. You had never heard about that beast before.

The cloud fairy looked really surprised that you had not heard about a hydra before.

"It's a sky demon with seven fiery heads and hundreds of hands."

The hydra seemed like an impossible creature to kill and besides it was not your fight. You had already wasted enough time.

This was a dilemma and you had to give a wise response. "This will only delay my quest," you said.

You watched as her lips hardened to a firm line and anger slowly crept into her countenance.

Turn to Chapter 31.

~ SUREFOOT ~

CHAPTER 80

The Cold Passage

The narrow hallway you just went through was unbearably hot and you had no intention of going into the hot passage. Besides, it looked extremely scary and you had no idea where it would lead. With that in mind, you chose to go through the cold passageway and brave the ice instead.

As you approached the cold passage, a flutter of air made you spin around to see a dark form descend from the ceiling of the cave and drop just in front of you. His massive eyes were in slits, studying you and a small ray of light from the ceiling reflected on the scales of his body, giving him a regal look. The huge dragon that had appeared in front of you was the guardian of the healing stone and he regarded you with a look that you couldn't place.

Smoke flowed out of his mouth as he said, "You chose the easy path."

"I was hot and I wanted…"

"The path to tread to victory is often filled with danger. You're a coward and as such, not worthy of the healing stone,' he said, coldly.

You tried to protest but he opened his mouth and set you on fire.

𝔄𝔡𝔳𝔢𝔫𝔱𝔲𝔯𝔢 𝔈𝔫𝔡𝔰 ℌ𝔢𝔯𝔢.

Cowardly Player!!!

You can return to Chapter 35 or start the game again from Chapter 1.

CHAPTER 81

I won't fight
a Child

❧

This magician has to be insane, you thought to yourself as you looked away from his cold, mocking eyes to the little, blonde boy standing in front of you. The boy's upper lip trembled and his eyes watered from unshed tears.

The flying men threw your spear at you and you looked at the weapon lying on your feet in disbelief. Everyone here had to be mad. There was no way they expected you to fight this little child.

"No, I cannot fight this innocent child," you screamed at Ishbatech, kicking at the spear that rolled to the feet of the magician. He smiled, looking at your weapon and gently picked it up and held it, studying the wooden handle and pointed tip. Immediately, you realized that you had just handed over your only weapon to the very person that might use it against you.

Ishbatech looked at you and your eyes met. It seemed like he could read your mind. He smiled and shook his head, disappointed in you. He nodded at the child, Arturech who walked confidently towards you, his eyes trained on you.

"I will not fight this child," you screamed this time.

What happened in the next minute was very fast. Arturech grabbed a sword from one of the winged men and ran towards you, waving the sword in your direction. You dove out of the way and he landed on both feet and spun around once more, coming in your direction.

Your eyes widened as you realized that the boy was well trained but still, he was a kid and you didn't want to fight him. He ran in your direction, twisting his sword left and right, which you dodged by anticipating his moves and turning in the opposite direction. Arturech cursed in frustration when he saw you were evading his sword and feigned a left move which made you turn to the right. You discovered too late that he had tricked you and slashing at you, he expertly ripped you to shreds.

There was no time to fight back.

Adventure Ends Here.

Looks are deceptive!!!

You can return to Chapter 11 or start the game again from Chapter 1.

CHAPTER 82

Drink the Water

The fight with T-rex was draining, but even more so was the death of Dusty. The hot, desert sun had further weakened you and you were extremely thirsty. After kneeling down beside the pool of water, feeling it and confirming that it wasn't a mirage, you cupped the water in your hands and poured it over your tired face and proceeded to drink it. The water tasted sweet and it felt cool to your mouth. You bent down and started gulping it greedily. Your eyes saw a red light in the depths of the pool that seemed to glow even brighter as it got closer. The water erupted in showery, silvery sprays in front of you as a creature with a woman's face and arms and seven snake-like tails, arose out of it.

The red glow you had seen earlier was from the long tentacles that sprang out of her hair and her green eyes gleamed evilly at you.

"You dare drink from my water?"

"I was thirsty and only wanted to ..."

"I'm Vanotica, the Queen of Zenoisa. This pool of water is the entrance to my kingdom and you shall be slain immediately for drinking from my pool without taking permission," she spoke, her voice rising in anger.

You made to get your knife but she was faster. One of her tentacles reached out for you, knocking the knife and it fell into the dark pool of water. Another tentacle came at you, but you dived out of the way, rolling on the ground. You tried to run away, but felt something grab hold of your heel. More tentacles wrapped firmly around your legs and they started to pull you towards the water. You screamed, stretching out both hands to grab hold of anything in the sand to prevent you from being dragged any further. Your hands helplessly grasped the soft sand. There was nothing in sight to stop you from going under the water. You felt more tentacles reach for your hands and clasp them to your side. With one final pull, they dragged you into the depths of the water, with Vanotica's voice ringing shrilly in your ears.

Adventure Ends Here.

Sorry, poor Game player.

Start again if you dare.

You can return to Chapter 37 or start the game again from Chapter 1.

CHAPTER 83

Vanotica's Tentacles

Her tentacles wrapped around you, squeezing hard as though they wanted to avenge the ones you had killed with your spear earlier. The tentacles on Vanotica's head rolled and curved and then in a coordinated move, flashed out in your direction as Vanotica screamed, pointing at you. You fought grimly with the numerous tentacles that attacked you on all sides. Vanotica screamed as you slashed another of her tentacles and she ripped the spear out of your hand, throwing it away. She leaned towards you and two more tentacles made for you, but you turned away as they landed by your side. This time, you held one of them and watched it squirm as you pulled with all your might. While fighting, you noticed that Vanotica was still in the pool of water and avoided coming out of it. You pulled with all your might and smiled with relief as her upper side fell on the soft sand. Her eyes opened in alarm and she yelled in dismay, letting go of your legs with her remaining tentacles, but you were too quick for her.

You fought with her. She might be stronger with the advantage of her numerous tentacles, but you were more cunning. With your legs free now, taking advantage of Vanotica's growing panic as she staggered to get back in the water, you pulled out your small knife from one of your boots and jumped on her neck as the tentacles started to wrap around you. You started slicing in a frenzy the tentacles that were trying to attack you. Vanotica screamed as you succeeded in pulling her completely back on the sand. She shrieked in fear and her few remaining tentacles tried to attack you, but their movements were getting slow. Vanotica was getting weaker as she watched her tentacles falling into the water, while you sliced them up. You dragged her out of the water completely and watched in surprise as she started to dry up. Her dried-up body started to crack and dissolve into a heap of sand. You coughed, with exertion from the fight and the dust that rose out of the body of the dead Vanotica, as she dissolved before your eyes. The cloud of dust was so much that it started to choke you. Rushing to the pool, you quickly started drinking. The water was very cool and satisfying. Suddenly, you felt a presence beside you.

You whirled around, knife in hand, ready to defend yourself, only to see an old woman. She was smiling at you with her sunken eyes, thin greying hair and a light, silk dress blowing in the desert wind.

She raised her hands up in surrender, with a kind smile on her face,

"I mean no harm. I only want to drink from this water," she said. Still holding the knife in front of you, you watched as she slowly knelt by the pool.

'Well done. I've looked for someone to destroy that lady for a long time. Now, I can drink water,' she said.

You stepped aside and watched her slowly cup her hands in the water and bring it to her lips. As she drank the water, some of the water trickled down her aged neck and you watched in surprise as gold lights started emanating from her body and she slowly transformed into a young girl. Her hair was sparkling blonde and she regarded you with ocean blue eyes.

You still had your hand on your knife and looked at the old woman turned young girl questioningly.

"My name is Marca. I was punished by Vanotica. She turned me into an old woman because she was jealous of my beauty. Now that I'm restored, I'll help you with anything you need."

You put your knife down slowly and said, "I am on a quest to the Mountain of Lanogoza. I need to find a way out of this desert."

"I'll show you a way out of this desert as a show of my gratitude."

She indicated that you follow her. After she walked with you some distance, she pointed at a huge hole in the sand.

The hole looked endless and you turned back to Marca, unsure.

"Where does this hole lead?"

"It will lead you to what you're looking for," she replied.

"Is this safe?"

"I owe you only gratitude and will not harm you in any way," she replied, smiling with her blue eyes-only showing sincerity.

There was no reason to doubt Marca. She could help you leave this desert. You thanked her and with a small wave, jumped into the hole. The hole disappeared and in its place the desert reappeared again. Marca smiled, walking away from where the hole used to be. You fell really fast, spinning in the dark hole that appeared to have no end. You screamed all the way, thinking that Marca might have deceived you to your death. Then you saw a bright light below. The hole opened up to a beautiful land full of pink, yellow and purple flowers and eventually you landed on a carpet of red roses.

Your abrupt entrance startled some ladies who were plucking the roses and they looked at you and stared up at the sky, wondering where you came from. You stood up and adjusted your pouch and waved at them but they moved away, chattering amongst themselves and stealing glances back at you. You decided to investigate this place that the hole had transported you to and noticed the entire garden was filled with tall, elegant, black-haired women dressed in white. You stood out, walking amongst them, and they stole surprised glances at you, because you were clearly a stranger.

A loud sound of a trumpet sparked off panic amongst the women as they started screaming and running in different directions. What could be the source of their panic? What was chasing them?

You wondered what you would do. You stood in the middle of the field, while the women ran across, some pushing you in the process, throwing away their baskets and running into their homes close by.

Will you join them and run? Turn to Chapter 26.

or

Will you wait and see what will happen? Turn to Chapter 11.

CHAPTER 84

Don't eat the Lad

❧❧❧❧❧❧❧ ❧❧❧❧❧❧❧

There was indeed a dilemma, with the hungry dragon that had starved for a thousand years and the young lad crying for his parents. The ancient dragon watched you slyly, with a glint in his green eyes and his tongue slithered out as he waited impatiently.

You definitely felt sorry for whoever that lad was and you had an answer for the ancient dragon.

"I have an answer to your question," you spoke.

"Okay, get on with the answer then, brave warrior."

"The dragon should not eat the lad."

"Why?" the dragon roared and you leaped back and put one hand back, holding the handle of your spear, just in case.

"Why, I ask?" the dragon roared again, this time louder than the first and you swallowed and began your explanation.

"I know the dragon is hungry," you spoke

"Yes. yes …," the dragon interjected impatiently.

"The dragon must have mercy on the lad. By doing this, it will be involved in an act so pure, and full of goodness that will cover for all the hunger the dragon ever felt."

The dragon just stared at you. An uncomfortable silence filled the room and then the dragon smiled, "Good and sensible advice. You just saved your life without knowing."

You heaved a sigh of relief when you realized that you were the lad in the riddle and had just saved yourself from being eaten by the dragon.

"You're brave and also wise. I shall carry you on my back to your people."

"Thank you, dear ancient dragon," you said, grateful for his help.

He lay his large head on the floor of the cave, allowing you to sit on his broad back.

"Hold on real tight, Princess. We won't want you falling off, now," he screamed and took off in the air.

It was amazing flying on the back of the ancient dragon. You watched in wonder as his magnificent wings spread out and he navigated mazes in the cave until he came out from one of the eyes of the mountain. As you circled around the mountain, you saw the flying horse still tied to the tree and asked if you could release the horse. The dragon obliged, descended to the entrance of the cave, spread his wings, lay down his head and you alighted from his back. The horse started to panic when it saw the dragon. The dragon's eyes glinted and he started to lick his lips. The horse started jumping from side-to-side, neighing uncontrollably.

"Please, you are scaring him," you said.

"What did I do?" the dragon asked, jokingly.

You walked up to the horse, talking soothingly as it started jumping from side to side, unable to fly away with the rope tying it to the tree, spreading its wide wings and flapping them around in alarm.

You walked towards the horse with your hand extended and talked to it. The horse eventually calmed down when the dragon walked lazily to the other end of the entrance. You calmed the horse down and eventually released it and it was too happy to fly in the air, away from you and the dragon. You turned back to the dragon and he asked with a smile, "Can we go now?"

"Yes, but you did not have to scare it like that."

"I didn't do anything to that horse. It looked tasty, though," he said mischievously, lying down as you climbed back on his back.

You continued your friendly banter in the air as the ancient dragon flew you across seven seas and seven mountains, back to your home in Omahi Village.

Congratulations!!!

Adventure Ends Here.

Wise advice

CHAPTER 85

Continue Flying

⤙⤙⤙⤙⤙⤙ ⤚⤚⤚⤚⤚⤚

You were already late and just couldn't stay back for anything. Not even when you noticed the clouds getting as black as night. You continued flying, although your bird senses kept warning you not to continue. A strong current of wind was blowing towards you. Your sharp eyes detected movement in the dark mass that was heading in your direction.

It looked like a simultaneous movement of wings that spread for miles out, blocking the sunlight and most of the sky. The wings, which belonged to some birds, were moving very fast in unison. You slowly realized that these were no ordinary birds, but cravuners. They were vampire birds that ate everything that moved and gave off a horrible stench but you were not able to detect the stench on time, in your bird form. There was no time to think. You had to get away and hoped they had not spotted you. That wish was farfetched, since it was an open sky and you were the only living creature flying at that time. Probably other birds had sensed their approach for miles and flown down to hide in safe locations.

You turned to fly away, but there were so many of them, blocking the light from the sky and once they noticed you, they gave chase. They had the advantage of flight and speed. You were just a bird only a few hours ago and despite all the defensive flight maneuvers you attempted, they eventually caught you and quickly ripped you to shreds.

Adventure Ends Here.

Next time, listen to yourself.

You can return to Chapter 107 or start the game again from Chapter 1.

 Death

I destroy you.

No matter what you are.

Be you rich or poor.

Young or old.

What am I?'

You listened to him say the riddle once again and smiled to yourself. There was no way you could be wrong about the answer that came to you easily.

Death is no respecter of persons, you thought. No matter your status, it had the power to destroy you. You smiled as you gave the answer.

Ishbatech smiled at you and immediately you were sure that you had said the right thing.

"I'm afraid, you're not so wise as I thought," he said, his smile fading away.

There must be something wrong. He probably didn't understand your response. How could he think that your answer was wrong?

He started to move towards you, his eyes hard and emotionless. With each step he took, you were getting weaker. He was definitely a powerful magician and this time there was no fighting whatever he wanted to do to you.

You tried to protest, but no words came out of your mouth. He pointed at you and you shrunk into the ground.

𝕬𝖉𝖛𝖊𝖓𝖙𝖚𝖗𝖊 𝕰𝖓𝖉𝖘 𝕳𝖊𝖗𝖊.

Please, try again, okay?

You can return to Chapter 25 or start the game again from Chapter 1.

CHAPTER 87

Refuse to Escape

·҉҉҉҉· ·҉҉҉҉·

Their laughter reverberated round the small cottage, sounding like a tempest to your bird ears. It made you unable to think and the thoughts of escaping seemed like a good one at this time, but somehow you decided to wait it out. The witches were not looking in your direction. They were deep in conversation, but you were not sure if you would find an exit on time. From where you stood looking around, there were no visible windows or doors that you could escape from. A soft growl just behind you made you turn back to see a slit of yellow eyes, as a black cat pounced, saliva dropping from its mouth at the anticipation of a sumptuous meal. You closed your eyes and anticipated your certain death, only to hear the cat hissing and meowing piteously. You looked up to see the cat suspended by a ray of light which seemed to emanate from the fingers of one of the witches.

"No, Guldrath, this is not your meal," one of the witches snarled and with a flick of her finger, sent the cat sailing halfway across the room. The cat picked itself up, shook its head in a daze and ran away without a backward glance, which sent the witches on another round of laughter.

Although given an opportunity, you had not made any attempt to escape and the witches noticed it.

"Why don't you try to escape, Princess?" the witch that had the light come out of her fingers asked curiously, as they hedged closer.

"I believe you brought me here for a purpose, and I want to find out what it is," you replied, bravely.

"Good and wise decision. We need to give you a test before we find you worthy of flying through the Western Sky," one of them said and another interjected.

"We are the three witches of the Western Sky and guard the passage through these airways."

'What am I expected to do?" you asked anxiously.

They smiled at you and looked at each other, slyly. You got a bit nervous in anticipation of what they intended to tell you and worried about how it would impact your quest. So much time had been wasted already and you wanted to return on time, to save your father. After whispering to each other again for a long time, they turned to you.

"There is a hole called The Forbidden Hole. We lost a key there and we want you to get it," one of the witches said.

You wondered if that was all you were expected to do. You felt you could get a key easily, but wondered why the hole was forbidden. However, another thought came to you as you realized that you would need to change from this bird form.

Looking at them you said, "In that case, I will need to change into my human form."

They shook their heads in unison, looking at you and one of them said, "You don't need to change your size. We need you in this size and form, to get into the hole."

You tried to shrug your bird feathers, but it wasn't easy, as it seemed like you were trying to flap it. They looked at you curiously and you said, "That is fine with me. How soon can I get on the quest? There was no point avoiding going on the witches' quest as you didn't see any other way out of this predicament. One of the witches stretched out her hand and you hopped in and they walked with you to the door. From the vantage point of her palm, you realized that escape was futile as they were no visible windows or exit points in the place, except a large metal door that was bolted.

The Witches of the Western Sky unbolted the door noisily and when they got outside, you observed that the cottage was on top of a grassy hill. They led you to a large oak tree, a few yards from the cottage. The tree was so tall that its long branches and leaves seemed to reach to the sky. You saw a hole in the tree, which they told you to go into. The hole was so small and was just right for a bird your size. Now you understood their inability to get the key, although how it fell into the hole was a mystery to you and they didn't seem ready to offer any explanation. The witch who held you in her palm dropped you at the mouth of the hole. You hopped around it and looked into the darkness of the hole, suddenly wondering what you would meet in there.

"Well, get on with it," one of the witches said. You turned to see them staring at you.

"Go on," the other added.

The third one looked at you coldly and spoke, "We had a deal, so get on with it."

Suddenly, you didn't seem as keen to get into the hole as you felt earlier.

~ SUREFOOT ~

There was something about the witches that left you a bit uneasy.

Turning around, ignoring their nasty glares and chattering, you faced the deep, dark hole in the tree and paused a bit.

Will you get into the hole? Turn to Chapter 52.

Will you use this opportunity to escape? Turn to Chapter 108.

CHAPTER 88

Throw Your Knife

✦✦✦✦✦✦ ✦✦✦✦✦✦

The volley of arrows was flying by your head and body, left and right and her growls of anger showed that she was getting angrier and even more frustrated by the minute. You sidestepped an arrow that just flew by your right and ran towards the opposite wall. Using the wall as a springboard to propel yourself in the air, you did a semi-summersault as you pulled out your knife and got ready to aim once you hit the ground. The series of movements you made, surprised Medusa. She stopped mid-way, mouth open, staring at you as you flipped in the air and landed in a kneeling position in front of her.

With a triumphant look in your eyes, you held up the knife and aimed it at that face contorted in a mixture of anger and surprise, but then realized your mistake too late. Her angry snarl slowly turned into a bitter smile. The snakes screeched, writhing frantically and trying to reach at you as her eyes turned into two holes of bright light that streamed from hers into yours.

Your mouth opened up to scream, but no sound came out. You were suddenly immobilized and couldn't move a muscle. Slowly, the light started to surround your entire body and you felt a hardening sensation from your legs, climbing up the entire length of your body. Your eyes opened up in fear as the feeling reached your face. Soon, you were standing wide-eyed, mouth open in a soundless scream, transformed into a statue made out of stone.

Medusa laughed evilly and slithered slowly towards you, her voice ringing around the hollow cave. As she stood directly in front of you, her snakes reached out to your face, crawling around it and licking it with their forked tongues. Her tail curved around your waist and with a shout, she snapped you in two and watched as your stone figure disintegrated to the floor.

She moved away to another section of the cave, having eliminated the most recent nuisance – an interruption to her quiet existence.

Adventure Ends Here.

Think, before you act, next time.

You can return to Chapter 8 or start the game again from Chapter 1.

CHAPTER 89

Throw down the Egg

⋯⋯⋯ ⋯⋯⋯

The old man looked at you expectantly, awaiting your response as you pondered on what he meant by passing through him. You were quite overwhelmed after the fight with the zepenter and the death of your trusty horse and being strangely transported to this land of magic, as the old man claimed.

"What did he mean by passing through him?" you thought to yourself and suddenly remembered the gifts the seer had given you. Between the feather and the egg, one of them had to prove useful. With that last thought, you felt for your pouch and brought out the egg, as the man watched with a thoughtful look on his face.

You held up the egg, threw it down on the ground and was surprised when the ground started to shake. The ground opened up and the old man and the land of magic disappeared into it. The mighty earthquake created a wide hole and you also fell into it. The wide, slippery hole started to close in and you found yourself sliding down it, with water pouring in from its walls, muddying you along the way. Screaming and rolling down the hole for a long distance, you were surprised when the journey ended with you falling into water.

You looked around and saw that you were in a pool in a dark cave and started swimming out of the water to the dry ground ahead of you. All of a sudden, you noticed that something which had wrapped your left leg was preventing you from swimming and pulling you underwater. You let it drag you in. When you opened your eyes and they got accustomed to the dark water, you saw a long, water snake. It had wound tightly against your leg and was stretching out towards your arm. It was planning to drown you and then feast on you and you were not going to let that happen. You brought out your small knife from the pouch around your waist and stabbed at the head of the snake. It started to loosen its grip as the water turned red with blood, but you continued to stab at it until it stopped moving.

Once you made sure it was dead, you swam out of the water before something else tried to attack you. You looked back to see the snake floating in the midst of its blood at the center of the shallow water in the dark cave.

There was no time to waste. You had to continue on your journey. As you made your way across the dark, underground passage, you heard a rumbling sound in front of you. You paused to listen and then realized that it sounded like someone's footsteps. You wondered if there were other humans in this cave so they could show you the way to the Mountain of Lanogoza.

Will you wait and meet them? Turn to Chapter 4.

Will you hide and see what's coming? Turn to Chapter 33.

CHAPTER 90

Bow and Arrow

here was really no time to be indecisive and you chose your weapon.

"I will take the bow and arrow," you said quickly.

"You are sure about that?" the cloud mother asked and you nodded.

You were quite a good shot and that explained your weapon of choice. You were in a hurry to leave the pink cloud so you could get on with your quest.

"I guess we have our weapon. Thanks, Cloud Mother," Mira said, taking one more bite of cake and sipping on her tea, then you both made your way out of the house.

Waiting patiently outside the pink cloud house was the flying horse that Ishbatech had given you and you climbed on it gratefully, patting its head. The cloud fairy stepped on her small cloud and floated away and led you up the sky towards the hydra's place of abode.

It started getting hotter as you flew up in the air and you could hear the heavy panting of your horse due to the strain of flying, the reduction of oxygen as you flew higher into the sky and heat from the sun.

"Are we there yet?" you asked. You started to sweat and were worried that your horse might pass out soon.

"We are here, now," she said, pointing ahead at pure greyness for miles on end. You looked down at the clouds below and the place felt like a large, empty void-like space. It seemed like you were all suspended in some weird way. Like gravity was there and then not there as the horse was just floating but he could control the direction it moved with its wings. Mira was wringing her arms in fear as she floated in front of you and the heat was so intense.

Then you heard it. A loud, piercing shriek that made the horse want to turn back. It sounded like the sound of one voice and many voices at the same time. You just managed to keep the horse under control after it started turning this way and that in panic. You managed to control it and Mira floated back to you.

"I wish you the best, Princess but I can't continue with you."

"Why?"

"My cloud will melt and besides, the hydra will kill me on sight. Good luck," she said quickly, floating away.

You tapped the horse and spoke to it gently, "It is just you and me, now. Do not be scared and do not let me down." The last words made you laugh as you clearly didn't want the horse to let you fall down to certain death. You urged the horse forward and the heat grew more intense. The hydra drew its power from the sun, so it made sense that it would live in this hot zone. The sky in this zone was dark, but suddenly became brighter as the hydra appeared from behind a dark cloud. Nothing prepared you for the sight of this monster, as its fiery heads reached towards you with flames pouring out of its red arms and body.

The beast appeared to be on fire, but it wasn't. Its forked tongue came out of its mouth and it poured fire in your direction. You directed your horse away. It neighed in pain as a flame of fire went past and singed the tip of its right wing. You turned the horse around and reached for your bow and arrow, hands shaking in fear as the beast made its way towards you. You struggled to put the arrow in the bow but the heat was so intense. The metal arrow was so hot that it burnt into your palm and you screamed in pain, while the wooden bow caught fire, burning into ashes before your eyes.

You looked up to see the hydra in front of you and the mouths in the seven heads opened up simultaneously as the hydra set you on fire.

Adventure Ends Here.

Clumsy Game Player!!!

You can return to Chapter 31 or start the game again from Chapter 1.

~ SUREFOOT ~

CHAPTER 91

The Hot Passage

᠁᠁᠁᠁ ᠁᠁᠁᠁

You were sweating at this time but decided to pass the hot passage. *There is no victory without a bit of pain*, you thought to yourself. Your legs landed on hot coals and you bit your lips to stop yourself from screaming. You continued for a while and the pain was excruciating. Though you wanted to stop this torture, you thought of your father. The face of your mother floated before your eyes and your hand unconsciously went to your neck, clasping the chain she gave you. A slight feeling of comfort passed through your tired frame and you continued, despite the gasps of pain.

All of a sudden, the next step wasn't as painful, and the next as well. The heat had suddenly disappeared and the coals vanished with a crumbling sound, into the ground. The walls of the hot cave started to shake. You fell to the side as the walls of the cave started to fall in and you began to spin, along with the particles of rock.

In a moment, you found yourself transported into a marble room. You looked around, trying to get your bearings after being circled in the air some few moments ago before being deposited in this room. A movement caught the corner of your eye. You pulled out your knife and spun around to see the huge ancient dragon come from behind a pillar in the marble room. The ancient dragon's scales sparkled with a silvery sheen. As it regarded you from behind deep, brooding eyes, you wondered if you had a chance fighting with this huge beast.

"There will be no need to fight me, dear princess as I mean you no harm," the dragon said with a sound of amusement in his voice.

You slowly brought down your hands that you had unconsciously raised, holding your knife in front of you and ready to defend yourself, though already exhausted from your adventures. He pointed at the center of the marble room. You had not noticed the stone table, but there it was, and right at the center stood a glass case with a pale stone inside it. You looked back at the dragon and he said, "Brave and worthy princess, you may have the healing stone."

You hesitated, unsure of his motive, but he encouraged you to move forward and you walked cautiously towards the center of the room. Looking at the ancient dragon that nodded at you, you opened the glass case and brought out the pale stone. It felt heavy to touch and you felt a warmth spread from your arms to your entire body. Once more, you heard the voice of the dragon fading into the distance.

"It will take you home, brave warrior."

You closed your eyes while you felt a rush of wind. Warmth encased your entire body and the wind lifted you. In the next few seconds, clouds, trees, mountains and seas rushed past at the speed of light and soon you were standing in a massive field of tall grass. Looking around, you recognized the huts in the distance and observed people walking around. Cradling the healing stone in your hands, you started to run towards your home. You couldn't wait to meet your mother, father and the rest of the villagers.

Congratulations!

Adventure Ends Here.

You have a lot to tell them at home!

~ SUREFOOT ~

CHAPTER 92

Reject Him

⁕⁕⁕⁕⁕⁕ ⁕⁕⁕⁕⁕⁕

Y ou found it amusing that Ishbatech thought you were so impressed by his achievements, you would want to remain here with him. Even if you forgot your quest and chose to remain here, you couldn't imagine living with someone as hideous-looking as Ishbatech.

You laughed in Ishbatech's face.

"How can I marry such an ugly man who is also cruel?"

Ishbatech looked at you with shock etched on his pale face and his eyes like angry slits.

"A girl as beautiful as I am cannot possibly stand looking at you," you continued, ignoring the warning look in his eyes.

He smiled. 'So, you're proud as well. You shall surely stand looking at me, because I'm a magician and I shall make it so.'

He pointed at you and you stood staring at him, unable to move from the spot and making no sound until the day you died.

𝔄𝔡𝔳𝔢𝔫𝔱𝔲𝔯𝔢 𝔈𝔫𝔡𝔰 𝔥𝔢𝔯𝔢.

It's bad to be proud!

You can return to Chapter 101 or start the game again from Chapter 1.

CHAPTER 93

Get to the Ship

The sunken ship loomed just ahead, but you were getting weaker. You tried to thrust yourself forward faster, using your fins to swim in a hurry towards your only means of safety. It seemed as though your fins couldn't move fast enough for you. The ship seemed close enough and then a rush of water pushed you from behind, caused by the movement of the shark as it snapped at you.

Flitting left and right to avoid the shark's open jaws, you had gotten close to the sunken ship when the shark propelled itself forward and caught you in its powerful jaws.

Adventure Ends Here.

Sorry, Game Player

I bet you were tasty!

You can return to Chapter 75 or start the game again from Chapter 1.

CHAPTER 94

Follow Her

~~~~~~~~~~~~~~~~~~~~

ooking around the dreary castle, you had no other choice than to follow her. How else were you going to find your way out of the maze of crumbling furnishings and numerous hallways? She started off towards the stairs where she had ascended from and turned around to be sure that you were following. You walked in her direction.

Each step you took towards her, you wondered if this was the right decision, as you could decide to leave the castle and find some other way to cross the road. You climbed up the creaky stairs that wound up in a spirally mode, leading to what looked like a tower (which was the highest point in the building). Your mind kept on rolling over stories told about a strange count that lived in a lonely castle and sucked the blood of his victims. You were not excited about meeting him, but it seemed you had no choice. *There has to be a passage to the other side of the road,* you thought, as you caught a view of the winding road that went sloping up the hill. But the castle was just right in the middle and there was no way you could climb over it. You intended to find your way across, with or without the help of the strange count.

The flight of stairs seemed endless and at last you alighted from the last set of stairs into a long, grey hallway. The walls were bare and had no wallpaper or paintings and there were no visible windows in this tower. She turned to look back at you and urged you to follow, as she glided forward to the left of the dark hallway. You felt the comforting coldness of the handle of your knife as you surveyed the environment for a possible means of escape, in case things turned south. The young lady seemed harmless enough, but you had no idea what was going to happen, since you hadn't heard any good stories about the owner of this castle.

She stopped suddenly, turned around and smiled, pointing at a section by the wall. Peering ahead, all you could see was a dark, rectangular-shaped object by the side of the wall and you looked back at her, curiously. She waved her hands to the object, indicating that you move closer and you walked cautiously to the strange object. As you approached the dark object, you realized that it wasn't an ordinary object. It looked like a coffin and that got you even more curious. Your hand pressed against the knife, taking comfort in the fact that you were ready to defend yourself, if necessary.

Someone was lying inside the coffin, his eyes closed and you observed him quietly, from his extremely pale face, to long, black hair that fell to the sides of his face. He wore a long, dark overcoat over matching black trousers and shoes and was a very handsome man. Though lying in a coffin, he appeared to be sleeping. You found all of this very strange. Why did she bring you to see a dead person? you thought. When you turned around, the girl wasn't there anymore. The castle was deathly still and each step you had taken caused a hollow sound to ring round the building. You could have sworn that you would have heard her if she had walked away. You turned your back to the coffin and the strange man in it and started looking around to see if she was lurking somewhere in the dark shadows of the huge hallway.

"What's going on?" you whispered to yourself. You heard a deep voice from behind you and turned around abruptly, pulling out your knife in defense and facing the source of the sound.

He was no longer lying in the coffin in some form of deathlike sleep. He was standing just behind you with a cold smile on his pale lips and staring at you with bloodshot eyes.

"You seek the healing stone, Princess?"

"Yes," you answered.

He moved very fast, almost like the wind, yet it seemed like he hadn't moved at all. You felt a wisp of air and he was by your side, his hand reaching to your pouch as he disarmed you of your knife. You were very flustered and moved back, hands raised, reaching to get your spear from your back. He smiled like before and the next minute, with a burst of air, your hands were clasping at nothing. He stood before you, holding your spear with a wicked, dangerous smile playing on his lips.

"You intend to attack me, Princess?"

You moved back slowly as he advanced, watching your every move. "No, I intend to defend myself."

"Defend yourself from me?" he asked, amused.

"Yes, if I have to," you whispered, as your back came against a wall. He moved closer and you could feel his breath on your neck, as if he were inhaling your scent. He took a long whiff, closed his eyes and smiled, opening them and looking into yours with an expression you couldn't fathom. The look was like the one a predator gives its prey before a hunt. It seemed like deep hunger and he gritted his jaw, like he was stopping himself from doing something and then turned away. You heaved a deep sigh of relief, as you were not yet sure how you wanted to fight your way out of this. The count was too fast for you and seemed to know your moves before you even acted on them. He turned around and, in a flash, took your spear that was firmly placed behind your back and threw it far away from him as though in contempt of the weapon. His cloak flew in the air when he turned round in a semicircle and he faced you, this time his face expressionless.

"Long ago, three healing stones were created. One was lost in the Sea of Eternity, the other was kept in the Mountain of Lanogoza, and the other one is with me," he said.

You looked at him, unsure and he indicated that you follow him. He watched as you hesitated and then he said, "If I wanted to kill you, I would have done that already."

You gave him a defiant look. "Why do you assume that I will be so easy to kill?" you asked, staring straight at him.

"I love your show of boldness, but I disarmed you easily. You have no weapons within your grasp to attack me with."

He smiled as your shoulders slumped in resignation. He walked away, knowing you had no choice but to follow him as he led you through the dark hallway to another empty, airless room. There was nothing else in the entire room when you looked around, except a stone on a silver pillow.

"This is the healing stone. You may take it and save yourself the journey to the Mountain of Lanogoza."

It seemed unreal that your journey to the Mountain of Lanogoza had been shortened by this visit to the count's castle, but there was the stone sitting just within your grasp. He was watching your every move with his expressionless gaze and that cold, mysterious smile playing on his lips and you wondered why he would just hand over the stone to you.

What was the end game? Did he have anything sinister planned for you? You had a nagging feeling of unease and doubt as you looked from the stone back to his ever-watchful gaze.

"Thank you," you replied.

Will you take this gift of a stone? Turn to Chapter 16.

Will you reject the gift of a stone? Turn to Chapter 67.

~ SUREFOOT ~

CHAPTER 95

Continue on Your Journey

The first drops of rain started to fall, pattering all around and the roar of thunder filled the entire dark sky, with bright flashes of lightning. They didn't deter you, as you felt that time had already been wasted and you had to make haste to get to the Mountain of Lanogoza. You were now in the form of a mountain wolf. What would a little bit of rain do to you? With that in mind, you continued on your way, bravely ignoring the rain and the splashes of muddy water, causing you to slip as you made your way down the mountain.

Your fur was soaked and getting very heavy as the unforgiving rain fell in torrents around you. You stopped under a tree, shook the water off and looked up at the sky to observe the elements, before proceeding. There was something strange about the sky as the clouds had gathered together in a weird billowing shape.

A loud sound of thunder, mixed with what would seem like laughter, reverberated through the air and you saw the clouds split into two. The source of the laughter was a man who appeared in the sky from the partition of clouds and his body seemed to be made up of dark clouds. With each movement as he laughed, the clouds making up his body jiggled and moved rapidly across his huge frame. He did not have any clothes on. A blue cloud around his waist was his only covering. His eyes and teeth shone like lightning and he looked at you with unconcealed anger.

"I'm the god of thunder and lightning. Nobody moves when I'm around," he said

He threw a thunderbolt at you, accompanied by lightning and you bolted out from behind the tree, which then erupted in flames when the lightning hit it. You started off down the mountain but he kept on throwing bolts of thunder and lightning at you, which you tried to avoid. Each of the lightning bolts fell at the sides of the mountain, narrowly missing you as you ran. This seemed like a game to him and he kept at it, throwing bolts at you and laughing at the narrow misses. You felt a flash of pain as something cut through your hind leg and you squealed, losing balance and falling off the mountain. The last thing you saw was the god of thunder smiling at you as he hurled a lightning bolt in your direction.

Adventure Ends Here.

Foolish attempt!

You can return to Chapter 49 or start the game again from Chapter 1.

Swim Away from The Water Demon

⊱⊱⊱⊱⊱ ⊰⊰⊰⊰⊰

As the water demon continued to pummel the boat, screaming and thrashing about, you dived away just in time as it made contact with the section you were in, breaking it into pieces. As you resurfaced, the waves pushed the particles of what was your boat in different directions and you struggled to remain afloat. You gasped as you coughed out water that had gotten into your mouth and nose when you dived in. The demon saw your head above the water and was soon heading your way. You held onto one of the floating planks as it moved in the water due to the waves caused by the approaching water demon. That beast was too big for you to fight. You knew you had to escape from it somehow and decided that you would trick it by swimming underwater away from it with the hope that it might lose track of you in the dark depths of the ocean.

You took a deep breath and went underwater, swimming expertly away from the direction of the monster. It seemed that your plan was working because you didn't sense the monster coming behind you but after a while, your lungs felt like they were going to burst. You were not used to holding your breath for so long. You scrambled to make it to the surface with powerful thrusts and kicks, pushing yourself to the surface. Your hand broke through the surface of the water and you came up, gasping for air.

Looking around, the demon was nowhere in sight and you wondered if your plan had worked and the monster had returned to the deep. The water around seemed to undulate and you looked down to see some strong underwater currents coming towards you. Something was heading your way very fast and you started swimming away in fear. The water demon was right behind you, expertly slicing through the water, covering the distance between the two of you very fast and reaching out its numerous hands to you, as your eyes widened in terror. It pulled one of your legs and you tried to resist by reaching for your knife in the pouch around your waist, but it wasn't there anymore. You might have lost it while swimming. The demon pulled you in and you took a deep breath before getting sucked into the water. Water bubbled past your ears with the force that dragged you in. Your eyes widened in panic as the demon kept going into the depths and you struggled to get away.

Images of your mother, father, your village went past your eyes as the demon went deeper and you passed by a school of fishes that darted away to let the demon pass. After a while, you started to lose consciousness as you couldn't hold your breath any longer and began to drown.

Adventure Ends Here.

Don't forget this is a water demon

It knows how to swim 😊

Learn to be brave.

You can return to Chapter 47 or start the game again from Chapter 1.

~ SUREFOOT ~

CHAPTER 97

Eat the Lad

꙳꙳꙳꙳꙳ ꙳꙳꙳꙳꙳

here was really no way around it. The dragon had to eat the lad. What did one expect from a hungry dragon? It is possible that it might not see such a tasty morsel for a very long time.

You felt this was the right response and noticed that the dragon was listening happily, nodding his large head until his forked tongue came out and he started to lick his lips with relish.

You started to get nervous as a thought strayed into your mind. You asked, "Are you the hungry dragon in the story you just told me?"

"Yes," he replied, laughing, his voice bouncing from all sides of the hollow cave.

'Where is the lad whom you intend to feast on?' you asked, suspiciously.

He stared at you without saying a word, an evil glint in his green eyes and realization leaped at you.

You turned around to escape, but he was too fast for you and blocked your exit with his large tail.

The last thing you saw was a ball of flame hurtling towards you from his wide-open mouth.

𝕬𝖉𝖛𝖊𝖓𝖙𝖚𝖗𝖊 𝕰𝖓𝖉𝖘 𝕳𝖊𝖗𝖊.

Don't give wrong advice next time!!!

You can return to Chapter 14 or start the game again from Chapter 1.

CHAPTER 98

The Form Changer

ippo was watching you with a smile on his gruff face. He lifted his pudgy hand and started stroking his beard as he waited patiently. The opening was just behind him and he didn't seem ready to let you go past him. It was a strange riddle indeed and you decided to give it some thought, if you intended to go past the angry hippo.

What is long and short?

What is fat and slim?

What is short and tall?

It was absolutely ridiculous for someone to assume two opposite forms. *Who else could assume so many shapes, if not a form changer?*

You smiled as you told him. "The answer to the riddle is a form changer."

He smiled as he said, 'Good, Princess."

Your face broadened into a smile when he spoke, but immediately his brow knit together in a frown as he coldly added, "I'm afraid you failed the test."

"Then, what is it?" you asked, confused. You were very sure that you had given the right answer.

"I shan't tell you," Hippo hissed.

"Okay then, I will try again," you said, but Hippo was shaking his head and slowly walking towards you. As he moved, his body started stretching out, his hands and legs elongating and filling the confines of the cave. Right before your eyes, Hippo transformed into a huge giant and before you could get over your shock and react, he reached out, grabbed you and tore you into pieces.

𝔄𝔡𝔳𝔢𝔫𝔱𝔲𝔯𝔢 𝔈𝔫𝔡𝔰 𝔥𝔢𝔯𝔢.

Sorry!!!

You can return to Chapter 57 or start the game again from Chapter 1.

CHAPTER 99

Descent into the Earth

⚬⚬

The hole gleamed invitingly and you were really tempted to check it out, to find out its hidden secrets. For all you knew, there could be gold in there and you would not only have continued your quest after giving the witches the key, but you could get rich in the process. It took all the strength inside of you but you decided to ignore the gleaming opening and continued your descent into the earth.

Commencing your flight into the dark underbelly of the hole, the sides of tree seemed to constrict and it appeared the tree had life and was breathing. The sides of the tree constricted and expanded with what would seem like each breath and you had to navigate through and avoid being squashed in the process. It was getting even darker and you wondered if you had made the right choice by picking this particular hole in the tree. Something ahead of you caught your eye. It was glittering in the distance, and you wondered if it could be the key the witches wanted.

As you approached, a part of the tree branched out towards you and you flew over it instinctively. You noticed that more parts of the tree were ripping out and stretching towards you. Flapping to the left, you avoided being ripped apart by wood that jutted out of the tree in your direction. The tree seemed to be attacking you from the inside and you started flying, avoiding being crushed by wood that was jutting out of the body of the tree and heading in your direction. You didn't expect what was happening. The witches simply told you to pick up a key. Why was the tree trying to kill you in the process?

The glimmer you had seen earlier was just in sight and already you could see the outline of a key lying at the bottom of the tree. The key was now within reach and you made to pick it up, when you felt a hard stem-like grasp on your little bird's feet. As it tried to drag you back with a burst of energy, you flapped your wings forward and picked the key in your beak. The stem let go and you fell forward, slamming against a side of the tree. Still with the key firmly in your mouth, you watched as the different protrusions of wood melted back into the sides of the tree. The key must have some type of power, since it stopped the tree from attacking you. *There must be a reason the witches want this key. This is no ordinary key*, you thought to yourself.

The key was still glittering in your beak and you made to fly back to the witches. The ascent up the tree was not as eventful as the descent into the old, oak tree. Pretty soon, you got to the section with the glowing hole and thought of stopping by to see what was in there. You remembered the tree protrusions that almost tore you apart and decided that you had had enough adventure already and wanted to get the key to the witches.

As you approached the surface, the darkness of the bowels of the oak tree slowly started making way for the light peering through the hole. You heard the voices of the three witches laughing and calling you out to hurry up and give them the key.

"Well done, brave warrior," the first witch yelled.

"You have indeed brought the key, hurry up and give it to us," the second witch added.

"You kept your word," the third said.

"Although we had our doubts," one of the witches said and they all started laughing in unison. At that point, you slowed down your ascent as you wondered if they knew the danger involved, when they sent you here. You wondered what the key was for, and why they wanted it so badly. They were still chattering and laughing amongst themselves when they noticed you were not flying towards them anymore and the glittering key wasn't moving towards the opening. You had placed the key by the side of the tree and hopped from side to side, deep in thought and the witches started to call out.

"Why are you stopping, brave princess?"

"Bring the key."

"We need the key."

"Why do you need the key?"

They paused for a bit and in unison started to call out.

"Just bring the key."

"What is this key for? What does it do?"

"Brave warrior, we thank you for going on our quest. Give us the key as you promised and we will explain everything you need to know about it."

You were not so convinced, but one of them said, "We will also help you on your quest."

You became confused about your next move. Was it wise to trust the witches? They had actually promised to help you with your quest. What will be your next move?

~ SUREFOOT ~

Will you go out of the hole and give them the key? Turn to Chapter 51.

Will you refuse to give it to them? Turn to Chapter 19.

CHAPTER 100

The Spear

Each moment you spent in the pink cloud house was time being taken away from your original quest. You hoped that your father was still alive and immediately made up your mind.

"I will take the spear," you said quickly.

"You are sure about that?" the cloud mother asked and you nodded affirmatively.

You picked it up and tested it. It was very strong and similar to your spear and you assumed it would make a good throwing weapon if aimed accurately. You trusted your aim and felt this was the best weapon to choose.

"I guess we have our weapon. Thanks, Cloud Mother," Mira said, taking one more bite of cake and sipping on her tea and then you both made your way out of the house.

Waiting patiently outside the pink cloud house was the flying horse that Ishbatech had given you and you climbed on it gratefully, patting its head. The cloud fairy stepped on her small cloud and floated away and led you up the sky towards the hydra's place of abode.

It started getting hotter as you flew up in the air and you could hear the heavy panting of your horse due to the strain of flying and reduced oxygen at this height.

"Are we there yet?" you asked as you started to sweat. You were worried that your horse might pass out soon.

"We are here now," she said, pointing ahead. Staring ahead of you, that area in the sky seemed devoid of life. The clouds were below and the place felt like a large, empty void-like space. It seemed like you were all suspended in some weird way, like gravity was there and then not there, as the horse was just floating but could control the direction it moved with its wings.

Mira was wringing her arms in fear as she floated slowly in front of you and the heat was so intense. Then you heard it. A loud, piercing shriek that made the horse want to turn back. It sounded like the sound of one voice and many voices at the same time. You just managed to keep the horse under control after it started turning this way and that in panic.

You managed to control it and Mira floated back to you.

"I wish you the best, Princess but I can't continue with you."

"Why?" you asked, alarmed.

"My cloud will melt if I continue with you. Besides, the hydra will kill me on sight. Good luck," she said, quickly floating away.

You tapped the horse and spoke to it gently. "It is just you and me, now. Do not be scared and do not let me down." That last word made you smile as you clearly didn't want the horse to let you fall down to certain death.

You urged the horse towards the sound of the noise and the heat grew more intense. The hydra drew its power from the sun, so it made sense that it would live in this hot zone. The sky in this zone was dark, but suddenly became brighter as the hydra appeared from behind a dark cloud. Nothing prepared you for the sight of this monster as its fiery heads reached towards you with flames pouring out of its red arms and body.

The horse started panting and acting fidgety, as the hydra rose up to its full height, blocking the sky with the heat growing more intense. The beast shrieked and threw out flames from its seven heads in your direction and the horse panicked, almost throwing you off its back. You managed to hold on tight and controlled the panicked horse, turning it back towards the beast. Your arms were becoming sweaty with the intense heat and you fought to control the horse, whilst reaching for the spear. The hydra's numerous arms were still stretching in your direction and you intended to take it out with one good aim of your spear to its heart. With the movement and fire burning in all directions, it was hard to tell where the beast's heart was, but you guessed that anywhere at the center where all the heads met would be a likely spot. You fumbled to get the weapon that you had tied in a cloth at the side of the horse and the minute your hand made contact with it, you screamed in pain. The heat had made the spear so hot that it burnt into the skin of your palm and you could smell your burnt flesh, but you held back tears as you grabbed it.

Your hands shook as you struggled to aim the hot spear at the hydra that appeared to be on fire but it wasn't. The forked tongues came out of its mouths. It poured fire in your direction and you directed your horse away. It neighed in pain as a flame of fire went past and singed the tip of its right wing. You turned the horse around, still holding the spear above your head, with your hand shaking in fear mixed with pain as the beast made its way towards you. The horse panicked as the hydra approached and you held on to the horse's back with both hands as the hot spear fell away and vanished in the clouds below.

You looked up to see the hydra in front of you and the mouths in the seven heads opened up simultaneously as the hydra set you on fire.

Adventure Ends Here.

Poor choice of weapon!!!

You can return to Chapter 31 or start the game again from Chapter 1.

CHAPTER 101

Success

I destroy you.

No matter who you are.

Be you rich or poor.

Young or old.

What am I?

You thought long and hard and after a while smiled, as realization set in and you said, "Success."

For a moment Ishbatech remained quiet and thoughtful, looking at your face with no expression in his cold eyes. You started to get anxious as the uncomfortable silence dragged. You shifted your feet from left to right, an anxious habit that you exhibited when you were preparing your mind for a fight. Reading your mind easily, he smiled at you and said, "You are indeed wise. The fact that one has been successful could cloud the person's reasoning and judgment."

Ishbatech's demeanor changed from a cold, calculating man to a friendlier personage of someone who was taking a friend around his home of abode.

You had passed his test and he didn't seem to think of you as a threat, anymore. He took you round his castle and showed you his vast kingdom on the Craggy Mountain.

Navigating through the dark narrow mountain passageways with Ishbatech and his winged men, they led you through an opening to a large field laden with flowers, slender stems and blue, bell-shaped flowers. The flowers were called mountain harebells and you wondered how they bloomed so beautifully in the heart of the cave. You didn't have to wonder for long as you noticed that the mountain was hollow in the center and opened up to the sky, so that plants could get rain and sunlight quite easily. The smell of fresh mountain air filtered through your nostrils and you looked around to see houses built from bamboo sticks, lying on top of each other. There were narrow steps leading like a maze from one house to another and beautiful, dark-haired women were holding baskets and singing.

You looked back at him in surprise and asked, "Are these the women from the beautiful village?"

"Yes, they are," he replied, watching them with amusement in his eyes.

"You… You killed them," you replied, confused.

"That is what it would seem like, but I bring them here and give them life."

"Why do you need to take them by force?"

"They wouldn't come if I asked them nicely," he replied, with an amused chuckle.

"Why do you need all of them, by the way?" you asked, more curious.

"I need them for my children," he said, pointing to a section of the cave where about twenty, tall muscled men were tilling the hard ground.

"They need wives and also need to have their own offspring," he said, pointing at some children playing in the field, away from the men.

You were surprised that you didn't notice the brown-haired children who were playing at the center of the field. They looked up at the group and smiled, waving to Ishbatech who nodded at them.

"Are these children also your creations, like Arturech?"

"No, they are offspring of my children. I need my heirs to rule over Craggy Mountain when I am gone."

You nodded as you observed some strange creatures that looked like half men and half bull emerge from one of the openings in the cave, carrying wooden planks across the cave to the houses by the sides. Everything was running effortlessly and peacefully here. Ishbatech seemed to wield so much power and was clearly in charge of his own kingdom full of creatures, which obeyed his every command. His mood was now more affectionate. He showered you with endearments and eventually asked you to be his wife.

"I have been alone for a long time and one as strong and wise as yourself will be a good companion to me." He further said that he was moved by your beauty and captivated by your strength and wisdom and begged that you remain with him. There was no way you could accept his offer; you certainly had not forgotten your mission.

You had to decline, but what will be your reason?

Will you tell him that you can't stay because he's ugly, wicked and cruel? Turn to Chapter 92.

Will you tell him that you have to find the healing stone? Turn to Chapter 58.

CHAPTER 102

Stop and Fight It

꧁꧂

The shadow of the figure stretched out against the wall as it approached, with the things on its head crawling about in different directions. You wondered what creature this was that had this shadow and was heading your way, but whatever it was, you intended to complete your quest. Nothing was going to stop you from getting the healing stone which was probably hidden in the dark recesses of this cave. Dropping the pouch on the floor, you whipped around, brandishing your knife and advancing towards the approaching creature with the aim of fighting it.

This was your final destination and nothing was going to get in your way. With that thought, you took a stand at the center of the passageway leading to the cave as the sound of screeching and slithering started to increase.

The creature came in through the bend and on spotting you, shot an arrow. You dove to the left as it swept past, narrowly missing your heart. You leaned against the wall and just rolled into a kneeling position when another arrow zipped past your head and hit the wall with a dull, *thwack* sound. You had to get closer so you could use your weapon on your attacker and you advanced in a surprise attack.

Screaming and raising your weapon, you leaped and rotated in the air and turned to look at the creature as it tried to string another arrow in its bow. Your eyes met and you quickly realized your mistake. Your eyes were locked with that of a woman, or what used to be a woman called Medusa. Legend had it that she was once a very beautiful priestess of the goddess, Athena. At the time the priestesses took a vow of celibacy, but Medusa broke it by having an affair with Poseidon, the god of the sea, which made Athena very angry. She had cursed Medusa, who transformed to this hideous creature with snakes sticking out of her head. What was even worse about the curse was that anyone she looked at turned into stone.

The snakes in her head screeched and moved rapidly on her head, stretching in your direction. Her face still looked beautiful, but she now had a wicked smile on her face. Her tail rapidly slithered towards you and her eyes shone with a bright light that emanated from her sockets as you landed in front of her.

The last thought that came to you was, *this is Medusa and anything she looks at turns to stone.*

Right now, she was looking at you!

Your mouth froze into a soundless scream as you gradually turned into stone.

𝕬𝖉𝖛𝖊𝖓𝖙𝖚𝖗𝖊 𝕰𝖓𝖉𝖘 𝕳𝖊𝖗𝖊.

Sorry, Game Player.

At least, you will be a statue!!!

You can return to Chapter 61 or start the game again from Chapter 1.

~ SUREFOOT ~

CHAPTER 103

Use the Egg

❧❧❧❧❧❧❧ ❧❧❧❧❧❧❧

The race down the hallway was never-ending and you were getting tired from the zigzag movements. You realized that after a while, you were bound to run out of luck with the volley of arrows that the angry and now screaming Medusa was throwing your way. A rude awakening to stir you to action came in the form of a blast of air to the side of your face, where an arrow flew past and slammed against the rough side of the cave.

The seer had given you an egg, along with the feather, and you hoped it would come in handy at this critical time and end this onslaught of arrows that was coming your way in rapid succession. The arrows could hit you at any moment, as the passageway started narrowing, leaving little room to maneuver. You took a sharp turn to the left and at the same time brought out the egg out of your pouch. From the corner of your eye, you saw Medusa slithering closer and stringing an arrow to her bow at the same time.

With no idea of how it worked, you held out the egg and threw it on the floor behind you. At the same time, you jumped ahead and rolled on the rough pebble cave floor and ducked behind a stone boulder, wincing at the sharp pains you received from the rough floor. Thick, grey smoke came out of the scattered pieces of the egg on the floor, separating you from the advancing creature. You coughed a bit as the smoke drifted through the cavern and up to the ceiling of the cave. The smoke rose along the walls of both sides of the cave and you covered your nose as you watched it go up in a thick curly mast towards the ceiling.

Initially, there were sounds and shrieks from Medusa and the hundreds of snakes on her head, but suddenly there was total silence. You waited until the last trace of smoke drifted away, and you peered from behind the boulder to see Medusa standing rigidly a few feet behind the boulder. The snakes on her head were frozen in different positions, like they were shrieking, with their forked tongues hanging out of their mouths. Her eyes were wide open but you avoided looking directly at them, and her mouth hung open in her final scream. She had turned to stone.

In life, Medusa had the ability to turn anyone that looked into her eyes into stone, but you didn't want to take the chance by finding out if it was true, now that she was dead. Making sure not to look directly into her eyes, you walked to her, observing up close her features, admiring the details of the scales on her tail, noting the way her tail curled up behind her head in the air, with her hands stretched to the side, like she wanted to embrace her long-lost friend. With that thought and a victorious smile on your face, you pushed her body to the floor. Medusa swayed to the left and slammed against a side of the cave. That action broke her neck, causing her head to fall off, rolling away and making thumping sounds against the uneven stony floor of the passageway. Finally, it settled against the wall at some far side of the cave hallway, propped up against a stone.

Time had been wasted on this fight with Medusa and you had to continue on your mission. *There has to be an exit out of this cave,* you thought to yourself. You hadn't a chance to find the exit, because you were running for your life from a deranged creature. Looking around the cave, you quickly sighted a light shining into the passageway. You cautiously approached it, observing a small opening and decided to make for it, wondering if it would lead you to the healing stone.

As you stepped into the opening leading to a cave with crystals jutting from the ground and the walls of the ceiling, an idea came to you, fueled by a niggling feeling. You looked back at Medusa's fallen head lying across the dark passageway.

Will you pick up the head? Turn to Chapter 106.

Will you save time, leave it behind and get the healing stone? Turn to Chapter 78.

~ SUREFOOT ~

CHAPTER 104

The Blue Stone

The blue, transparent stone had a strange glow inside of it that lit up the cold floor where it lay and you knelt down once again to look at it. It seemed like small translucent balls of liquid floated inside of it and your eyes grew wide with wonder just watching the images dancing within the stone.

This had to be the healing stone, there was no question about it. How else could you explain the magical and almost captivating nature of this stone and the sensation of happiness that it gave you? This was the result of your searching; you had finally found the healing stone and you could now return home to save your father. Stretching out your hand, you held the stone and lifted it up, watching the balls within the stone dance around. You spun around, causing the liquid in the stone to swirl with the movement.

"This is the healing stone," you said, unable to contain your joy at finally reaching the end of your quest.

The dragon stepped out of the shadows and marched slowly towards you with a smile on his ancient face, which made you even more certain that you had chosen the right stone.

"You impressed the count with your wisdom," he said, stopping just in front of you.

You nodded, still looking at the stone as the balls seemed to be floating faster.

"Yet, you don't impress me," he added coldly and you looked up in alarm. "Well done, Princess. You have proved to me that you are as empty and transparent as what you have picked. You're not worthy of the healing stone. Farewell."

"Wait...," you screamed, as the balls in the stone kept on spinning faster and faster and your hands became very hot. You dropped the stone and it broke in a thousand pieces, sending blue light to every corner of the room.

You looked up to see the massive tail of the dragon heading your way. You had no time to avoid it and he slammed you against the wall of the cave. The impact caused all your bones to shatter with a resounding crack that reverberated down the dark hallways of the cave.

Adventure Ends Here.

Wrong choice!!

You can return to Chapter 67 or start the game again from Chapter 1.

CHAPTER 105

A Place to Hide

The door opened abruptly and you immediately knew your life was in danger. The look of absolute terror on the merman's face was enough to make you realize that what was coming through that door was something you were not ready for at the moment. You decided to find a place to hide. This was not your fight and you didn't owe the merman anything. Although you felt a bit sorry for him, you didn't know what was coming through that door and you had to save yourself.

You quickly darted into a cupboard in the corner as the sound of someone approaching increased. From your hiding place, you watched as the mermaid queen swam in, looking very angry.

Her long, purple hair, held down by a diamond sparkling crown, twirled around her beautiful but visibly enraged face. Her green, massive, scaly tail fluttered in anger as she looked around the room, searching for something or someone.

"You tried to get help from that cowardly princess," she yelled.

"What princess?" the merman king asked in alarm.

'Princess Surefoot in fish form, of course. I hear everything and see everything."

"I don't know what you're talking about." King Octan shook his head in protest.

"I thought I had cured you from loving anyone else, after what I did to that stupid blonde."

King Octan screamed and made to attack her, but she laughed and pointed at him. He stopped in his tracks and held his hand to his throat, being strangled by a force you couldn't see.

"Well, you will both die together," she screamed, and the cupboard you were in started shaking and disintegrating right in front of your eyes.

Adventure Ends Here.

Sorry!!!

You can return to Chapter 71 or start the game again from Chapter 1.

CHAPTER 106

Pick Medusa's Head

⟶⟶⟶⟶⟶ ⟵⟵⟵⟵⟵

That niggling feeling was something that you were familiar with. A feeling of dread and caution that most times you couldn't place a finger on, but overtime had come to trust. "There is wisdom in listening to your heart," your mother would whisper to you. You remembered her kind eyes and smiling face and fingered the necklace that she had placed so lovingly on your neck when you were leaving Omahi Village. It seemed like ages that you had left and you wondered how she was faring back at home. Was your father still alive? Did the council decide to make Nadum the new chief?

You were not going to let that happen. You had to complete your mission and get home on time to save your father. Turning around with renewed resolve, you marched towards Medusa's head, careful not to look directly into her dead, but still open eyes. As you stood in front of it, you observed her head frozen in death and held one of the snakes that was outstretched in your direction, with its mouth open in a frozen shriek. Holding the head carefully in front of you, you made your way to the opening again. This time, you looked around the room you had just entered. Your feet made contact with tiny crystals on the floor and the entire space was lit up by a colorful light. This place filled you with a sense of wonder and you fixed your eyes on the glass casing at the center of the room.

The light glinted off a glass casing sitting on a flat, elevated stone slab at the center of the room. On closer inspection, you observed that the single ray of light coming from the ceiling reflected on the glass casing. The effect was a burst of pink, orange and purple colors, reflecting off the glass and shimmering on the stalactites and stalagmites hanging from the ceiling of the cave. For a moment, you were distracted by the beauty of the colors jumping off the walls and the cave ceiling. You were immersed in a sense of peace, then you noticed there was something in the glass casing. You moved closer to inspect it, still holding Medusa's head firmly in your left hand.

As you approached the glass casing, your face broadened into an excited smile as finally, there in front of you was the healing stone of Lanogoza. Protected by a glass casing sitting on the flat, plain stone slab, there was nothing magical about the stone itself. It looked very simple, like a regular stone and was as large as a big, ostrich egg. You slowly stretched your hand towards the casing. Then, you felt it, a low energy like a tremor passing from the stone to your fingertips and down, like a sharp current to your toes, and immediately you dropped your hand.

You carefully placed the head of Medusa on the floor. This was definitely the famous healing stone of Lanogoza. This was the end of your quest and you were going to collect the stone and return back to your people in Omahi Village. With your hands shaking, partly from excitement and the tremors radiating from the healing stone, you reached out again for the casing. Your fingers had barely touched it, when you felt something hard hit you across the chest and face, tossing you half across the room. You miraculously avoided being impaled by a crystal jutting out of the side of the wall. You lay there for a bit, out of breath as you observed a figure rise from a dark corner of the crystal room.

Hidden by the shadows, watching you all this while was the guardian of the stone, the ancient dragon. You shook your head as you tried to catch your breath, realizing you had allowed the excitement of seeing the stone to take away your sense of judgment. Quickly scrambling to your feet, you berated yourself for not remembering that the stone was being guarded. The dragon had hit you with his tail like it would a pest whilst you were standing by the stone, and he was heading your way again. His huge size blocked the light from the hole in the ceiling and the cave momentarily lost all its magical colors. You looked up and all you could see were two wide, red eyes staring at you with hate.

The dragon did not take his eyes off you and all of a sudden, his huge tail made for you. You deftly jumped away and he narrowly missed his target. You rolled away and leaning against the wall, quickly scanned the room for Medusa's head that you had dropped when the dragon flung you across the room. The head was not damaged, but it was just in front of the approaching dragon, who looked very upset that you were putting up a fight.

The ancient dragon roared at you, his red eyes stared angrily into yours and blew flames of fire at you, which you avoided by rolling away. The heat of the flames scorched a side of your hair as it passed by you, torching the wall that you were leaning on. The dragon was momentarily taken aback as you screamed and charged at it and it took a step back, watching you jump and land just a few meters away. The dragon threw his head back and you could see his neck bulge as he got ready to burn you. You got to a kneeling position in front of the dragon, at the risk of being burnt at any moment, and quickly brought out Medusa's head, pointing it at the dragon.

You almost dropped Medusa's head in fright as the snake you were holding suddenly came to life and started twisting and trying to grab your hand. A bright white light emerged from Medusa's eyes, aimed at the dragon that was staring in your direction. His mouth opened wide and you could see smoke flowing out of his huge snout as the flames were about to emerge.

The light from Medusa's head was reflecting in the dragon's red eyes and all of a sudden, he raised his wings, poised to fly. He started to roar and the sound was so loud that the crystals started to shake and fall off the ceiling like rain. You jumped left to right to avoid being impaled to the ground, avoiding the glass like daggers but still positioning Medusa's face to face the dragon. The wings of the dragon froze in the air and you watched, surprised, as he started solidifying from the tips of his wings, across his entire body. You dropped Medusa's head to the side and as you looked at the massive ancient dragon, you saw that he had turned into stone.

In his death, you had to admire this creature which was a very formidable beast. The wings were large and stretched almost across both ends of the large cavern and his tail stood tall, up to the top of the high arched ceilings. His eyes stared at you in a mixture of surprise and anger. After you were certain that you weren't in any immediate danger, you walked wearily towards the slab.

Thankfully, the falling crystals had not destroyed the glass casing and you imagined it was due to the energy from the stone. The crystals had formed a circular pattern around the casing but other than that, it was untouched. Ignoring the electric tingling as you touched the casing, you gently lifted it up and retrieved the stone. It felt very cold to your touch and a sensation that you couldn't describe went through your arm. You quickly placed it in your pouch and turned away from the slab.

With one last look at Medusa's fallen head and the huge, forever-frozen statue of the ancient dragon, you began the long journey home, hopefully in time to save your father and your people.

Congratulations!!!

Wise Game Player

~ SUREFOOT ~

CHAPTER 107

Flying

You flew with the wind under your wings, effortlessly and gracefully. After gliding about playfully, you remembered your quest. You suddenly realized that you had wasted so much time enjoying the rudiments of flying for the first time. It seemed almost wonderful to find out that you could use your wings this well.

You focused on your journey and continued on your quest, heading west. The skyline was a bright orange and you couldn't help but notice how the rays of sunlight bounced off the clouds. Looking down, you could see vast green lands with a sprinkling of tall trees. The horizon ahead started to take on a darkish hue. Something was blocking out the beautiful orange from the setting sun.

Whatever it was, it didn't seem right and it appeared that your bird senses agreed with you as well. It wasn't night yet, so what could the creeping darkness that appeared to be moving in your direction be?

Will you drop down on a tree and observe this strange darkness? Turn to Chapter 44.

Will you continue flying, since you are already late? Turn to Chapter 85.

~ SUREFOOT ~

CHAPTER 108

Try to Escape

This was not your original mission and you had no idea what to find in that dark hole in the tree. The witches were probably hiding something from you. How did they lose their key in there? What are the chances that they even had a key in that hole? What if they were leading you to your death in some sort of sick game? Their voices got louder as they started shouting at you to get into the hole.

"Stop your wavering."

"What's keeping you?"

"Get into the hole and retrieve our lost key, you idiot."

That was the last straw. You didn't owe the ugly witches anything. This was an opportunity to escape and you decided to take it. You flew above the hole and into the air, soaring between the gnarly branches of the oak tree and finally breaking through to the sky. You were so relieved to have gotten away from those horrible witches who definitely had a plan to destroy you. It took some time before it finally registered that your wings were flapping, but you were not moving. You turned mid-air to see the three witches on their different broomsticks, looking at you in great anger and disappointment

One of them had her finger pointed at you and you were suspended in the air, not able to move forward or backwards, although your wings were flapping frantically.

"You gave your word," they yelled in anger.

One of them pointed her crooked, magic stick at you and a huge ball of flame hurtled towards you.

𝔄𝔡𝔳𝔢𝔫𝔱𝔲𝔯𝔢 𝔈𝔫𝔡𝔰 𝔥𝔢𝔯𝔢.

Learn to keep your promises, dear adventurer.

You can return to Chapter 87 or start the game again from Chapter 1.

CHAPTER 109

The Departure

The drums were beating far into the night as the entire village prepared for a special Omahi Fire Dance Celebration. The celebration happened on rare occasions like this one. The villagers were expected to sing and chant prayers for you, asking the spirits to guide you safely on your way. Your mother came into your hut as you lay on the bed, waiting for the celebration to begin.

"They are ready for you," she said and watched as you stood up and accompanied her outside.

Two women wearing white wrappers tied on their chest smiled at you and bowed as your mother stepped aside to let you pass. The women led you into the heart of the celebration. You watched the entire village filled with women, children and men standing in two lines and allowing you to pass through their center. Everything appeared to happen in slow motion and you watched the faces in the crowd. The women and children looked on with a sense of pride and joy. In the eyes of the men, you sensed surprise that you would attempt such a feat. Your eyes met Nadum and this time, he did not look away. You wondered what he was thinking but you had to focus on the celebration.

Ahead of you roared the large bonfire and the sparks erupting from the flames leaped up to the sky. The drummers beat their drums in unison and a frenzy, their faces serious as their sweaty palms hit the drums in a beat that is known to summon the spirits. The seer stood in front of the flames and beckoned on you to come closer. You walked towards him.

As you got closer, the two women held your hands on both sides and led you to the seer who stood tall and regal, with a faraway look in his eyes.

"Andogun, we seek you this night," he screamed, his hands lifted to the sky, as you came closer.

The women let go of your hands and stood beside you, as you watched him closely.

"Andogun, the fire god, we come to you and present our daughter Surefoot to you. Guide her, great spirits, on her quest to the Mountain of Lanogoza," he yelled, his hands high up in the air. You could see his eyes whiten and protrude as he stared at the sky.

The bonfire crackled and the flames split into two as a sign that the spirits had responded to his call and everyone screamed and started chanting.

"Protect her," the seer screamed.

"Protect her, protect her," everyone chanted.

The seer looked down at you and pointed at the flames and the two women held your hands. You knew what was expected of you. You had seen it done once or twice before. If the gods did not protect you, the flames from the bonfire would kill you. The women held your hands and led you to the bonfire and you raised your head in defiance as you felt the heat of the flames before you even got closer. The women gently pushed you into the bonfire and you fell in, closing your eyes in anticipation of the pain, but the flames engulfed you like a blanket of protection.

The flames crackled and roared in your ears and you suddenly went into a trance. Images leaped at you, and they seemed so real that you could even touch them – snow-capped mountain peaks, tall edifices, pale-skinned people reaching out to you and then you suddenly came back to the present. To the sound of singing, clapping and the flames. You opened your eyes and smiled. Your eyes met those of your mother and she smiled in relief as the seer cried out.

"Andogun the fire god has accepted our petition and sacrifice. Surefoot will go in peace."

The entire crowd erupted in shouts of happiness. They started dancing around the bonfire and the seer asked you to come out of the flames and join in the celebrations.

A while later, the shouts of warriors mixed with laughter from the women and children faded away into the night, like the dying embers of the bonfire. You were now in your hut and proceeded to pack your pouch with everything that you needed to embark on the quest. The room was very simple and bare and you looked around at all the items of clothing neatly arranged there. A single, small bed at the side of the only window. A large bundle of fur lay on the bed, a relic from the bear you had fought and skinned some time ago.

Your mother was beside you, watching with eagle eyes as you packed, ensuring that you left nothing of benefit. In true motherly form, she made sure she filled your pouch with dry meat and bread.

"Thanks, Mother," you said, watching her gently placing the food items in the pouch.

Now to the weapons, you thought as you held up your spear and tested it. The edges looked sharp and you examined it closely, looking at the small pieces of strings tied on it. Each string you had meticulously tied was for every person you had killed in battle. The colors of the strings mattered too. Red was for a warrior defeated in battle and green for every successful hunt. Over the years, you had a lot of green strings on your weapon and it was seen as a mark of respect for every Omahi warrior.

After placing small knives and daggers in different hidden compartments of your belt and pouch, checking your arrows and the string of your bow, your mother spoke to you. "You have to go to bed, child. It is almost daylight and you will need to be strong when you leave."

"Yes, Mother," you agreed.

She gave you a warm embrace and left the hut. You lay on the bed for a while before drifting into a troubled sleep. You woke up to someone shaking you and looked up to see your mother smiling at you with sad eyes.

"Wake up, Surefoot. It is time to leave."

You stood up and quickly cleaned up and changed to fresh clothes and joined your mother who was waiting outside your hut.

Two young girls wearing short wrappers tied around their chest were approaching both of you at the hut, leading your faithful horse. You thanked them and patted your horse which nudged his face towards you

as you stroked him lovingly. Dusty you named him, when you first picked him out of eight other horses your father had brought, whilst trading with the neighboring Zanzu tribe across the plains, when you were just fourteen.

Dusty stood out with his gleaming black coat and you fell in love with the beautiful creature. Your father taught you how to ride this graceful horse and he had been your constant companion for a long time now. The horse had joined you in battle as you fought against raiders coming to steal from your land. Dusty never shied away from battle. The screams, slashing of knives, flying arrows and the sight of blood didn't drive him away, like it did most horses. He stuck by you through thick and thin and would also participate in the battle by striking down your attacker with his heels, if he sensed you were in danger.

"Surefoot my daughter," your mother said, snapping you out of your reverie.

You turned to look at your mother who seemed to have aged overnight. Her eyes had worry lines but she managed a brave smile and pulled you into a hug like she didn't want to let go. After what seemed like a while, she detached herself from you, slowly put her hand to her neck and removed her necklace. Your mother had always worn this necklace for as long as you could remember and right now, she reached out and quietly put it around your neck.

You shook your head. "Mother, I cannot take this. It was given to you by your mother and her mother before her."

"Yes indeed, my child. And now, I feel the time has come for me to give it to you for protection," she said smiling, and looking up at you with a sad look in her eyes.

"Thank you, Mother," you replied, with a tear rolling down your cheek.

You wanted to say something but immediately got distracted by the sound

of singing and clapping. A small group of people had come to say goodbye and they were singing your praises and calling you a brave warrior. Some of the women you had grown up with, who had joined you in fighting battles. You hugged them and kissed some of the little children on their foreheads. Four other warriors started approaching on their horses and you could see Nadum in the lead.

You waited and the singing quieted down as the men got closer and Nadum said, "We are here to accompany you to the outskirts of Omahi Village."

They nodded in greeting to Queen Cohahi, who acknowledged their greeting with a nod as well.

"As is our custom, we appreciate the gesture," Queen Cohahi replied while you remained silent.

"I would like to see Father," you said to her.

"I am afraid you do not have a lot of time … the chief…," Nadum said and his voice trailed off when you looked at him.

Your mother held your shoulders and whispered to you, "I am afraid that he is right. Your father will be fine. I will watch over him. Just make sure you come back to me."

You wanted to protest but the men were watching and you knew she was right. Instead, you hugged your mother tight and turned back to mount Dusty. A quick kick to the sides and the horse flew expertly away, as the crowd of villagers shouted praises and calls of goodbyes to you. In the midst of the voices, you could hear the shrill voice of your mother.

"Come back to me, Surefoot. Come back with the healing stone."

With determination etched on your face, you pushed the horse forward and galloped away, accompanied by the four warriors, two on each side.

The healing stone was part of a legend told to children as nighttime stories under a bright, moonlit sky. People had journeyed there, lured by the promises of what the healing stone could give. Legend said that the stone was capable of curing any sickness and giving unimaginable wealth and long life to whoever found it. There were seven friendly tribes across the plains and each tribe had different stories about how several adventurers died in the course of trying to get the stone. Some versions said that the adventurers had never been seen again. Some stories mentioned that the adventurers had actually returned but people couldn't see them, anymore. They had just heard their voices.

You remembered that your father's younger brother, Strongheart had attempted the journey to make a name for himself. Everyone, including your father, had warned him not to go. It had happened six years ago. He had never been seen or heard from, anymore.

You looked ahead with determination, and shook the thoughts of Strongheart from your mind as you listened to the sounds of the horses' hooves pound the hard earth. Though no one had ever returned from the journey, you intended to come back. The life of your father and the future of the entire village depended on you finding the healing stone.

As you rode away, you thought of the path you would take.

Will you go east? Turn to Chapter 9.

Will you go west? Turn to Chapter 55.

Will you go north? Turn to Chapter 37.

Will you go south? Turn to Chapter 24.

~ SUREFOOT ~

Original Manuscript Cover sketch by author

Initial draft written in March 2001

Other Books Written by the Author

Echoes of my Heartbeat – A collection of poems

Talo – An African love story

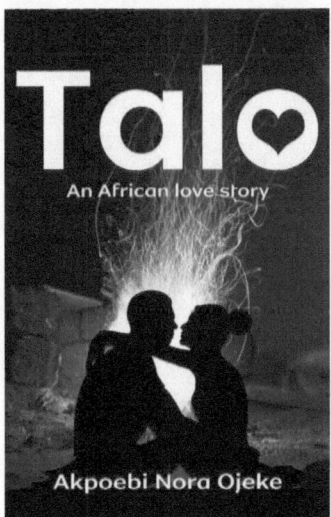